MAYA
Symbiogenesis Book One

Pete Barber

LEGAL STUFF

ISBN: 978-0-9855230-6-0

Symbiogenesis: Evolutionary change by the inheritance of acquired gene sets.

… *Lynn Margulis*

DEDICATION

I have obsessed over the premise of this story for more than ten years. That my wife remains with me after reading the finished novel speaks volumes for her love, but perhaps reflects poorly on her judgment. Book Two is coming soon.
Run, Joyce, while you still can!

CHAPTER 1

Margaret navigated the trailer park's rutted track and pulled up in front of a gray single wide trailer. When Cliff's Harley wasn't outside, she let out a relieved sigh and flexed her fingers off the steering wheel. A dozen barking mutts hurtled toward the vehicle and crowded her door. One mongrel, his fur caked in Georgia red clay, lifted onto hind legs and slobbered on her side window, scoring his nails down her paintwork. She climbed out and shooed the pack with her purse, and they scattered in a cloud of dust and yips.

Bypassing the trailer's front door—Cliff had nailed it shut when the hinges broke—she skirted his rusty '58 Chevy. Hood raised, no wheels, no engine, the vehicle had been perched on axle-stands long before Patsy had moved in with him. According to Cliff, once he rebuilt it they'd have themselves a fifty-thousand-dollar classic.

Fat chance.

The wooden steps at the side entrance slewed sideways as she climbed. The door was open a few inches. Margaret pushed it wide and shouted, "Patsy?"

She backed down to ground level. Just in case he *was* there.

Margaret visited most days after work. Especially today, Friday, because she couldn't come on weekends, when Cliff was home. She climbed the steps again and raised her voice. "Patsy, it's Momma. Can I come in?"

A soft mewling—like a muffled cat's meow—came from within. *Surely, the silly girl hasn't gotten a kitten.*

The trailer was an unfinished DIY project: a rectangular box with a narrow hallway of unfinished drywall that ran along the outside wall—bedroom, bathroom, and living room off to the right, kitchen at the end. She stepped inside. A blanket of hot air enveloped her. July in Atlanta without A/C, but Cliff wouldn't waste beer money on a busted heat pump. *He* wasn't seven months pregnant.

Stopping in the windowless space—the bare bulb had blown weeks ago—Margaret let her eyes adjust. And listened.

The strange sound repeated.

Something about the tone set her arm hairs on end.

She called again, "Patsy?"

Ahead, the bedroom door gaped open. A ceiling fan buzzed and ticked, and when it threw a shadow across the doorway, Margaret's heart fluttered and she froze.

One hand at her throat, she edged forward and peered in.

Empty.

The stink of tobacco and liquor oozed from the room. On the carpet, a dark patch glistened. A thin brown line progressed through the doorway and along the hall. At the living room it stopped.

A low groaning sound pulled her forward. Her pulse revved. *Patsy!*

She clambered over a pile of dirty laundry, grabbed the living room doorknob, turned, and pushed. The door jammed. And her daughter squealed.

A pink nightgown poked through near the floor. She bent low and said into the crack, "Patsy, what's wrong?"

She made out shallow panting.

In-out.

Patsy mumbled.

"I don't know what you're saying, sweetie."

In-out.

Margaret squeezed two fingers through the gap and touched the warmth of her daughter's back. "Are you cramping?"

In-out. In-out. Then Patsy croaked, "Call 911."

Margaret sprang up, yanked the cell phone from her purse, and punched in the code. With the device pressed to her ear, she ran through the kitchen and out the rear door.

The operator picked up. "911. What is your emergency?"

"It's my daughter. Something's wrong. She's pregnant. Due in nine. No. Eight weeks."

In the backyard, Margaret dodged through a tumble of torn trash bags, black with flies and reeking. The living room's patio doors lay wide open, but the curtains were drawn.

She climbed onto the milk crate that substituted for steps and slipped through the drapes.

Her hand shot to her mouth and smothered a scream.

The 911 operator said, "Ma'am. Is there an intruder?"

"Send an ambulance. Quick." She gave the address and dropped her phone and bag on the floor.

Her daughter was lying on her left side, back humped against the hallway door, knees high, hands gripping her belly. A swelling on her cheek narrowed her eye to a slit.

Between Patsy's legs, a white bath towel was saturated with dark-red blood.

Margaret crouched and touched her daughter's shoulder, softly, with one trembling finger, as though she might break her. "I'm here, baby. The ambulance is on its way. What happened?"

Stupid question. Cliff had happened. He had never wanted kids. And since she'd gotten big in the belly, he didn't want Patsy either. In Patsy's second trimester, it was Margaret who drove her daughter for a sonogram because her *boyfriend* was too stoned to climb out of bed. When the technician traced two fuzzy outlines on the screen, Patsy had squealed like a five-year-old on Christmas morning. "Twins, Momma!" Yes, twins. Thrilling for Patsy. The final straw for Cliff. "He'll feel differently once he holds them," Patsy had said. "I love him, Momma. And now he'll love me back."

Love? What did a seventeen-year-old know about love?

Patsy tilted her head and peeked through her right eye. The watery smile that glanced off her lips was instantly replaced by a grimace of pain.

"Momma. Ah. Ah. Ah!"

A contraction rippled the material of Patsy's nightie, stretched over her swollen stomach.

How long has she been like this? Should I move her? Her older daughter had been an army medic. She would know. Margaret retrieved her phone. The operator was still talking, reading questions in a flat voice. Margaret hung up and punched in Lauren's speed dial. Voicemail picked up. She left a message: "Lauren. Emergency! Patsy's hurt bad. Call me back."

Standing over Patsy's prone body watching helplessly as life gasped and wheezed from her daughter, Margaret pinched the skin on her arm until it hurt. This was her fault. She should have been stronger, should have made Patsy come home. Should have... should have....

Outside, sirens sounded.

"The ambulance is here. I have to move you from the door so they can get in." Grabbing Patsy's arms, she pulled, and her daughter screeched—an inhuman keening sound. Margaret dropped to her knees.

"I'm sorry, baby."

Smoothing crusty, blood-matted hair from her daughter's face, she sobbed along with her—head shaking, eyes blurred—an old woman whose weakness had let this happen to her youngest child.

"Mrs. Doolan?" a man called out in the hallway.

"In here," she shouted. "Go through the kitchen and out the back door. This way's blocked."

Patsy cramped again. She bent forward and dry-heaved. More blood seeped onto the towel.

Margaret's stomach knotted and churned. Her body vibrated as though she were plugged into a wall socket. She squeezed her daughter's shoulder and stared at the closed drapes.

Willing them to open.

Hurry.

CHAPTER 2

When Lauren Doolan's phone rang in the left breast pocket of her lab coat, Dr. Maya Arrunsen let out an exasperated sigh.

Damn it! Lauren returned the safety razor to the instrument tray, stepped away from the stainless steel workbench, and turned off the tripod-mounted video camera. When she pulled out her phone and saw her mom's face on the screen, she shook her head, switched the device to airplane mode, and returned it to her pocket. How often did she have to tell her not to call during work hours?

"My mother. Sorry," Lauren said.

The doctor, seated next to the workbench in her wheelchair, treated Lauren to a withering glare.

Maya Arrunsen was angry.

Maya Arrunsen should not be at work.

Maya Arrunsen had cancer.

Lauren took a long, steadying breath before switching the camera on again. Although she'd adjusted the equipment moments before, she rechecked the lens's orientation. The scene, projected on a computer monitor positioned to her right, showed an open-topped glass cube, similar to a small aquarium, which rested on the stainless steel work surface. At the center of the glass box, a white mouse was crammed into a rectangular plastic container. The rodent's head poked from a circular hole in the front and its tail from another at the rear. Immobilized, the creature's whiskers twitched nervously. A half-inch-wide band of white fur on the mouse's back protruded from a slit that ran the length of the container.

"Test subject—" Although she knew the animal's code by heart, Lauren followed procedure and leaned close enough to read the identifying ear tag: "—*FM104*. Female mouse, six weeks old." She read today's date from the bottom of the screen, "July 16th." After waiting for the clock's second hand to reach a whole number, Lauren called out, "Start time, sixteen hundred hours."

With her latex-gloved right hand, she retrieved the safety razor, and in six strokes shaved a strip of fur from the mouse's back, exposing its pale pink skin.

Lauren placed the soiled razor in the empty instrument tray to her right. With a plastic vacuum tube, she sucked up the stray hairs before swabbing the freshly shaved skin with a local anesthetic. The animal did not need to suffer. From the sterilized instruments in a tray to her left, she selected a scalpel. Holding the knife between thumb and forefinger, she made an incision beginning at the base of the skull and ending at the tail. The cut exposed the rodent's spine. As adrenaline spiked its nervous system, the mouse trembled and jerked. Blood flooded the gash. Although the animal struggled, the container constrained its movement.

The digital timer on the screen ticked away in one-hundredths of a second.

"Fifty seconds. Incision complete."

Blood pooling on the mouse's back spilled from the cut and seeped into the surrounding white fur, turning it pink.

As Lauren tapped a function key on the laptop, screen magnification increased. At ten times normal, the screen filled with a close-up of the bleeding gash. A skin rippled and formed on the surface. She noted the time again: "Seventy-nine seconds, clotting commences." *That was fast!* Thrilled, Lauren glanced at the doctor, but her boss remained intently focused on the experiment.

The mouse's frantic heart pumped blood, which the fast-forming membrane sought to contain—a life struggle in miniature. Half an inch below the mouse's head, a blood bubble broke through. In seconds, the thickening surface sealed the breach and stemmed the leak.

The color of the gash darkened to ochre, then brown, and finally black. Lauren zoomed out until the mouse was again center stage. A dark exclamation point now ran along its spine, obscuring the incision.

The crust covering the cut cracked and cratered. Disturbed by the mouse's muscle spasms, a large scab bridged upward near the tail and broke loose from the animal's back. Along the length of the healing cut, other splits and crevices lifted and flaked. With the tip of one finger, she scrubbed the cratering scab, which crumbled and scattered from the mouse's back. A neat, pink line of scar tissue covered the wound.

Arrunsen insisted on scientific detachment during experiments. But this recover rate was unprecedented, and Lauren struggled to hide the excitement in her voice. "One hundred ten seconds, lesion sealed."

Lauren popped the catch on the container and eased the front panel off the animal's head. The mouse wriggled free from its plastic prison, scurried to a water pipette embedded in the wall of the aquarium, and began to drink, replacing the liquid it had bled out.

Lauren again increased magnification, focusing on the mouse's back. White hairs sprouted from the shaved skin. Like a time-lapse photographic sequence, in twenty seconds, hair covered the scar, and the mouse became whole. Only bloodstains and congealed scabs encrusting its fur remained as witness to what had occurred. The screen froze on the image of a healthy mouse. "One hundred eighty-four seconds, repair complete." She turned off the camera.

The tiny effort required to manipulate the toggle controller and reverse her motorized chair from the workbench caused Dr. Arrunsen to wince. In a hoarse whisper laced with her strong French accent she said, "The recovery was *trés rapide.*"

Lauren smiled. The woman was a master of understatement. "An order of magnitude faster than *MM091*. But why?"

Arrunsen leaned back in her chair and fixed Lauren with tired eyes. "Try not to think of *FM104* as a mere mouse. Like you and I, her existence results from three thousand million years of DNA refinement." She smiled. "Nature does not like to be rushed. And yet—" The doctor wagged a finger at Lauren to reinforce her words. "—stumbling in the dark, we have tripped over an evolutionary branch that may not have occurred naturally for thousands or millions of years. Perhaps never. *FM104's* accelerated

recovery shows us that evolution has more to offer us mammals."
Arrunsen folded forward. Her back arched and heaved as a
barking, dry cough shuddered through her. After the spasm ended,
it took her thirty seconds of face-wincing shallow breathing to
recover. Red faced, she leaned back in her chair and continued in a
whisper. "Unfortunately, my retrovirus targeting protocol is crude,
and I am modifying a DNA strand of over three million base pairs.
We know that one correct splice exists. *FM104* may be a second.
There may be others, or not. Only time will tell if today's viral
arrow struck the bull's-eye. Based on the specimen's rapid healing,
perhaps we have exceeded our expectations." The doctor gave a
Gallic shrug, dipping her lips and raising her eyebrows. "Or
perhaps not." She turned from Lauren, pointed a trembling finger
at the aquarium, and addressed the mouse: "Now try not to die
over the weekend, one-zero-four." Arrunsen's slight smile failed to
flatten the dark rings underlining her eyes. She pulled in a raspy
breath and sighed it out.

"You should rest," Lauren said.

"No rest for zee wicked. Now, don't forget to call your
mother." The doctor patted Lauren's arm and winked—an apology
of sorts for her earlier outburst. "I'll finish up here."

Lauren frowned. Maya Arrunsen didn't look capable of
opening the lab door, let alone returning the specimen to its cage.
But she wasn't about to argue and risk the sharp sting of the
doctor's temper again. "Thank you, Doctor. Have a nice weekend."

Already focused on her laptop, Arrunsen didn't reply—
probably didn't even hear the words.

After discarding her gloves, Lauren washed up and returned
to her office to log the results of the one-hundred-third attempt to
reproduce an anomaly. Seven months earlier, a female mouse
infected with a military-grade retrovirus had delivered a litter of
five babies. The mother and her offspring should have died, but
one pup survived—a female who demonstrated remarkable healing
traits; she was cataloged as *FM001*. Dr. Arrunsen nicknamed the
mouse Eureka. Sadly, it proved an overambitious name. Although
subsequently infected mice had displayed enhanced healing traits,
they all died within eight hours of contact with the retrovirus. But
logically, if survival occurred once, it could again. Multiple attempts
to breed *FM001* had failed. Closer examination revealed that the
mouse lacked a womb.

Maya Arrunsen believed that duplicating Eureka's capabilities in a fertile specimen could open the door to a new branch of medicine. But unless she unlocked the DNA combination, the doctor's dream would never be realized. Maybe today's mouse would provide the key. Lauren shook her head clear and focused on her work. Emotion clouded judgment. Logic, method, process. In the six months she had been working at Pharmacon for Maya Arrunsen, Lauren had learned much, but that lesson overrode all others.

Lauren's phone vibrated. Mom again.

She pressed *talk*.

CHAPTER 3

Lauren arrived at the Atlanta Medical Center ninety minutes later, wrung out from the stress of weaving through Atlanta's rush-hour traffic in a blind panic. She slammed her hand against the steering wheel and screamed as she followed a conga line of cars up six levels of the hospital's parking deck before finding a space—more time wasted. After taking the stairs instead of the elevator, she sprinted along the sidewalk to the Emergency Room entrance. A receptionist gave her directions. "Your mother's in the surgical waiting room."

It's my mother's fault Patsy's here. How many times had she told her mom to get Patsy out of that shit-hole trailer and away from that no-good drunk? "She won't listen," her mother had said. For God's sake, Patsy was seventeen, a child.

Lauren followed the wall signs, twisting and turning through the corridors. With every step, her fury grew. On the third floor, a nurse pointed to a glass door on the far side of a waiting room. A half-dozen people, their faces drawn with worry, watched her pass. She reached the door and yanked it open. Her mother sat alone in a twelve-by-twelve windowless room with her elbows on her knees, face buried in her hands. "What happened?" Lauren snapped.

Her mother lifted her head. Her mouth opened then closed again. She blinked rapidly as though waking from a coma. "He beat her."

"Of course he did!" Lauren screamed. Blood roared through her ears. She pointed an accusing finger at her mother. "You should have brought her home as soon as she fell pregnant."

Her mother glared at her through narrowed mean eyes. Her lips formed a tight, hard line. "At least she *wanted* her babies."

Lauren rocked backward, poleaxed by the venom-laced words. The air took on substance: brittle, unbreathable. She couldn't move, couldn't breathe, couldn't swallow.

Margaret's face crumpled in pain and her shoulders dipped lower. She shook her head. Cheeks sunken, home perm disheveled, her gaze drifted sideways until it fixed on the blank wall. She whispered, "I don't know why I said that, Lauren. I'm sorry."

The door closed with a soft click and shut out the hospital sounds, leaving the two of them in a silent tomb. Tears leaked from her mother's eyes and wet her cheeks. Her fingers trembled as she dug in her purse for a Kleenex. No more words came. The woman was defeated. Lauren took a deep breath, steadied herself. For her mother's sake, she had to be the better person. She crossed the room, sat close, and draped an arm around thin shoulders. Margaret leaned into her and released a guttural cry that sent shivers skating down Lauren's spine.

Although desperate for information, Lauren waited until her mom's grief became low and soft before asking, "How is she?"

"They took her into surgery." Margaret rubbed at a long streak of dried blood painted like a brush stroke down the front of her green-and-white-checked work coveralls. "I rode with her in the ambulance, but she never woke up. I signed consent papers. They're going to do a cesarean."

Lauren jerked upright. She hadn't given a thought to the babies. She was focused on her sister. "How long?"

Glancing at the wall clock, her mom said, "About an hour. They rushed her straight in."

Lauren swallowed bile, and a shudder of nausea washed through her chest and settled in her belly. If they'd cleared her sister for emergency surgery on arrival, the prognosis from the ambulance crew must have been terrible. Lauren's throat constricted; she couldn't catch a breath. "What about Cliff?" she croaked.

"He left her lying there. I've never seen so much blood." The tears returned.

Lauren again waited for her mother to gather herself. Waiting was all they had right now.

"Did you see him?"

"He wasn't home. I found her in the living room."

"Why didn't she call?"

"No phone."

"Well, she *had* a phone." Lauren had bought her sister a new pre-paid two weeks ago. Cliff had probably pawned it. "How long had she been lying there?"

"That's why I called. I thought you'd know."

Lauren pulled away and barked, "How the hell could I know?"

Her mother recoiled, turned away, and stared at the floor.

"Sorry." Lauren rubbed her mother's back. This was how it had been since she could remember—the daughter looking after the mother instead of the other way around. She softened her voice. "Go on. What were you going to say?"

"The cut on Patsy's lip had clotted. I thought you'd know what that meant."

"Damn, she must have been lying there over an hour." Lauren shook her head. *Now what?* After this, Patsy would *have* to move out of the trailer, away from Cliff. That, at least, was a good thing. "Look, Mom. I'll wait here for the doctor. Go and freshen up in the restroom. It's just along the hall. Drink water; stretch your legs. Do you have your phone?" Her mom nodded. "Go on now. I'll call if I hear anything."

Head bowed, Margaret Doolan sleepwalked to the door and left Lauren alone with her anger. Patsy wouldn't want to testify against Cliff. But she had to, had to stop him from moving on and abusing another naïve girl.

Her mom returned ten minutes later. "Better?" Lauren asked.

"Yes."

Her mom's tight smile, thin face, and button nose reminded Lauren of her sister. She and Patsy had both inherited Margaret's dirty blond hair and blue eyes, but for Lauren the family resemblance ended there. Her short, stocky build came from her father—at least that was what she'd been told, having never met the man who deserted the family before Lauren's first birthday. At least Patsy's baby-daddy had given her long legs. Unlike Lauren, she didn't resemble a short, square character in a Legos movie.

12

They waited for another hour with only the soft whirring of the wall clock to break the silence. Finally, Lauren asked, "Have you had anything to eat?"

Her mom shook her head. "Not hungry."

"Me neither, but we need something. Wait here. I'll check out the cafeteria."

When Lauren returned with two sodas and a couple dried-up sandwiches, a uniformed policewoman was in the waiting room speaking to her mother.

Lauren yanked the door open. "Why didn't you call me?" she snapped.

Her mom stared at her with glassy eyes and shook her head.

The police officer introduced herself then finished taking a statement from her mom before asking Lauren if she knew what had happened to Patsy. Lauren wanted to scream out that because of bad parenting, instead of being in high school, her sister was having sex and playing house with a twenty-eight-year-old loser! "Clifford Jarvis is the one you need to interview. He'll be able to tell you *exactly* what happened."

"Thank you, Ms. Doolan. We're already looking for him."

"Well. Good."

After the police officer left, Lauren sat close to her mom, removed the wrapper from a turkey sandwich, and persuaded her to take a bite. Blaming her for what happened to Patsy wasn't fair. The problem ran deeper. Her mother wasn't a stupid woman, but she had left school at fourteen, forced to work after Lauren's grandfather ran off. And Margaret was only sixteen when Lauren was born. The pattern repeated across generations. A pattern Lauren had been destined to follow until she chose to break the mold. A familiar nausea stirred her stomach. She shook her head to banish the memory of the terrible choice she had made. Perhaps after this, once she was well, Patsy would come to her senses too.

Her mom fished a Kleenex out of her purse and blew her nose. She pulled in a deep breath and let it out as a long, faltering sigh; then she said, "Will you pray with me, Lauren?"

What good would prayers do? Would God turn back the clock and save Patsy from the horror of being beaten and left to bleed out on the floor like an animal?

Her mother rose and turned and knelt. Elbows on the chair, she steepled her hands. Lauren stared at the bald spot forming at her mom's crown. The woman had lived a tough life. If she found solace in religion, what was the harm? Lauren knelt beside her.

"Dear Lord," her mom whispered, "please spare my little girl. Patsy has strayed from your path, Lord, but she's young. In time, she'll come back to you. Please, Jesus, she—" A hopeless sob caught in her throat.

"Amen," Lauren said, and her mother turned to her, clearly surprised to see her kneeling there.

Margaret reached out and stroked Lauren's cheek. "Thank you," she whispered, then lowered her head and screwed her eyes shut. Her lips moved in silent prayer.

The door opened.

Lauren sprang to her feet.

A young man in green scrubs with a stethoscope dangling at his neck entered the room. A disinfectant-filled draft wafted Lauren's face. She read his blank expression, a tourniquet twisted around her gut. The door clicked shut, and the clock whirred. She swallowed hard to keep down her sandwich.

Using Lauren's arm for leverage, her mother tried to stand, but she swayed and stumbled, forcing Lauren to hook an arm around her shoulders and guide her to a seat.

Lauren straightened again and faced the medic. African American, mid-thirties, the whites of his eyes were shot through with red veins; his cheeks were hollow with exhaustion. He said, "Both babies survived, although they're very weak, especially the girl. We've admitted them to the neonatal intensive care unit."

Terror gripped her. She stepped forward, grabbed the front of his scrubs, and pushed him back toward the door. "What about my sister?"

His eyes went wide, and he raised his palms. "I'm sorry. We did all we could, but her injuries were too severe. She'd lost a lot of blood. If we'd reached her sooner—"

Lauren staggered back. "Patsy's dead?" That couldn't be what he meant.

"I'm sorry, yes. The mother died two hours ago. We've been working on the twins."

"Are you sure?"

A puzzled frown wrinkled his forehead. "I'm sorry."

Lauren's legs trembled. She locked her knees. From behind, a keening sound came from a place deep inside her mother. It bounced off the walls and echoed around the room. It set Lauren's teeth on edge and raised the hairs on her neck. She reversed. The backs of her legs hit the chair, and she slumped into the seat next to her mom, shaking her head. How could this happen? How could this be? Patsy was a child. They should have saved *her*.

The doctor cleared his throat. She glared up at him—this man who had failed her sister. "You can leave."

"I'll send the patient advocate along," he said.

"Don't bother."

The door shut, and Lauren stared through the opaque glass panel at the doctor's blurry green silhouette as it receded, willing him to stop, to return and tell her he'd made a mistake, got his patients' names confused. When he rounded a corner and his shape disappeared from view, she turned to her mother. Margaret's eyes were closed and her head hung low, chin on her chest. Soft sobs escaped her lips as her body rocked up and down. Like a drooping wing, Lauren's arm lifted and slipped around the broken woman's shoulders.

Her baby sister was lying on a gurney somewhere without the spark of life. She'd never see her cheeky grin again, never hear her over-loud laugh, never exchange birthday gifts or gossip. She shook her head. It wasn't possible.

The patient advocate knocked before entering—a stocky woman with a round face and a voice laden with sympathy. She introduced herself as Dorothy and explained that the police suspected foul play, so the coroner wanted to undertake an autopsy.

"No shit," Lauren said, and felt guilty when the kindly woman winced.

"The babies are in the NICU—a boy and a girl. You can see them through the window if you'd like."

Lauren didn't give a damn about the babies. They were the reason her sister was dead, and they carried Clifford Jarvis's genes. No good could come of them.

Her mother said, "I'd like that," and stood. Lauren followed suit. What else could she do? The patient advocate led them out.

They marched in single file behind the woman. Lauren's footfalls sounded distant. People she passed looked gray and ethereal. Corridors blended one into the other until a wall on her right gave way to a long glass partition. The advocate stopped and pointed. Lauren moved to the side and cupped her hands against the window to shield the reflection of the overhead lights.

In the dimly lit room, dozens of plastic isolators positioned on stands set to an easy working height were arranged in rows. Ten feet from the window, a nurse wearing a facemask had her hands thrust through two holes in the side of one of the plastic boxes. Three poles holding multiple IV drips and a monitor flanked the incubator.

From where they stood outside the NICU, their voices couldn't disturb the infants, but still Lauren whispered, "They're so small." Lauren had never had a child, but she'd held babies. These tiny objects were fetuses.

"The boy"—Dorothy pointed to the isolator the nurse was working at—"weighs three pounds two ounces."

To the left, in a second isolator, the other twin lay on her back, head turned toward them. Tubes snaking out of a pink plastic disk that obscured the baby's lower face connected her to a machine and a series of drips hanging from a metal pole. "And the girl?" Lauren asked.

"Two pounds ten ounces. She's very frail." The woman's brow creased with concern. Dorothy was a ball of empathy, well suited to her job. "Right now the ventilator is breathing for her."

"Will they make it?" Lauren's words hung in the corridor like solid blocks she couldn't take back and whose sharp edges she couldn't soften.

Dorothy offered a tiny smile. "This is a terrific hospital. We'll do everything we can. Your babies are getting the best treatment available. It's a good thing they are so far along."

"Far along?" Lauren asked.

"Oh, yes. We get much younger babies in here. At thirty weeks, they are better equipped to fight through the trauma of suddenly finding themselves outside their momma's womb."

A small squeak off to her left was the only warning Lauren received before her mother crumpled to the floor.

They got home at ten o'clock and Lauren ordered-in pizza, which they hardly touched. After giving her mother an Ambien and making sure she got to bed, Lauren stretched out on the sofa, turned on late-night TV, and tried to switch off the thoughts circling in her head. A dark shadow soiled the place in her heart where her baby sister should have been. They hadn't been close for a long while. Cliff had made sure of that. Isolating Patsy from friends and family was part of his method, his control. But this was different. Now Patsy wasn't there and would never be there again. It was impossible to comprehend. And there was nothing Lauren—fixer of family problems—could do to change the situation.

But the babies *were* here. They were real. Who would take care of them? Cliff? She supposed he had paternal rights. The law was an ass. Imagine handing those innocent children to that sleazebag, to the man who killed their mother. But if there were no witnesses, who could prove murder? Who would press charges? Surely, the DA would follow up.

Dorothy had explained that the infants would need weeks of care before they would be strong enough to leave the NICU. But what then? Her mother scraped by on a supermarket cashier's pay. Who would pay the hospital bill? And how could her mom raise two children if she wasn't working? Would her mom even want to? The last thing *Lauren* needed was to become a mother. She'd had that opportunity once before. She'd made her choice—a desperate, difficult choice. If Patsy had chosen the same path, she'd be alive right now and those two babies wouldn't exist. Lauren's career was on an upward trajectory. She loved her downtown Atlanta apartment, and she needed her salary to pay the rent. Heck, she already picked up her mother's power bill every month. They *both* needed Lauren's job.

Not a word had passed between them on the drive home, but Lauren was certain the same worries were whirling in her momma's head. Maybe the adoption services could step in. Weren't there always childless couples looking for babies?

The smell of coffee and the clink of cups roused Lauren from a fitful sleep. The wall clock read six a.m.

Her mom shouted from the kitchen, "You want your coffee through there?"

She swung her legs off the couch and stretched. "No. Let me swill my face and have a pee, and I'll join you."

When she returned, her momma sat at the table, staring out the window. Lauren took the chair opposite and picked up her drink. "Thanks. Did you sleep?"

"Uh huh, thanks to that little pill you gave me."

They sipped and stared and silence stretched between them like a screen. Lauren sucked in a deep breath. This had to be faced. "What about the twins?"

Her momma dragged her gaze from the window and looked at Lauren with misty eyes. "I can't think of anything else. They're so small, so innocent." She sighed and focused on her cup as though the brown liquid held the answer.

Lauren steeled herself to broach the idea of adoption. But her mother spoke first her voice sad but determined. "I think it's in God's hands. If he wants them to live, they'll live. And if they live, he'll help me look after them." Margaret lifted her head, and Lauren saw resolve in her gray eyes. "Whatever *he* decides. But they're family. And family looks out for family."

Lauren had considered the possibility that the twins might not pull through. The babies looked so tiny, so fragile, so not ready for life. At the hospital, she'd read the doubt in Dorothy's eyes. The patient advocate didn't think they would make it, and the woman had plenty of experience. Her mom was right. Wait and see was the best approach—no point in tackling problems before they appeared. With forced lightness she said, "Come on. Get dressed, and I'll treat you to breakfast on our way to the hospital." As Lauren stood, her mother reached across, gripped her daughter's forearm, and squeezed. "Thank you for always being the strong one, Lauren."

Her throat tightened. She swallowed, and blinked away the mist in her eyes. Margaret had never acknowledged Lauren's unspoken role as the one who handled things when they went wrong.

But helping with her momma's power bill or buying her sister a cellphone was one thing. Fixing Patsy's twins was something else entirely. A step too far, even for her.

CHAPTER 4

Lauren turned on her office light and put her purse in the top drawer. It was 7:45 a.m., and Maya Arrunsen was already bent over a workbench on the far side of the lab. Lauren cleared her throat as she approached so she wouldn't startle the woman. "Coffee?"

The doctor rotated her chair and removed her surgical mask. "Wonderful."

Lauren studied her boss's gray face. "Were you here all night?"

Arrunsen swatted the question away with a wave of her hand. She pointed to a flat screen displaying the exposed brain cavity of a dissected mouse that was pinned to a specimen tray on the doctor's left. "*FM149*," the doctor said by way of explanation.

Lauren bent to the image and narrowed her eyes. "Anything interesting?"

"The anomaly is more apparent at one-hundred magnification." She pressed a key on the laptop.

The image changed to show a network of filaments encasing the magnified brain tissue as if the organ had fallen victim to an infestation of spiders. "The strands of mitochondria are consistent with the last three specimens. But once again, they curtail before reaching the spinal cortex."

"The repetition shows that your targeting is accurate," Lauren said. The doctor had hypothesized that the modified virus she introduced to her specimens, altered the mouse's DNA in a manner that triggered the construction of a secondary nervous system that permitted the mouse to control healing functions normally handled autonomously.

"The repetition is a step forward, but—" The doctor pulled off her gloves and massaged her neck. She looked up at Lauren. "—how about that coffee."

"Sure." Lauren headed to the kitchen.

When she returned with two drinks, Arrunsen had closed down the computer. The doctor accepted the mug. "Thanks, how are the twins?"

It had been six weeks since Patsy's death, and Arrunsen never failed to ask for a status update. Perhaps because of her own medical challenges, the tragedy had penetrated her hard outer shell.

"Both still in the NICU. Joshua continues to improve."

"And Susan?"

Lauren broke eye contact. "No change."

Maya patted Lauren's arm. "Don't lose faith. Babies are tougher than they seem."

Lauren smiled. "Thanks."

"I'm all in. Can you finish up for me?" She waved her hand at the workbench.

"No problem."

"Okay. See you tomorrow morning for—?"

"*FM150*," Lauren said. "I'll be ready."

Dr. Arrunsen rolled out of the lab, and Lauren began tidying the previous experiment. She welcomed a free day to tackle the mound of filing stacked on her desk.

Late that afternoon, Major McGeehan stopped by. Other than a passing hello in the elevator or hallway, she rarely saw the man, and she couldn't remember him ever visiting Maya's lab. Lauren had served under him at Fort Bragg during her second four-year stint in the army medical corps. Before she left the military, he'd moved to the CDC and now acted as their military liaison at Pharmacon where he headed up Maya Arrunsen's primary project. He had sought Lauren out for the role as Arrunsen's personal operations assistant, and he'd been blunt about his motivation: "I need Doctor Arrunsen focused one hundred percent on my work, and she's being distracted by this damn mouse. I want you to handle her *pet* project, so she's free to work on mine."

Lauren was at her desk, and after the obligatory pleasantries, he asked, "Where is she?"

"Went home early this morning. Pulled an all-nighter."

"I see." The major stroked his graying goatee, a recent addition, and in Lauren's opinion a poor fit for his round face. She remained silent because he appeared to be struggling with what to say. Finally, he asked, "What's your opinion of her Eureka project? You can speak freely, Lauren."

That was unexpected. "I think it's very exciting. I mean, the science is way above my pay grade, but the doctor has explained the basic concepts. And *FM001* is living proof that the potential for rapid healing exists. Dr. Arrunsen is making progress. We've recorded enhanced healing in thirty percent of the last fifty-five trials."

He nodded, but continued with the beard stroking. "The specimens all died?"

"Yes, sir."

"Humor an old man, Lauren. Explain the concept to me."

"Okay. Well, as Maya, sorry, Doctor Arrunsen says, most functions essential to keep a mammal alive, content, and sexually potent happen without its knowledge—even you and me, Major. For instance, if you had to think about every muscle movement needed to breathe or pump your heart or figure out how to send clotting agents to stem the blood flow at a cut, you'd spend your days bumping into walls and getting nowhere, right?"

The major smiled. "Go on."

"The retrovirus inserts itself and changes the mouse's DNA structure. The changes appear to manifest as a secondary nervous system through which the specimen exercises control over a range of bodily functions normally handled on autopilot. Because they are managed through a parallel network, the control doesn't overload the specimen's conscious mind. The result is a mammal that can micromanage its autonomous systems." Lauren smiled. "Without bumping into walls."

"So she's creating a breed of super mice?"

"Enhanced might be a better definition. The specimens already possess antibodies to combat infections, and mechanisms to clot blood, heal cuts, and repair broken bones. The command and control mechanisms for those capabilities are present in every mammal's brain. Maya believes Eureka and the other specimens who accepted the modified virus can *direct* those autonomous functions. None of the healing processes demonstrated by an infected mouse is extraordinary. If I cut Eureka with a scalpel or infect her with a disease, she amplifies her existing autonomous abilities. The same way a mouse controls the speed at which it runs, a *modified* mouse can control the speed with which it grows skin or clots blood, or attacks and destroys cancerous cells. The difference is in the speed and method of control."

"Thank you," he said.

"But aren't you familiar with the premise?"

"As I explained when I recruited you, my focus lies elsewhere." He shrugged.

"I understand." Lauren didn't *want* to know why McGeehan's group was modifying deadly viruses. She suspected it was a military project that fell into a politically gray area for the CDC, which was why they contracted the work to Pharmacon.

"May I?" He pointed to the seat beside her desk.

"Of course."

He sat. "I need to share something with you."

He fixed her with a hard stare. Heat flooded her neck and cheeks. Although she was a civilian now, she was still uncomfortable with this level of scrutiny from a senior ranking officer.

"Do you believe Maya's hypothesis to be provable?"

Lauren blew out the breath she'd been holding. She had assumed he was going to speak about Dr. Arrunsen's *other* project and that unsettled her. Because Maya was so obsessive about the Eureka project, Lauren mentally partitioned that *other* work in a place where she didn't have to face the likelihood of what it entailed. With the major sitting here, she couldn't avoid her conclusions. But she could talk about the healing retrovirus all day; she was a believer. And on those occasions when she lost faith, Eureka slept in a cage on the far side of the lab, capable of demonstrating the power of rapid healing if Lauren were inclined to use a scalpel.

"Yes, sir. I do. After all, one and a half million years ago, our ancestors were hunter-gatherers with a life expectancy of twenty years. They hadn't even discovered fire. Advances in communication have exponentially accelerated our species' advancement potential. A half million years from now, surely our future selves will be far more capable than our twenty-first century selves. The DNA changes in Eureka represent an evolutionary leap forward. If *FM001* were fertile and her offspring possessed those healing capabilities, her gene line would have significant natural advantages for survival and would prosper. Eighty million years ago, humans and mice shared a common ancestor. Some mouse genes are ninety-nine percent similar to human genes. If Dr. Arrunsen can replicate the autonomous-healing DNA and transfer the enhancement to humans it could give our race a shortcut to an evolutionary future where diseases no longer dictate when we will die." Lauren tilted her head. "But why ask?"

The major took a few seconds before speaking his mind. "Very well… last week, Doctor Arrunsen requested to be relieved of her duties outside of the Eureka project. Initially, I refused. My deadlines are fast approaching, and she is a key member of my team. When I recruited you, I explained your purpose was to free up her time so I could have more of it."

Lauren straightened. Perhaps this was about her after all. Perhaps she was about to lose her job. "I believe I've achieved that objective, sir."

He leaned back in his chair and filled his chest. When he next spoke, his voice was weary, carrying a weight he didn't wish to bear. "Yes, Lauren. You have, admirably. But yesterday Maya received bad news from her oncologist—end-of-life type bad news—leaving me no option but to grant her request and to change your objectives. Maya is no fool. She knows this—" he waved his hand at the lab, "—is a Hail Mary pass. But I'd like you to assist her in any way you can."

Hot tears welled in Lauren's eyes. A band tightened around her chest. She opened her desk drawer, pulled out a Kleenex and blew her nose, buying time. After a deep breath, she asked, "I didn't know the cancer was that advanced. What about chemo?"

"Apparently, that door closed many months ago."

"So the Eureka project was her solution all along?" The consequences seeped into Lauren like a damp fog. She wiped a clammy hand across her cheek. Tears were close. If she'd known, she would have worked longer hours. They could have accelerated the experiments. "I should have done more."

"Nonsense. You did everything Dr. Arrunsen wanted."

"How—" Lauren's voice choked off. She swallowed the cotton in her throat. "How long?"

"Weeks, not months."

"If she'd only confided in me." Lauren covered her mouth.

"She's a proud woman. But I know you'll help her any way you can."

"Of course."

CHAPTER 5

Two weeks later, on Saturday afternoon, Lauren looked on while her mom fed Joshua. They were in a small ward adjacent to the NICU. The boy, still only five pounds, nestled in his grandmother's arms and sucked on a bottle of formula. Margaret eased the nipple from his lips and passed the bottle to Lauren, who held it up to the light. "An ounce and a half." She turned to the pediatric nurse. "Are you sure the nipple's not too small—he seems to be working awfully hard for his dinner."

The RN, a slender Asian woman, glanced up from changing the covers in the boy's crib. "We can certainly try a larger hole. It's difficult to judge with one so premature. But it's a good sign, Ms. Doolan. Joshua is growing stronger every day."

The first forty-eight hours had been touch and go for both infants, then Joshua had started to improve. After six weeks, he'd gained enough strength to leave the NICU, and now that he was taking milk orally Joshua should continue to improve, although the doctor said it might take twelve months to reach average weight for his age. How high functioning he'd be was still in doubt because of the head trauma he had suffered. "The brain is a remarkable instrument, Miss Doolan," Dr. Pavan had said. "Joshua may catch up on all fronts. The only certainty, however, is that he's past the worst."

On hearing this, Lauren's mom had nodded sagely and said, "He's in God's hands, Doctor."

Pavan had looked quite put out, and Lauren sympathized with the man. After years of study to learn his trade and then working his ass off to save Joshua's life, it must have stung to know that, in Margaret's mind, God, and not Doctor Pavan's medical skill, was responsible for Joshua's survival.

Grandma teased the nipple back into Joshua's mouth and he clamped on.

"If only Susan would catch up," Lauren said with a hopeful, questioning lift in her voice.

Head down, the nurse finished with the crib. Her silence was deafening.

"Could I hold her today?" Lauren asked. Physical contact had been limited to poking her latex-gloved hands through holes in the side of Susan's isolator.

"I'm sorry, Ms. Doolan, Susan's still too weak to be handled."

"Are there any plans to move her from the NICU?"

The nurse discarded her gloves and rubbed in hand sanitizer, preparing to leave. She answered without meeting Lauren's eyes. "You'll need to speak to the doctor."

But Lauren didn't want to ask Dr. Pavan *that* question. She was too unsure of the answer.

Watching the twins through the viewing window on the night of Patsy's death, Lauren had felt distant, disconnected. Unspeakable grief for her sister left no room for babies. But things had changed; emotions had shifted. Cliff had murdered Patsy, of that Lauren was sure. And if not for modern medicine, he would have ended Joshua and Susan. Her sister wasn't here, so Patsy's responsibility now passed to Lauren. She would never abandon these children to the tragic lifestyle that had broken and eventually killed their mother. They deserved to be loved and cared for, deserved a family. Above all, they deserved to choose their own life path.

Margaret put down the feeding bottle and eased Joshua onto her shoulder. Maybe because he was more available, or because he was the boy she'd always yearned for, her mother had connected with Joshua. But baby Susan was Lauren's mission. Nine years earlier, she chose an army career over a teen pregnancy. That decision had left an open seam in her heart. Every day spent with Susan sewed one small stitch to seal the scar. To lose her now would be as devastating as losing Patsy. Worse—Patsy had made decisions, poor ones, but they were hers to make. Like the life that had been extinguished from Lauren's womb, this child had no choice. But if Lauren hadn't made her own desperate decision, she wouldn't now have the ability to help Patsy's children. So perhaps this was destiny.

Four weeks earlier, Lauren had moved out of her downtown Atlanta apartment—her first place of her own—without a backward glance. Compared with Susan's life struggle, the sacrifice seemed inconsequential. Moving back in with her mom, sleeping in the room where she'd grown up, was a reversal she had never contemplated. But the twins had changed that. The twins had changed everything.

Lauren left her mother with Joshua and visited Susan in the NICU. She sat beside the incubator and watched the baby's tiny chest rise and fall. She caressed her little girl's bare leg with a latex-gloved finger.

But she didn't ask for Dr. Pavan.

"I'm off to church," her mother said.

Sitting at the kitchen table, Lauren glanced up from her Sunday newspaper. "Okay."

Her mom hovered in the doorway. "Are you sure you won't come? There's a *healing* service today."

The audacity of the question triggered a surge of anger. She'd told her mother often enough what she thought of Reverend Freddie Morgan, pastor of New Beginnings Church. While she and Patsy were growing up, their mom could barely make food and rent on the pittance the grocery store paid her, but she never failed to hand over a tithe to the church. "You know how I feel about you giving money to that charlatan."

"You shouldn't speak like that about the reverend."

Lauren slammed her paper on the table. "Reverend of what, exactly?"

Her mother adopted her pious face—lips pursed, eyebrows raised in judgment—not Lauren's favorite look. "They are darkened in their understanding due to the hardness of their heart."

"Quote the Bible at me all you want, but once the twins come home and I'm the family's sole breadwinner, this has to stop." Lauren pointed a finger at her mother. "And where does it say in the Bible that a mother should steal food from her children's mouths to pay for a church membership?"

Her mother reared back and jutted out her chin. "I don't know where you get these ideas from. For your information, I've already spoken to the deacon about our new arrangement, and she told me once I leave my job, I can continue as a member without paying a tithe."

"Well, good. Have a nice time." Lauren snatched up her paper, and her mom left. She should know better than to get involved in these arguments. Her mom *totally* believed that severe illnesses were *healed* through prayer, and Lauren *totally* did not. There was no logic involved. There was no common ground. And there never would be.

When her mom returned from church, Lauren had lunch prepared.

"There was a wonderful *healing* today," her mom said.

Lauren took a big bite of her sandwich and used the chewing time to calm herself.

Margaret apparently mistook the silence for a green light. She continued, "And the congregation prayed for Susan. After the service, I spoke to the reverend, and he agreed to lay hands on her and Joshua as soon as we could bring them by."

Lauren swallowed her mouthful, and with a steadiness to her voice that belied the anger bubbling inside said, "We are *never* exposing the twins to that crook."

Margaret winced and tears glazed her eyes. Lauren felt like a bully, but there was a limit to how much of the woman's blind belief in this superstitious nonsense she could tolerate. If her mom received inner peace from attending church, that was up to her. But the twins were off limits. They finished lunch in silence.

At two thirty, Lauren parked at the hospital and walked with her mother to the NICU. By now, they were on first-name terms with the nursing staff, who greeted them like old friends when they entered the baby floor. Joshua was in a small ward reserved for babies who had recently graduated from the intensive care unit. Currently, he was the only occupant. Margaret headed there to give him his afternoon feed, and Lauren wandered over to the nurses' station for an update. "How're they doing today?"

The head nurse looked up from her tablet and smiled. "The doctor thinks Joshua will be well enough to leave the hospital next week."

"Wow! That's great news. And Susan?"

The smile faded. Her expression transformed into a noncommittal mask. The detachment in the nurse's eyes shivered through Lauren's belly.

"Doctor Pavan will be here at four thirty. He's asked to see you."

Lauren cleared her throat, buying time to steady her voice. "Of course. Is something wrong?"

The nurse's lips pinched together as though she were squeezing a small seed. "The doctor can explain in more detail; better to wait, okay?"

"Okay. Thanks." On cotton legs, Lauren made her way to Joshua's room.

Her mom said, "What's wrong? You look as though you've seen a ghost."

Margaret seemed so fulfilled, sitting in the nursing chair, cuddling her tiny grandson as he slurped his bottle. How would her mom handle the news that Lauren believed was coming in a few hours? How would Lauren handle it? Perhaps she'd misinterpreted the nurse's body language. "I'm fine. I'll just say hi to Susan. You okay here?"

"Sure, off you run, honey." Her mother smiled. "It's okay to have a favorite, you know. You were mine, and it didn't do you any harm."

Lauren stopped as though she'd run into a wall, turned. "I always thought Patsy was your favorite."

"Patsy needed me more."

"But you were so angry when I joined the army."

Her mom shook her head. "It hurt when you left. And Patsy gave me hell for weeks. She blamed me for pushing you away."

Lauren swallowed the rock in her throat. "Is that why Patsy moved in with Cliff? Was that my fault?"

Her mom looped her arm around Joshua so she could hold the bottle in one hand. With the other, she reached up and took Lauren's fingers. Looking into her eyes, she said, "Never think that. None of this is your fault. Patsy was willful, and I'm the one who wasn't strong enough. I know why you did what you did. You didn't want to end up like me. And I don't blame you."

She was right. But the words made Lauren's decision sound selfish and cold. Should she have stayed home to look after her mother and Patsy? But how? And with what? On a shelf-packer's pay?

Her mom squeezed Lauren's fingers. "I'm proud of how you've built a life for yourself, become your own person, landed such an important job. And your sister was too."

"Patsy told you that?"

"She talked about following your example, of joining the army like her big sister when she was eighteen—until Cliff got in the way."

Lauren spun around and headed for the intensive care unit with tears welling in her eyes. She had been her mother's favorite.

And now Susan was Lauren's.

Once she'd donned a gown, mask, and latex gloves, the duty nurse let her into the NICU. Grabbing a chair, Lauren headed for Susan's isolator and settled beside her niece. She pushed one hand through the hole in the side of the box, and with her latex-covered finger softly stroked the baby's cheek. Bending close to the side of the plastic, she whispered, "Hello, Susan. How are you today?" The child remained unresponsive. Her chest lifted and fell with the regular rhythm of the respirator as it forced air through the pink tube plugged into her mouth.

Last week, Susan's face had twitched when Lauren touched it. A thrill of excitement had surged through her chest, stolen her breath, and made her believe her baby was coming back from wherever she was. Like one of those coma victims in the movies who awoke after months in a vegetative state. Her niece never repeated the reaction, although each time she laid a finger on the child's face, Lauren's heart thumped with anticipation and hope.

The heart monitor bleeped away. Too fast, it always seemed to Lauren, but when she had challenged the doctor on the topic, he explained that an infant's heart rate should be high. Plastic tubes dripped nourishment through Susan's nose and saline into her bloodstream. Like an occupant of *The Matrix*, Susan wasn't really living. She was *kept* alive.

But for how long?

When the nurse tapped Lauren's shoulder, she jumped with fright. She'd been in that faraway place where Susan's cherubic features lit up with a toothless smile and her eyes—chocolate brown, the nurse had informed her, because Lauren had never seen them open—sparkled with intelligence and mischief.

"Doctor Pavan is here to see you." The woman pointed to the adjacent room. Through the window, Lauren saw her mom holding Joshua and standing beside the doctor, talking.

"Okay, thanks." After one last hope-filled stroke of Susan's pale, sunken cheek, Lauren withdrew her hand and turned away. Weak-kneed, she headed across the NICU. A band of fear wrapped her throat, making breathing difficult. Her feet moved—left, right—but lightheadedness made the room appear ethereal. Like Susan.

Once out of the NICU, Lauren removed her gown, mask, and gloves and followed her mom and the doctor to a small consulting room. He closed the door behind them. Air wheezed from an overhead register. When he spoke, his voice sounded flat, as though he were delivering a practiced sermon rather than a patient update. "Joshua here—" He cupped the boy's head in one hand. Replete from his bottle, the baby remained asleep, snuggled against his grandma's breast. A thin line of spittle had escaped his open mouth and left a dark spot on her blouse. "—is our star patient. But I think he's seen enough of the hospital. I'd like you to take him home on Tuesday."

A broad grin lit her mom's face, and she squeezed and rocked her grandson. They had bonded, and the joy of taking him home to care for was writ large in her expression. Lauren clamped her back teeth together. Jaw locked and tight, she waited.

"Sometimes," the doctor said.

"Ah." The sound came from Lauren, high and squeaky and unbidden.

Pavan gave her a fatherly smile. "Sometimes, despite our best efforts, a premature baby can't transition from the womb to the world outside." He faced Lauren as he pronounced a death sentence on her niece. "Both babies suffered internal damage, but the trauma marks on Susan's skull indicate she was closest to the abdominal wall during the attack. She suffered an interventricular hemorrhage."

"Sorry, doctor?" Margaret squinted up at the man.

He smiled and faced Margaret, clearly relieved to discuss diagnostics and not emotions. "The blows caused bleeding inside her brain."

Margaret's hand moved to her mouth. "Oh, dear."

He returned his focus to Lauren. "I'm sorry, but I see no possibility for recovery. My recommendation is to switch off her life support systems and let nature take its course."

He touched Lauren's arm. The contact triggered tears that welled and then spilled down her cheeks. She'd known this was coming, but when it did, his prognosis was so raw and his voice so cold that the words numbed her mind.

Susan deserved better, so much better. She deserved a mother, deserved a life, deserved a chance, not a no-good father who stole her beauty with his boots.

"I'm sorry, Miss Doolan, but we can do nothing more for Susan."

Joshua opened his eyes. He twisted and strained in his grandmother's arms, so she had to readjust her grip. Then his face screwed into a grimace, and he started to cry. Margaret bounced and shushed, but the cries grew louder, more insistent, as though he sensed what the doctor had said about his sister.

Still with one hand on Lauren's elbow, Pavan softened his voice. "Why not spend time tomorrow saying goodbye, Ms. Doolan. I'm sure you'll have a lot of questions. I've arranged an end-of-life conference at four p.m. with Susan's neurologist and your patient advocate." He glanced at her mother. "I'd like you both to attend." Lauren felt her head nodding yes, but anger boiled inside. She had to get out of the room before she exploded. Lauren yanked her arm from the doctor's fingers, spun around and left the room, banging the door behind her.

This wasn't right.

This wasn't fair.

She reached the hospital parking lot with no recollection of how she had arrived there. The sun blasted down. A hot wind twisted and swirled a cloud of dust and trash in a concrete corner to her left. Ahead, a low wall surrounded the hospital's formal flower gardens. Lauren headed there, sat, buried her face in her hands, and sobbed out her grief.

Eventually, her mom found her. She draped a thin arm around her daughter's shoulders. Lauren looked up briefly before covering her face again, staring into her fingers, trying to conjure a reason to contradict the doctor. Down deep, she had always known Susan wouldn't make it. Denial and love had fed her hopes. Pavan was right—damn him. The isolator, the care, would help someone else's baby, a baby with more fight, strong enough to struggle past its injuries and come back to the light.

"I'm sorry, Lauren," her mom said. "Perhaps it's for the best. Maybe she was suffering. How can we tell? I know you don't believe, but she's going to a better place. Like the doctor said, Susan needed a miracle, and only God performs miracles. If it was the Lord's will to save her, he would have."

Lauren whispered into her fingers, "There are no miracles." But that wasn't true. She *had* witnessed a miracle of sorts. Springing to her feet, suddenly aware of being short of time, she said, "Come on, Mom. You need to prepare Joshua's room. I'll drop you at home. I have work to finish."

"On Sunday?"

"Yes."

CHAPTER 6

One hour later, the security guard at Pharmacon's outer gate checked Lauren's ID before lifting the barrier and waving her through. Absent the weekday crush of vehicles, only a couple dozen cars were in the lot, so she parked close to the entrance to Building C. Lawnmowers droned, and the thick air smelled of gardenias and fresh-cut grass.

She hurried to the door and swiped her key card to gain entry.

With her fingers mentally crossed, Lauren strode through the corridors and swiped again to access the main lab. She made a beeline for the vivarium that contained female mouse *162*—Dr. Arrunsen's latest experimental subject. If the mouse had survived. If Maya had finally cracked the genetic code, that could change everything.

The tank appeared empty until Lauren saw the rodent's tail poking out from beneath a small straw nest it had constructed in one corner. Hope ticked up her pulse, and she leaned close to the top of the vivarium and tapped her nails on the glass. When the mouse didn't react, she pulled on latex gloves, lifted the lid, and disturbed the straw with one finger. *FM162* was curled up in the corner of the tank, stiff and dead. The full weight of Susan's plight closed on Lauren like a casket lid. One hundred sixty-one times she'd hoped, and one hundred sixty-one times those hopes had been dashed. But today wasn't about career advancement. Today was about family. The failed experiment was a punch to the belly. Her knees jellied, and she leaned against a stainless steel workbench for support. Even if the mouse had survived, Lauren's plan was a long shot. But now? A cold cup of hopelessness spilled onto her scalp and shivered down her body. Did it even make sense to continue?

The proof that the impossible did happen, that Maya Arrunsen's experiments were justified and hundreds of mice had given their lives for a worthwhile cause, resided at the far end of the laboratory. Despondent, Lauren drifted across the room and peered into the oversized cage with its "Eureka" nameplate attached to the top bars. The large white mouse, *FM001*, stood on hind legs, gripping the bars, whiskers twitching as though in greeting. Lauren selected an almond from a tin of snacks. The mouse's vivid violet eyes followed her every move; the rodent had seen this movie before; she knew how it played out. "Here you go, Eureka." She poked the treat into the cage. *FM001* grasped the nut in both paws, positioned it vertically, and gnawed at the sharp end.

The mouse was an anomaly whose survival had spawned an unusual research protocol. Instead of seeking a solution to disease through experimentation, Doctor Arrunsen's challenge was to reverse-engineer and duplicate what Eureka had already achieved.

Lauren rolled her neck and rubbed tension from her forehead. The mouse nibbled the nut and studied her. The close attention Eureka paid to the goings-on in the lab could be unnerving. Steve Babbington, the lab manager, called her "creepy eyes," but Doctor Arrunsen believed the violet irises were a key marker, a clue to what had changed in *FM001*'s DNA.

Lauren turned from the mouse and opened a two-foot-square fridge mounted on the table near the cage. She removed a tray of vials and scanned the labels until she found one marked *FM104*. The mouse treated with this version of the retrovirus had shown the most rapid healing results, *and* she had lived for nine hours—ten percent longer than the next best specimen had. But still she had died. Baby Susan weighed three pounds, six ounces. The ampule contained 2cc. Nowhere near enough. Meager hope faded. The blanket of despair wound tighter, crushing her chest. Her hands were clammy, the room stuffy.

In the hallway outside the lab someone laughed. Lauren froze, ampule in hand, caught in the act. She could lose her job, and worse. Her pounding pulse thrummed blood through her ears. The consequences of what she intended to do slammed into her—a little late. She spun around. Stared at the door. Groomed her hair with her fingers. The laugh sounded again, but quieter—moving away. She exhaled the breath she'd been holding.

The risk of discovery forced her decision. Lauren pierced the stopper with a hypodermic needle and extracted the serum. After covering the tip with a safety cap, she placed the loaded syringe into a plastic baggie and slipped it into her pocket before dropping the empty vial into the sharps container reserved for biohazard waste.

When she turned back to the workbench and saw that she'd left the fridge gaping, Lauren let out a nervous laugh. "I'm not a very competent burglar." As though it understood the words, Susan's only glimmer of hope, still standing on its hind legs, stopped eating and locked intelligent eyes with hers. Lauren closed the fridge and slipped a second almond through *FM001*'s bars.

"Wish me luck, Eureka," she whispered, and headed for the door.

When Lauren arrived home, her mom had dinner ready.

"Let me take a quick shower, first." Lauren grabbed a soda from the fridge and tucked the plastic bag containing the syringe behind a six-pack of yogurts at the back of the top shelf. Kept cool overnight, the serum should be fine unless the virus had been damaged on her drive home. Could it survive a one-hour trip to the hospital? Did it even matter? Likely not, but that wasn't the point. The point was to try. Maya Arrunsen, the smartest woman she knew, had thought it could work. If Lauren didn't try, for the rest of her life she would regret her inaction. And the act of trying kept hope alive and thoughts of Susan's death at bay.

After her shower, as she passed her mom's bedroom, a change snagged her eye. The furniture had been rearranged. Lauren went in and stopped beside Joshua's crib. She touched the blue mobile suspended above the neat blue bedding and made it rotate and chime. The second crib, the one with pink coverlets that she and her mom had placed there weeks ago, when their hopes had been high, had been dismantled and put away. The symbolism stung like a face slap. For a religious woman, Margaret's faith seemed lacking. Susan's crib should still be standing beside

Joshua's. There was still a chance. Lauren spun out of the bedroom and marched into the kitchen. "You're all ready for *Joshua*, I see."

Her mom had her back turned, plating their dinners at the stove. She missed the sarcasm.

"Who would have dreamed it would happen so quickly. I mean, when I saw him through the window that first night after Patsy I—"

Her mom paused to wipe a sleeve across her face and took a few deep breaths before bringing their food to the table. A drawstring cinched Lauren's throat. She shouldn't blame her mother for moving the crib. Maybe that was her way of handling the situation. This was tough for them both. "Mom. Sit. Eat."

Margaret took her place and stared at the table. "I moved Susan's crib."

Lauren took a steadying breath. "I noticed."

"Only to the hall cupboard. I couldn't stand the thought of it laying there beside Joshua, empty."

Lauren reached across and squeezed her mom's arm. Margaret was avoiding the shadow of what they were losing and focusing on the joy of gaining a life they had thought lost. It made sense. Her mom had tried everything she knew to help Susan—even if New Beginnings Church's collection plate *was* the main beneficiary. "You're right."

Her mom looked up, met Lauren's eyes, and smiled. "I can hardly believe he'll be here in two days."

"Me neither."

Lauren turned in early and took a sleep aid. She needed to be fresh tomorrow, and without pharmaceutical help, her mind would bounce around all night thinking of Eureka, scouring remembered test results for missed clues or a crucial parameter overlooked.

And dwelling on what was stored in the fridge.

Monday morning, she called human resources and took a sick day. She and her mom arrived at the hospital at nine fifty. Lauren wore scrubs, partly for ease of access to the hypodermic concealed in her right pocket, partly to blend in—she wanted to draw as little attention to herself as possible.

She waited while her mom lifted Joshua from his crib and settled him on her knee. Still thin of face and limb with an unsteady head, Joshua had begun to respond to human contact, especially his grandma; he clearly knew her, even if only as a feeding machine.

Her mom settled him in the crook of her arm and looked up. "Lauren, don't take this the wrong way. I can't… I don't want to visit Susan."

Lauren didn't press. Everyone has the right to say goodbye in their own way. "I understand, Mom. You look after Joshua." Tears welled in Lauren's eyes as she prepared to leave the two of them, to carry out her mission. Was Joshua's fate better than Susan's? The boy was growing. The crisis was over, and he would survive, but what life prospects did he have? According to Pavan, only time would tell, but the cautious manner in which the doctor had delivered those words told Lauren he anticipated problems for the boy.

Margaret looked up. "I thought you were going to visit Susan?"

Lauren had been standing stock still, staring at Joshua. The question snapped her reverie. "Sure. I'll see you for lunch."

As she turned, her hand brushed against the syringe in her pocket and her heart bounced. If someone caught her with the drug, she would be in a world of trouble. She'd lose her job for removing the specimen from Pharmacon. She'd never work as a medical technician again. She'd be back to stacking supermarket shelves, if she was lucky. And God only knew what the authorities might do if they caught her injecting a premature baby with a serum derived from an experimental retrovirus and stolen from a federally funded research project. And in a neonatal unit to boot. They'd lock her in prison for sure.

Janet Simms opened the door from inside the NICU. "Hi, Lauren. Sorry. I didn't hear you knock. Have you been waiting long?"

Lauren had been standing, not knocking. "I just arrived."

"Come on in. You know where to find her."

"Thanks, Janet."

Stepping into that room was like leaping off a ledge without knowing how steep the drop was or what lurked below.

"You've dressed the part today, I see," the nurse said.

"Huh? Oh—" She struggled to catch a breath. The scrubs had prompted the opposite response to the one she had intended, drawing attention *to* her. Simms tilted her head, awaiting an answer.

"I have to work later," Lauren said.

Simms frowned. "Oh?"

"The scrubs seemed easier."

"Anyway, enjoy your visit." Color flooded the nurse's face. Obviously realizing the insensitivity of her comment, she spun away. All the staff would know this was Lauren's last visit. Tonight, the isolator would be turned off. Tomorrow it would be sterilized, and a new baby would take Susan's place.

Her niece was at the far side of the ward. Lauren weaved through the other incubators and settled into her usual chair beside Susan's plastic cube. She stared at her niece's thin face, watched her chest go through the motions, and listened to the heart monitor's familiar pulse. Reaching through the sidewalls into the incubator, she touched her niece's cheek, for once unsure if she desired a reaction. If Susan showed signs of life, would Lauren have the guts to try the serum? Could she carry the guilt of speeding her niece's death? Except for Eureka, every test specimen had died within hours of treatment. The retrovirus wasn't ready for animal trials let alone a human one.

But no cheek-twitch complicated Lauren's impending decision to take a wild gamble with Susan's life.

"What life?" The words came from her unbidden and aloud. Lauren checked over her shoulder. The nursing staff were busy with a new arrival. With her back to the room, Lauren had unfettered access to the infant. She hadn't pondered the *when* of the planned act. Worrying about the *if* had consumed her thoughts.

But if there *was* to be a when. It was now.

Another furtive glance behind showed no one near, no one paying her any mind. Lauren withdrew her arm from the isolator. She took a deep breath, retrieved the baggie from her pocket, and concealed it in her lap. After opening the Ziploc, she gripped the needle tip's safety cover through the plastic then put her fingers inside the bag and slid the syringe out, tip bared, leaving the cover behind. She held the hypodermic in her palm, secured with her thumb.

The piercing, high-pitched screech of an alarm triggered on the isolator to her left. Lauren jerked upright, fumbled the syringe, and it took two attempts to trap it against her thigh. Alarms went off all the time in the NICU, but why now?

She looked around.

Janet Simms was striding toward her, only ten paces away.

Lauren turned in her chair and slipped the baggie into the pocket farthest from the nurse. She moved both hands to her lap.

Simms reset the alarm and scanned the dials on the baby's monitor.

Lauren stared straight ahead at Susan, both hands covering the hypodermic, back rigid, shoulders locked.

Janet moved closer until she stood directly behind Lauren's chair. "I'm sorry to disturb you, but will your mom be coming into the NICU?"

"My mom?"

"We're short staffed. My assistants need a break, but it'll leave no one to open the door for a while."

"I—" Lauren cleared her throat. She didn't turn, fearful of what her eyes would betray. "That is, she prefers not to come in today."

Janet paused. "I understand. I'll leave you then, to your visit."

"Yes, thank you."

Instead of moving away, the woman bent low and peered into Susan's isolator. She seemed about to speak, but instead, reached down and patted the back of Lauren's hands.

Lauren's heart rate was outpacing Susan's monitor. The heat in her face was sure to fire up red blotches on her neck and cheeks. The nurse gave her a sympathetic smile, spun around, and made her way toward the other staff.

Lauren took deep breaths trying to calm down. She felt like a criminal. She was a criminal. When she lifted her hand from her lap and eased it through the lower access hole, nearest to Susan's leg, her fingers trembled so violently that she struggled to grip the syringe.

Breathe.

And breathe.

And breathe.

She glanced around. The assistant nurses had left. Simms was alone on the far side of the room, engrossed in her work. Lauren slid her hand lower until the needle's tip was adjacent to Susan's thigh.

Easing the hypodermic from her palm, she angled it to allow a side penetration into what little muscle existed on her niece's wretched body. She gritted her teeth and pushed the needle tip half an inch into Susan's leg.

Then she depressed the plunger.

And sent 2cc of an untested drug into Susan's body.

As soon as the syringe emptied, she withdrew the instrument and grabbed the baggie from her pocket. Her trembling fingers struggled to guide the safety cover over the needle tip. Once secured, she slipped the hypodermic into her pocket. One last look at Simms—still busy. Lauren sighed out the breath she had held throughout the procedure, and her shoulders sank three inches as the muscles unwound.

Staring at the pallid, unmoving face of her niece, hot flashes of guilt roiled her. Who was she to play God with another human's life? What if she'd hastened Susan's death? Maya Arrunsen had sought a solution, but even she hadn't considered this version of the serum a risk worth taking—she was waiting for something better. But Susan couldn't wait. Lauren shook her head, trying to stop the mental jousting, stop the pointless swaying from one side of the argument to the other. Doctor Pavan was the one who should feel guilty. Pulling the plug on Susan was business as usual for him, a commercial decision, the best use of resources, cutting his losses. To him, the baby was already dead. Hadn't his decision forced Lauren to take this dire action?

No.

This had been her decision. Hers alone. And she would have to live with the consequences—no way to spread the blame.

Lauren bent toward the plastic cube and whispered, "I'm sorry, sweetie." And her eyes filled with hot tears of remorse. She reached a hand into the isolator and stroked Susan's cheek with the back of her gloved finger.

And the baby flinched.

Lauren jerked back in surprise, then leaned in, close to the side of the isolator. She narrowed her eyes and scanned for further movement, but Susan's face remained flat and lifeless.

Lauren reached in and again touched the baby's cheek—nothing. She had imagined the response—wishful thinking. She pressed, firmer, enough to dent the skin—nothing. Hope evaporated.

She stroked the area where the hypodermic had penetrated. Susan didn't react, but Lauren's eyes widened.

Crap.

A red blotch marked the injection site. The staff would notice. Panicked, she rotated in her chair. The nurse was still occupied. When Lauren turned back to the incubator, Susan's left leg, the one that had received the dose, jerked twice. Three heartbeats later, the right leg mimicked the movement. Lauren cursed under her breath. She should have observed the exact time of injection. But she didn't.

Why?

Because she hadn't expected the serum to work.

Susan's arms went through a series of jerky movements, like a marionette whose puppet master was simulating a nightmare by twitching at its strings.

Something was going on inside Susan. This couldn't be coincidental. The drug was affecting the baby. But what effect? If the result corresponded to many of the mice she'd observed, she might be witnessing Susan's death throes.

The enormity of what she'd done stole her breath. She leaned back in her chair and gripped her thighs to stop her hands from shaking. The room swam out of focus. She dug in her nails.

The baby settled. Spasms over, her expression calmed. The wrinkled skin that affected a permanent frown on Susan's forehead, so familiar to Lauren after weeks of staring at the child and memorizing her every fold and mark and pore, seemed less defined.

Lauren stroked Susan's cheek again. The baby's arm twitched and then lifted. The elbow flexed; her fist balled; she reached toward the spot that Lauren had tickled, and attempted a crude rubbing motion.

Hot damn!

The twitching and jerking began again and spread throughout Susan's body. This was no wish-fulfilling delusion. But if the serum was working a miracle, would the miracle last? Why should *this* experiment come to a successful conclusion when the others had ended in death? If Maya Arrunsen's hypothesis about accelerated autonomous functioning was correct, how would those changes translate to a human cortex? Lauren had no way to estimate the effects on a human subject, no way to guess what was going on inside Susan Doolan's body. But something *was* going on.

The folly of what she'd done threatened to overwhelm her. A buzzing started in her ears, and she forced a series of deep breaths, fearful that she would pass out. Like Shelly's Dr. Frankenstein, by endowing life where there was none, had she created a monster? And if so, would her creation survive? Lauren buried her face in her hands. She wanted to fill her lungs and scream. Why hadn't she thought this through?

"Are you all right?"

Lauren sprang up and almost toppled from the chair. The woman laid a hand on Lauren's shoulder. "I'm sorry. I didn't mean to frighten you. You seemed upset. Is everything okay?"

Unable to hide what was happening in the incubator, she had to hide the reason. "Silly of me. I thought Susan moved."

Simms shifted her focus to the isolator, and her eyes widened. She leaned close to the cube. "Good grief!" Susan's limbs were straining and stretching. Her left hand reached toward her mouth, vainly clawing at the breathing tube but unable to master the concept of grasping. "How long has she been like this?"

"A few minutes. At first just tiny movements, so small I couldn't be sure. You do see it, right?"

"I most certainly do." Janet checked Susan's readouts on the life support machine. "Her blood pressure is rising."

"I've never seen color in her cheeks before," Lauren said.

"I'll call Doctor Pavan." Before she left, Janet squeezed Lauren's shoulder and grinned. "Perhaps this is the miracle your mom has been praying for."

Shaking from a concoction of anxiety and relief, Lauren leaned close to the plastic box and whispered, "Hang in there, Susan. Fight for what's yours. Don't let anything take this from you." The spasms of twitching and jerking had given way to a slower rhythm, something more familiar. Susan was stretching her arms and grasping at air, moving like a newborn as she mapped her surroundings and tested her abilities.

Then for the first time, the baby's eyelids flickered open.

And when she stared up at Lauren, Susan's vivid violet eyes gleamed like beacons.

CHAPTER 7

The covers on the cot that the nursing staff placed in Joshua's ward so Lauren could stay the night remained unruffled. Except for a bathroom break, she had never left Susan's side in the NICU. When midnight passed and the baby's vitals were still optimal, hope swelled. Once her niece passed the nine-hour point, they were in uncharted territory. By five p.m., over twenty-four hours after the retrovirus had done its work, Susan had made a believer of Lauren, and she went home to shower.

When she pulled into the driveway, her mother opened the front door and ran down the path. "Is she?"

Lauren sprinted to meet her. She grabbed hold and clung to her mom like a lifesaver. Between sobs and faltering breaths, she gasped out her news. "Yes. Yes, Momma, she's okay. No, she's better than okay, she's good." Not since childhood had Lauren bawled in her mother's arms. They stood in the front garden, and her mom stroked Lauren's hair until the tension of the past twenty-four hours was wrung out of her.

"Come on," her mom said, "a hot shower and some soup. Then off to bed for you."

Lauren didn't argue.

She was back at the NICU by eight the next morning. Susan's vitals were close to normal. Her cheeks were pink, her eyes wide, alert, and filled with intelligence. At nine a.m., Lauren left the intensive care area, and from Joshua's ward she called Pharmacon and asked to speak with Doctor Arrunsen. She couldn't tell the doctor what she'd done, but she couldn't go into work, couldn't bear to leave Susan's side.

Major McGeehan picked up Maya's line.

"Oh? Major. I was looking for Doctor Arrunsen."

His sigh was audible. "Sorry, Lauren, she's not here."

"Is she okay?"

"I'm afraid not. She collapsed at work yesterday. She's been admitted to Wellstar Community Hospice."

Lauren grabbed a chair and slumped down. Phone pressed to her ear, she bent double like a balloon emptied of air. "I... I'm at the hospital with Susan."

"I'm sorry. Is everything okay?"

"She's doing much better, but I wasn't planning to come in today."

"There's nothing to do here right now. Look for me tomorrow and we can discuss next steps."

"Thank you, sir."

She hung up and stared at the floor. How cruel. How unfair. The woman responsible for saving Susan's life was losing her own. Unless. Lauren stripped off her scrubs and gloves. "Problem at work. I have to leave," she said to the duty nurse.

Three hours later, walking through the atrium of Wellstar Community Hospice, Lauren glanced in the window of the gift shop, but dismissed the idea—Maya Arrunsen wasn't the teddy bear type. No. Direct and to the point was the only way. The doctor had chosen hospice rather than undergo chemotherapy. She preferred to "die with dignity." But that was when she had no alternative. Maybe, now, she did.

When Lauren entered Arrunsen's private room, the doctor was sitting up thanks to the elevated angle of her mattress, but her eyes were closed. An untouched plate of food on a tray to the left of the bed gave the room a cafeteria smell. Although Lauren had seen the woman a few days earlier, Maya had lost weight. Translucent skin draped her cheekbones and stretched around eye sockets so prominent that the outline of her skull was visible. Lauren had known about the cancer for months, but an up-close look at the way it had ravaged this vibrant woman churned her stomach and stole her confidence. Coming here was a huge risk.

But without Doctor Arrunsen's brilliance, Lauren would be attending Susan's end-of-life meeting with Doctor Pavan. She owed her the same chance.

The chair screeched as she pulled it close to the bed. Arrunsen opened her eyes and tried a smile. "Lauren." The word came as a whispered croak.

"How are you, Doctor?" As soon as they left her lips, she wanted to snatch back those stupid words. Anyone with half a brain could see how the woman was. Arrunsen, seeming to read Lauren's mind, fixed her with rheumy eyes, and waited.

Direct and to the point. "They were planning to take my niece off the life support machines."

"I'm sorry… When?"

"Today."

Arrunsen frowned and tilted her head. "But?"

"But she has recovered."

Arrunsen's smile creased the paper-thin skin of her cheeks. "That's wonderful news."

"The improvement in Susan's health was so rapid that her doctor called it a miracle." Lauren widened her eyes and raised her eyebrows, trying to convey her message through body language, frightened to expose her role by speaking the truth. But Arrunsen's gaze drifted from Lauren's face, and her head slumped until her chin rested on her breastbone. Her eyelids closed and her breathing faded to a soft rasp.

"Doctor?" Lauren raised her voice. "Doctor!" Maya's eyelids cracked opened, and with an obvious act of will, she lifted her head and refocused on Lauren.

"Doctor Arrunsen. Yesterday Susan had brown eyes. Today they're violet."

Arrunsen blinked three times. Lauren could almost see her forcing the words through the fog of end-of-life drugs. She reached out a hand and squeezed Lauren's fingers. "How?"

"*FM104.*"

When Arrunsen rocked forward, Lauren thought she had started coughing, but instead, a soft gurgling laugh shook her frame. She patted Lauren's arm and whispered, "Brave girl."

This was the moment. Lauren's chest tightened. She couldn't draw a breath. She glanced behind. They were alone. She dipped a hand into her purse, retrieved a plastic bag containing a hypodermic syringe, and held it in Maya's line of sight. Inches from Maya's ear she whispered, "I used all the *FM104* serum, but I brought *FM105* with me."

Arrunsen pointed to the water jug on her bedside table. After tucking the plastic-wrapped needle under the bedcovers, Lauren half-filled a glass and pushed in a straw. The doctor lifted her hand, which trembled for a few seconds and then flopped onto the bed. Lauren moved the drink near to the doctor's mouth and guided the straw to her lips. Maya sipped, then again, before waving the glass away. She sank back into her pillow; her face sagged, and she wheezed in a shallow breath, sounding as though she'd run a marathon.

Lauren whispered, "Tell me what to do, Doctor."

A wry smile settled on the old woman's lips and she said, *"Quand t'as rien, t'as plus rien à perdre."*

Shaking her head, Lauren frowned.

The doctor patted Lauren's hand; the touch of her fingers reminded Lauren of a baby bird's fluttering wing. "Bob Dylan." Breathless, she panted. Each inhale came with a wince; each exhale rattled like punctured bellows. "It means," she said, "When you've got nothing, you've got nothing to lose." The doctor turned her arm over and raised her sleeve, exposing her bare forearm. "Give me the syringe."

Lauren slipped her hands below the covers and extracted the hypodermic from the baggie. Recalling the last time she played out this drama, anxiety cramped her stomach. This was different—somehow worse. She had been protecting Susan, protecting her from a system that had already proclaimed her time of death. But this act seemed wrong. Maya Arrunsen was adult, aware, complicit. The shared risk should be easier to manage, but instead, her decision was drenched in doubt.

The doctor accepted the syringe and pressed it against her wrist. The tip indented her skin, but her grip failed and the instrument slipped from her fingers and rolled across the covers in slow motion. Lauren's hand shot out and caught the needle by the tip—millimeters from sticking herself. Nausea washed through her. She dry heaved and swallowed, dry heaved and swallowed. When she regained her composure, her throat stung from acid bile.

With half concealing, glassy eyes that swam in and out of focus behind drooping eyelids, Arrunsen locked then lost, locked then lost eye contact. Then she pointed one trembling finger at Lauren. "You," she wheezed. Her eyes drifted sideways, and the lids closed. Her head slumped forward, and her breathing shallowed.

Lauren hid the syringe beneath the covers again, leaned in, and hissed in Maya's ear, "Doctor... Doctor!"

Arrunsen exhaled a stale breath, and then for ten long seconds her chest didn't rise. Panic gripped Lauren and lodged in her gut like a hardened mass. She straightened and frantically scanned the woman's face for signs of life. Finally, the doctor sucked in a wavering breath that gurgled in her chest. The sound stood Lauren's arm hairs on end. It was the sound of a woman on her deathbed.

"Doctor?" Lauren said.

"Is everything okay here?"

Lauren snapped upright and turned her head, eyes wide, a rabbit caught in a snare. The nurse standing behind her—a tall African American man in green scrubs—raised an eyebrow and waited. Did he suspect something?

She coughed and cleared her throat. "Yes. Of course. Everything's fine. I'm a colleague... a friend. Doctor Arrunsen drifted off in mid-sentence. I was—"

His face softened. "It's nothing personal. The pain meds make her sleepy."

Lauren nodded. Heat prickled her face and neck—if he'd come in seconds earlier... "I'll sit with her a while if that's okay." She reached across and laid her hand on Maya's arm, using her elbow to protect the place where she'd secreted the serum.

The nurse moved around the bed and took Arrunsen's pulse. "Sure. Stay as long as you want. I'll be out of your hair in a moment." He updated Maya's chart. "I'm Robert." He tapped the plastic name tag pinned to his chest. "Buzz if she needs anything."

"Thanks." Lauren's forced smile froze on her face. Robert left, and she took a dozen deep breaths to calm herself. After checking to make sure he'd gone, she shook Maya's shoulder—perhaps a little roughly—but couldn't wake her.

The decision towered before her.

For Susan.

Beneath the covers, Lauren gripped the plastic bag and pulled out the hypodermic, unshielded. In one swift action, leaving no room for second thoughts, she pierced the doctor's forearm and depressed the plunger. After expelling the serum, she returned the syringe to the bag and stuffed the evidence into her purse.

Maya slept on. Lauren stood and paced the room. She peered outside into the empty hallway. Her cheeks burned. She moved back to the bed and again shook the doctor, but she remained asleep. Lauren lifted the chart from the bottom of the bed and checked the morphine regime. Perhaps out-cold was a more accurate assessment than asleep. She replaced the chart and leaned in close to the doctor. "Come on, Maya."

Arrunsen's right arm jerked upward and slapped Lauren's chest. Lauren backed away. The motion repeated and then spread to both arms. Maya's head jolted upright. Color flooded her cheeks. Her eyes sprang open—pale blue, filled with life—and stared directly at Lauren. "It's quite logical." The doctor's voice was pitched high, excited.

"Logical?" Lauren asked.

"Yes. If not for the attack on your sister, Susan would still be floating around in her mother's amniotic fluid. In effect, she is closer to a fetus than a fully formed human baby. How much does she weight?"

"A little over four pounds."

"Exactly. A fetus. So was Eureka... How ironic." She threw back her head and let out a forced maniacal laugh.

"Excuse me?"

"Our friend Major McGeehan is trying to figure out how to construct a non-infectious, targeted killing agent, and he's inadvertently created the exact opposite."

Lauren blinked a couple times as she assimilated that information. "Should you be discussing this with me?"

Maya smiled and patted Lauren's hand. "Of course not, my dear."

The way the doctor's eyes scanned the room—left, right, up, down, pausing only for a fraction of a second between moves—unnerved Lauren. "But you're not a fetus," Lauren said, "and the serum seems to be working. Does that mean—?"

Arrunsen's hands shot to either side of her head and she let out a piercing scream. A terror mask transformed her face. Beads of sweat peppered her forehead.

Robert rushed into the room. "What happened?" He focused on the heart monitor. Erratic blips stormed across the screen. An alarm triggered and he silenced it. Arrunsen's pulse read one seventy-three.

"She woke up and started rambling. Then she screamed." Lauren stood and backed away from the bed.

Arrunsen's body was jumping and jerking around as though she was trying to evade a thousand jabbing needle pricks.

Robert hit the panic button.

Maya's body arched up, arms outstretched, hands grabbing like claws at some invisible substance. Her breath sawed in and out with a high-pitched whine. The heart monitor squealed then flat-lined. Her body collapsed like a punctured tire, and she slumped into the mattress.

Back pressed hard against the wall, Lauren was terrified. The retrovirus had only entered the doctor's system fifteen minutes earlier, and yet the chaos had seemed to last for an hour.

Robert picked up Maya's limp wrist and felt for a pulse. A second nurse burst into the room followed by a woman in a white coat—Maya's doctor, Lauren assumed. The doctor glanced at the monitor. Then focused on Lauren. "Who are you?" she snapped.

"A friend."

"Robert. Get her out of here."

He skirted the bed and took Lauren's arm. "This way."

She let him guide her into the hallway. "What happens now?" Lauren asked.

"Nothing. Doctor Arrunsen has a DNR on file."

Lauren tilted her head, questioning.

"Do not resuscitate. It was her wish that CPR not be attempted in the event of a heart failure."

Icicles slid down Lauren's back. Her legs buckled, and Robert wasn't quick enough to catch her. She dropped to her knees and threw up.

She had killed Maya Arrunsen.

CHAPTER 8

After Lauren collapsed in the hospice hallway, a patient advocate, older than Dorothy but cut from the same cloth, had taken her to the cafeteria. They sat for over an hour. Lauren talked about Doctor Arrunsen's brilliance. She talked about Susan and Joshua and her mother and Patsy. Her words tumbled like water from a rain spout. The kindly woman listened. Then she reached out and laid a hand on Lauren's arm. In a voice filled with knowing, she said, "Maya Arrunsen came here to die. You happened to be in the room, but you are not responsible. If there had been a medical solution to her cancer, she would have tried it."

Hearing the truth spoken aloud assuaged her guilt. Lauren had depressed the plunger on the syringe, but Arrunsen had wanted to take that risk. Although the serum failed to save its creator, Arrunsen died happier for knowing she had saved Susan. The next day, Lauren completed her niece's birth certificate application. Memorializing Susan's secret savior, she named the baby Maya Susan Doolan. When Maya was older, Lauren would share with her the significance of her name.

One week later, Janet let her into the NICU. "She's waiting for you." The knowing smile that lit the RN's face sent a nervous tingle through Lauren's chest. Today, for the first time, she would hold her baby. She and the nurse walked together to the isolator. "Maya suits her," Simms said. "I never saw her as Susan." Without the ventilator and feeding tubes, Maya Susan Doolan looked more like a baby and less like a science experiment. "Go ahead. Pick her up."

Lauren stared into the plastic cube, then spun around, suddenly unsure of herself. The nurse grinned and laid a reassuring hand on Lauren's shoulder. "It's okay. She *wants* to be held. It's been awfully lonely lying there all these weeks." Lauren lifted the top of the isolator, and eased it back on its hinges. Leaning over, she reached toward the baby. Maya was so small, so fragile. What if she hurt her? Lauren pulled back. "Perhaps you should—"

"You go on now, Miss Lauren." The nurse chuckled, obviously enjoying the moment. "Sometimes a cuddle is the best medicine, you know."

Lauren slipped her hands under the infant and lifted. Once she cleared the plastic prison, Maya opened her eyes. Deep-violet irises locked onto Lauren and torrents of fear and anguish and pain poured from the infant and buffeted Lauren like physical blows. Her hands weakened and her knees wobbled under the brutal onslaught.

Simms placed her palms below Lauren's, supporting the baby. "Are you okay, Lauren?"

Maya narrowed her eyes; a tiny frown of concentration wrinkled her forehead; then her face softened, and she smiled. Calming waves washed over Lauren. Her nervousness melted away, and her grip tightened. "Yes, of course. I've got her now," Lauren said, pulling Maya close and snuggling her against the soft cotton blouse she'd worn in anticipation of this moment. Unconditional love burst forth from the baby and saturated Lauren. The emotions pulsing through her were an order of magnitude stronger than any previous life experience. Never had Lauren felt as fulfilled as she did right now.

Janet tapped Lauren's arm. "Let's take her through to the ward; I have her crib ready."

Lauren's head snapped up. "Can't I hold her for a while longer?"

"Of course," she said in a soft voice. "Once I get you two situated, I'll bring over a bottle. She's due a feeding."

Lauren followed the nurse, intently focused on her footing lest she bumped into something, or worse, tripped and sent her precious bundle crashing.

Settled in the chair beside the same crib that Joshua had occupied before his discharge, Lauren gazed into Maya's eyes and Maya gazed back, and a silent conversation of love and understanding began. A conversation that Lauren knew would last until her final breath. This miracle child, this crazy, risky experiment had earned her right to life. And Lauren would make sure she lived it to the full whatever her limitations might be.

The nurse returned with a bottle containing four ounces of formula. "Try her with this." She handed over the milk and laid a hand on Lauren's shoulder. "Be patient, now. Don't expect too much. She's very new at this. Even an ounce will be a great achievement." She gave Lauren's shoulder a squeeze and smiled. "Will you be okay?"

Lauren couldn't wait for Janet to leave her alone with her baby, but she kept her voice even and polite. "Yes. Thank you."

The nurse spun away to care for the dozen other preemies who teetered between life and death. Lauren whispered, "But you're not one of those anymore, are you, baby girl?" Maya's eyes moved constantly, mapping Lauren's face. It seemed odd to have to teach a baby to suckle, but quite normal in a premature birth. The nurses had been introducing the concept to Maya all week and assured Lauren her niece had latched on quickly to the concept of oral nourishment. When the tip of the nipple touched Maya's lips, a small frown wrinkled her forehead. Lauren expressed a drop of milk and teased the bottle back and forth. Pink lips parted, allowing the nipple in. The frown deepened, and then the baby sucked. Her eyes widened as though surprised. "Good girl." After a few more frowns, and a toss of the head, Maya began to eat.

How quickly Lauren's attitude to the twins had changed. And especially to Maya. Hard to imagine that her first instinct had been to seek out adoptive parents. No longer. She sat in the nursing chair, staring at her baby's beautiful face, memorizing every pore and fold, marveling at the beauty of her eyes, ensuring her onesie was straight, smelling the newness of her. This child needed her, and that knowledge no longer frightened Lauren. Maya needed a mother, and Lauren willingly volunteered.

When Maya dozed off, Lauren laid her in the crib and tucked her in. She grabbed a sandwich from the cafeteria and hurried back to the ward. Then she called home to check on her mom and explain that she planned to stay late so she could feed Maya again. In the background, Joshua was screaming.

"How long has he been awake?" Lauren asked.

Her mom sighed. "Over an hour. I've tried everything to calm him."

Lauren looked down at Maya, sleeping, replete with milk, content. Cutting off a limb would be easier than leaving her now. But Joshua had already suffered two seizures. The first qualified as the most terrifying experience of Lauren's life: limbs rigid, eyes wide, foam spilling from his mouth. For five minutes, Joshua had jerked and spasmed as though otherworld demons had taken possession of his tiny frame. She couldn't risk a recurrence while her mom was home alone.

"Don't worry, dear. You stay. We'll be fine. I'm sure he'll stop crying soon."

"If you're sure." Lauren hung up the phone, stomach churning with guilt, but she stayed, and Maya took two more ounces before she put her down for the night.

Car windows wide, Lauren sang along with the radio on the drive back. But when she reached home and climbed from her vehicle, harsh reality struck. Josh's screams echoed down the garden path. She ran to the door and let herself in. Her mom was pacing the living room, jogging the baby boy whose cheeks glowed like red balloons. For a little tot, he made a fearsome noise.

"Mom... Mom!"

Her mother spun around; her face tight as a wrung-out washcloth. Lauren tossed her coat on a chair and held out her arms to receive him. The exchange distracted Joshua for a heartbeat, but then he filled his lungs and wailed again. Lauren shouted to be heard. "Did you eat dinner yet?"

"What time is it?"

"Ten thirty. How long has he been like this?"

Her mom sighed. "Since, oh—" She shook her head.

"Never mind. Go. Make yourself a sandwich. I've got this."

Margaret turned and walked away, shoulders crushed inward, head bent. Lauren jiggled her nephew up and down, but the crying became more insistent. What a contrast to her earlier experience with Maya. "Shh, little guy. Your sister'll be coming home soon, and you don't want to be shown up, do you?"

For a five count, Joshua stopped screaming and locked big brown eyes on Lauren, studying her face, then he flinched and screamed again. How long could they survive this?

CHAPTER 9

"Two hundred dollars from Margaret Doolan." Deacon Nina Morgan cranked the lever on her black leather recliner until she was almost horizontal. She held the check high for him to see.

Her husband sat across the living room crouched over his polished wooden desk. A reading light illuminated a scattering of papers. Close to his right hand, ice cubes floated in a tumbler of bourbon. Without lifting his head, he asked, "Should I know her?" He continued to scribble in the margins of his pad with a black Mont Blanc pen.

"You should. According to the note, she's been a member of New Beginnings Church for ten years!" She held a page of lined paper at arm's length, squinted at the handwritten note, and read aloud: "Express our gratitude for my granddaughter, Maya's miraculous recovery."

"Happy we helped," he said. Then he whispered to his desk, "Even happier to see the check." He snickered, picked up his drink, and raised the glass to her before taking a long pull. "Ah!" He smacked his lips.

Nina screwed up her face; she hated that annoying noise, and he made it often enough.

She slapped the back of her hand against the letter. "Damn, Freddie! You know who this is?"

He peered over his reading glasses and waited, lips pursed, impatience painted on his face. The strong jawline was still there. The espresso-colored skin. The deep-brown eyes. The long lashes.

But the unkempt clothes, greasy hair and stubbly face—they weren't part of the original fairy tale. No one stayed the same. That she understood. She had changed, too—hardened. But whose fault was that? She narrowed her eyes, studied him, studied herself. What did she feel? Love? That horse had run its race, ridden into the ground by lack of money and prospects. And his off-hand treatment of her right now—that glowering condescending look—boiled her blood. A two-hundred-dollar check wasn't peanuts. He should be more supportive. Try to work out how to get more checks instead of spending them in the liquor store. "If you don't like it, do something about it," her mom always told her—easily said.

She yanked the lever and *thunked* her recliner upright. "The girl who got beaten to death earlier this year, this came from her mother. She spoke to us before the service two weeks ago and explained she'd have to withdraw her tithe because she's leaving work to care for her grandkids."

He shook his head—still clueless.

"The Doolans! Come on, Freddie. Make an effort. It was all over the news. Her seventeen-year-old was pregnant by some loser who beat the crap outta her then disappeared. The doctors saved the babies but lost the mother. Maya was one of the preemies."

He blinked.

She swatted at him with her hand. "Go back to your booze."

He laid down his pen, straightened his back, swiveled his chair to face her, and executed a dramatic sigh. "Okay. *Nina*. What did we cure?"

She skimmed the words on the page. "Wait. I just had it. Okay, here: Two Sundays ago, forty-eight hours before the doctors planned to take her off life support, you led a prayer for the girl at the eleven o'clock service. She recovered. The doctors are baffled. A miracle for sure, her grandmother says."

"A miracle indeed." He rolled his neck, making an audible crack that elicited a wince. He took another sip.

Nina glared at him. This was like pulling teeth. "Says here the girl had never opened her eyes before."

Smirking, he said, "He shall maketh the blind to see."

Digging in her purse, she pulled out a pair of reading glasses, and studied the note.

Freddie returned to scribbling on his sermon.

"She'll be at the service on Sunday to thank you in person."

"Who?"

"Son of a bitch, Freddie. Focus! The grandmother of the kid you cured is who!"

He perked up. "Is she bringing the baby?"

She shook her head and pursed her lips. Freddie was a terrific showman, electric and exciting on the stage. That's how she fell in love, sitting in the front row, drenched by his charisma, gobbling up emotion-laden words that he dispensed like candies. When he walked into a room, every woman's head turned. The silver in his hair had made him look distinguished; age was no obstacle to love—even the twenty-year gap between them. But strip away that thin veneer, and underneath, her husband was self-centered and dumb as soup. Truths she discovered only *after* they'd exchanged vows. "The kid's in intensive care, just escaped death, and you expect her to show up for the eleven o'clock in her Sunday best?"

"Huh. Okay, I guess not." He looked to the ceiling then snapped his fingers. "Do we have any pictures of the baby?"

"Margaret Doolan's phone number will be on file. I can call and check."

"Get me before and after images. He stared at the page of notes and drew a firm line through a couple paragraphs. I'll change Sunday's pitch to emphasize God's special love for infants." A smirk spread across his face. "The Lord works in mysterious ways."

"The Lord will need to step up his game if we're going to make next month's rent on the new church building."

Her husband scowled at her, threw back the remains of his drink, and slammed the empty glass on his desk.

When her phone rang and she didn't recognize the caller's number, Margaret suspected another newspaper reporter. Even three months after Patsy's death, they still called, trying to find out if the twins' father had shown up. The police hadn't traced Cliff, maybe never would. The schemes he got involved in didn't require a social security number, and he never used a credit card, at least not one of his own.

A woman's voice, somewhat familiar, asked, "Mrs. Doolan? Mrs. Margaret Doolan?"

"Yes."

"This is Deacon Nina, Reverend Morgan's wife from New Beginnings Church."

"Oh!"

"I called to thank you for the generous donation I received in the mail, but mostly to thank you for sharing the remarkable story of Maya's *healing*. Although the church helps many sick children, often, once their ailments are cured, their families forget how inspiring their experience can be for others."

"Well, Lauren and I… That is, after Patsy—" Margaret's throat clamped tight, and from the tiny airway that remained, a strangled squeak escaped and a series of sobs racked her chest. Unchecked emotions swamped her mind, and she bawled like a child over the telephone to a woman whom she saw only from a distance at church each Sunday. It took long, painful minutes for the sorrow-tide to ebb. "Sorry, Deacon. I don't understand what happened."

"I think I do. May I call you Margaret?"

"Of course."

"Margaret, this is why the reverend and I chose our mission. I feel blessed to have shared your torment. A broken heart requires healing just as your granddaughter's illness did. At New Beginnings Church we minister to the bodies *and* to the hearts of our flock."

"Thank you, Deacon."

Although embarrassed by her outburst, Margaret stood straighter. The deacon's sympathy and the simple act of venting her grief soothed like warm cocoa.

"How is Maya?" the deacon asked.

"Still in the hospital. Although each day she grows stronger. She's breathing unaided now. If she continues to improve, we may have both twins home in a few weeks."

"That's wonderful news. I hope you're still planning to attend this Sunday's service?"

"Yes. Provided Lauren, that's my other daughter—" Speaking the name of her living daughter triggered another embarrassing bout of sobs and tears. The deacon waited—so thoughtful and caring. Margaret gathered herself. "I'm sorry, I don't know what's wrong with me today."

"Not at all. I understand. I hope Lauren can join you; she is most welcome at the service."

"My daughter is a nonbeliever, but she'll watch over Joshua for me so I can come."

"We'll expect you, then. Perhaps we could share the good news of Maya's recovery with the congregation. Many families who attend our services face challenges with their children's health. How inspiring for them to witness the power of God's healing hand."

Margaret suspected that Lauren wouldn't approve, but her daughter wouldn't be at church, so she wouldn't know. "I suppose that'd be okay."

"I wonder, Margaret, do you have any photos of Maya from before her *healing*? The reverend always says a picture is worth a thousand words. But if that is too sensitive…"

"I have a picture of her in the incubator, but you can't see her face because of all the tubes… Oh, wait. I have a better one since they took the IVs away."

"Wonderful. Can you email them both to me? The comparison will make it clear how God's grace has helped her."

"I suppose so. Yes."

"Thank you so much. Reverend Freddie will be delighted. Be sure to come forward at the end of the service and receive his personal blessing. Have a blessed day."

The call had been a complete surprise, and after hanging up, Margaret Doolan felt better than she had for weeks.

The Lord works in mysterious ways.

CHAPTER 10

"What harm can it do?" Margaret collected Lauren's breakfast plate.

Lauren shook her head and narrowed her eyes. "Would you stop?"

"Look how much better Maya is."

Arms folded in a tight knot, Lauren's expression was flat as a cold iron. "There might be many reasons for Maya's recovery, but Reverend Freddie Morgan isn't one of them."

"Come with me. Attend today's service. See for yourself."

"You'd better get going or you'll be late." Lauren returned to her newspaper—discussion over.

Margaret took the dishes through to the kitchen. When the congregation had prayed for Maya, her granddaughter had recovered within days, but Joshua was proving a more difficult case. If the reverend touched her grandson, actually laid hands on him, Margaret was convinced he could also be *healed*. But there was no moving her stubborn daughter, and Margaret couldn't push too hard. Without Lauren how would they eat and make rent?

She climbed into her car and punched the church's new address into her GPS. For ten years, a rickety wooden building—a converted firehouse—in a depressed, blue-collar part of town had been home to New Beginnings Church. But the city of Atlanta had bulldozed the "projects," and now the old church stood alone amidst rubble and decay reminiscent of a bombed-out Middle East city. They had been losing members. Something had to give, and so the reverend had struck a deal for a vacant Kmart store closer to downtown. Today's service was the first at the new location.

Margaret parked alongside a few dozen cars near the big-box store's front entrance. Once the anchor had closed down, the adjacent retail outlets had followed. The strip mall was desolate and empty, fronted by acres of concrete with more than a few weeds poking through the cracks. But it was still an improvement on the old location where parishioners feared having their vehicle's tires stolen while they were at the service.

A church member with an artistic eye had covered the sign above the entrance with white paint. Then in tall blue letters they had hand-painted "New Beginnings Church."

A larger venue meant more members and more tithes. The reverend was such a gifted preacher that it was sensible for him to expand, but Margaret would miss the communal feeling of the old building even if it did have a leaky roof and funky A/C.

A young man dressed in a blue T-shirt, white slacks, and sporting a name tag that read "Junior Healer" met her at the entrance. The grinning teenager shook her hand. She didn't recognize him. "Welcome to New Beginnings Church; may God be with you," he said. This was new, and Margaret didn't much like the formality.

"Visitor or member?" he asked.

Margaret's back straightened and she glared at him. "Young man, I've been a member of this church for ten years."

"Well. Thank you," he said and quickly moved away from her.

After crossing the lobby and passing through the secondary doors, where Kmart greeters would have stood, she halted a few paces inside the steel-framed building. The shelves were gone, replaced by thousands of plastic picnic chairs laid out in neat rows. Large air-conditioning pipes crisscrossed the high ceiling. Suspended mercury lights cast sharp shadows. The space was huge and empty and unwelcoming.

Thirty minutes until the service, and a couple hundred worshippers waited in their seats, clustered in front of a raised stage positioned against the wall farthest from the entrance. With a sinking feeling in her stomach, she headed for the group. Just when she needed the church's support, was it doomed to fail? Margaret nodded and smiled at the many familiar faces she saw, found herself a seat to the rear of the congregation, and listened to the undulating buzz of quiet conversations. Folk were speaking in hushed tones: uncertain, uneasy. Thank heavens Lauren and Joshua hadn't come today. This didn't even feel like her church.

The stage was a hundred feet across and fifty deep. A middle-aged man in a suit climbed the side steps and guided a boy to a set of bleachers positioned at the back of the stage. The child sat on the lower-level bench next to three girls while his guardian returned to a seat near the front of the hall. The children huddled together, staring at the congregation with cow eyes. In the old church building, the reverend called the sick children to him during the service—something else that had changed.

At eleven o'clock, a high-pitched squeal rattled four large speakers suspended from the roof supports. Margaret glanced behind. A couple more rows had filled. In a space equipped to hold thousands, maybe three hundred souls had gathered. The meager congregation covered their ears while a technician sitting behind a control panel in the center of the auditorium tweaked a few dials to kill the shrieking feedback.

Reverend Morgan rose from a seat in the front row and climbed the steps onto the stage. His blue and white robe flowed behind him as he strode across the platform. The reverend was a well-built man, but the scale of this new meeting place dwarfed him; today, he looked smaller and thinner. He stopped center stage, faced the auditorium, and held his arms high, palms out. Two large screens suspended above him flickered to life and filled with a close-up of the preacher's dark face. His eyes were squeezed shut.

"Let us give thanks to the Lord for blessing us with another day on this Earth of His creation."

The speakers crackled, and a long organ note sounded. Everyone stood. The reverend led, and three hundred voices joined him in singing "How Great Thou Art." Finally, by closing her eyes and surrendering to the music, Margaret received some of the comfort she sought. But when the last verse finished, the final organ note lingered in the empty space, and the hollow feeling returned. The preacher lowered his arms. "Amen," he said and opened his eyes. They shone from both screens—chocolate brown and clear. His black hair, groomed and slick with hair gel, topped a handsome face—at least, Margaret though so. As people took their seats, the scrape and squeal of chairs echoed through the empty building. When they had settled, the reverend said, "Today is a *healing* day."

"Halleluiah… Praise The Lord… Amen…"

"But first let us reflect. This year, the power of your prayers has guided the Holy Spirit to grant healing and succor to these suffering souls." The reverend unfolded a piece of notepaper and slowly read names from a list. As he mentioned each individual, an image of a child appeared on both screens. Applause broke out from some segments of the congregation when they recognized friends or family, giving testament to the *healing* they had received. Finally, the roll call stopped, and the left screen filled with the image of Maya that Margaret had emailed to Deacon Nina. Seeing her granddaughter in the isolator surrounded by tubes and monitors triggered memories that misted Margaret's eyes and tightened her throat.

"This, brothers and sisters," the reverend said, "is Maya Doolan, granddaughter of Margaret Doolan, a longstanding member of this church. Margaret, if you are with us today, please show yourself."

His words acted as a starting gun, and Margaret's pulse rate went to the races. Face burning, she sank lower in her seat. A woman in the row behind tapped her shoulder and hissed, "Get up, Margaret."

On jelly legs, she stood, praying the reverend wouldn't ask her to speak in front of so many people.

From the stage, Reverend Freddie smiled at her. "God bless you, Margaret. Brothers and sisters, this poor woman's daughter was attacked and beaten to death by a savage."

The congregation murmured. A few raised their hands high and closed their eyes, their lips moving in silent prayer. "Tell the truth, Reverend," someone to her left shouted.

The reverend's voice strengthened. "Margaret's youngest daughter— a child of seventeen years—was taken from her family by a monster."

"The devil's work," a powerful gravelly voice cried out from the rear of the church.

The reverend raised his pitch a half-octave, driving home his message. "Margaret's youngest daughter—beaten and bloodied and left for dead—carried in her womb two unborn innocents!" The hall fell silent. The preacher paused and the last word resonated as though it had substance. "This child." He pointed at the screen. "This child, Maya Doolan, was assaulted before she left her mother's body." He paused, and then into the stunned, hushed hall he whispered, "The doctors did what they could."

"That's right," came the booming voice again.

The preacher slowed his cadence. "They told Margaret: medical science can do no more."

"Amen to that... Tell it true."

"They told Margaret: we must switch off Maya's life support machines."

"They told Margaret: your granddaughter's life will be forfeit." The last word, said with harsh force, bounced off the rear walls and transported Margaret back to the stuffy hospital room where Dr. Pavan had delivered his deadly prognosis. Her stomach cramped as the dread of losing her precious little girl once again swamped her heart. Her knees wobbled, and she grabbed the seat back in front of her.

The congregation waited, their eyes locked on the screen, locked on Maya.

"Margaret Doolan," Reverend Freddie said, "is a founding member of this church. She approached me for a *healing*. Many of you were present at that service in the old church hall. Together, we prayed to the Holy Spirit. We entreated him to show mercy. We begged that he spare this innocent child, beaten and battered before she breathed a breath."

"If it's His will," the man behind shouted.

The reverend gave a nodded signal, and his arm shot up and pointed to the empty screen to his left. He scanned the faces of his congregation while a few scattered pixels appeared on the screen, then more, until they resolved to form a second image of Maya—still in the incubator but without the IVs and breathing tube. A rumble of voices rippled across the hall.

"The doctors were baffled," the reverend said. "A miracle they called it." He flung both arms wide and high, stared to the heavens and filled the hall with his voice. "And yea I say unto you, this *was* a miracle, the miracle of Spiritual *healing*. God heard your prayers. As it was with Lazarus, so it was with Maya Doolan. *He* decided it was not her time. *He* brought her back from the grave to live the life *He* intended."

"Amen... Halleluiah."

Tears spilled down Margaret's cheeks. Those seated close by reached out and touched her as though the spiritual power that saved Maya could be transferred and captured for their own use. A close-up of the reverend's face replaced the before image of Maya surrounded by IVs and equipment. His chocolate eyes focused on Margaret, and he softened his voice. "Tell us, sister; how is your granddaughter?"

Margaret cleared her throat. "Good," she croaked.

"Praise the Lord," the reverend said, and the congregation echoed the words.

The service continued—the mood far lighter, joyous even. They sang hymns. They chanted prayers. Through the familiarity of the rites, Margaret felt more at home in the new hall. Reverend Morgan laid hands on the four children seated on the bleachers. When Deacon Nina began the collection, the before and after images of Maya again displayed on the screens. The preacher exhorted his parishioners to give generously and aid the growth of the church. "The Lord has commanded me to expand my mission, to reach out and guide his healing spirit into the lives of the many other children suffering in our community."

Margaret folded and pushed her donation through a slot cut into a wooden handle covering a collection bag—another difference from the open plate she was accustomed to at the old church building. She deposited twenty dollars that she could ill afford.

But what price could be put on Maya's health?

Once the hall cleared, Nina Morgan left the Junior Healers to clean up, and drove from the parking lot to the rear of the church, where she collected her husband.

He sank into the passenger seat and sighed. "Man. That was crazy. Coordinating the audio-visual aids was a challenge, but I'll get better. How did it play from the auditorium?"

Watching him from the wings, Nina had once again felt the rush of pride and admiration in her husband—the wellspring from which her love had grown years ago, before they married. This was *her* man. *Her* man held everyone in that hall in his sway, moved them with his cadence, left them hanging on his every word. Freddie was an artist, a showman. No one was better once the curtain went up. "You were terrific, Freddie; you should've heard the buzz as people were leaving. The images of baby Doolan really rocked them. The take is bound to be up on last week."

"What about attendance?"

"Three twenty-six."

Freddie frowned. "Is that enough?"

Anger at his naivety flooded her mind. Worry washed in and swilled away her belief in him. "How can you ask that? You know we need more tithes just to make the new rent payment, and that's before we think about the equipment lease."

"The finances are your responsibility."

He snapped the words out with an accusatory tone, as though she were to blame, as though she were the one who had committed to the huge building and expensive technology.

She glared at him, and he looked away, unable to meet her gaze. "We agreed to move from the old building, but I told you this Kmart made no sense. It's too big."

"God spoke to me," he said. "When he commands, I must obey."

That was his justification for setting them on the path to the poorhouse. God had told him to sign the lease. Really? Well, God had better hurry up and fill those seats. He laid a hand on her wrist. She snatched her arm away and pulled into traffic.

CHAPTER 11

Five Years Later...

Lauren's foot vibrated. Bent forward, hands on knees, body tense and torqued, she sat in Dr. Pavan's office. To her right, her mom knelt at a low table, watching Maya assemble a Lego house. Maya wore a pink T-shirt, pink shorts, and matching pink Nikes; Lord, the child loved pink.

Joshua, the diametrical opposite of Maya's intelligent exuberance, slouched in his stroller to Lauren's left. He had fallen asleep on the drive over, thankfully, because when Joshua wasn't sleeping or eating, he was unhappy. Although most of the burden fell on Margaret, difficult didn't begin to describe the challenge of raising Lauren's son

A third surgery to unblock a shunt that syphoned excess liquid from Joshua's brain had lessened the severity and regularity of his seizures. But each procedure sapped a piece of his essence. His life force was being peeled away one layer at a time. He had lost his appetite, and because his diet had never progressed beyond milk and pureed food, he was rail thin. Like a boxer punished with jabs and blows for nine rounds, to Lauren, Joshua appeared ready to give up the fight.

They were awaiting the results of his latest brain scan.

Pavan opened the door and entered the room, accompanied by the odor of antiseptic and aftershave. He held a chart in his hand.

Maya sprang to her feet and spun around to face him. "I've built a house." She lifted the Lego project for the doctor to admire.

He beamed. "Why hello, Maya." He bent low and squinted to better study her colorful creation. "I see you have. It looks very sturdy. And how is my little miracle today?"

She giggled and blushed. "I'm well, thank you. And how are you, Doctor Pavan?"

His eyebrows lifted, a reaction to which Lauren had become accustomed; Maya's diction and mannerisms were often more suited to an adult than a five-year-old. "I'm well too. Thank you for asking."

With a grunt of effort, Lauren's mom stood. She patted Maya's head. "Play with the blocks a little longer, sweetie, while we talk with the doctor."

Pavan's face glassed over as he glanced at Joshua's stroller.

Reading his eyes, Lauren moved beside her mom and took her arm. "Do you have the scan results, Doctor?"

He nodded, checked his clipboard, and then met Lauren's gaze. "I'm sorry, Ms. Doolan, but the shunt is not balancing the pressure in Joshua's brain. To replace the device a fourth time would be too traumatic. Simply put, he lacks the physical strength to recover from another surgical procedure."

"But he's been so much better since the last operation," Lauren's mom said.

Pavan gave a slow, considered nod. "I fear the changes in mood, the calmness you've reported, are signs that his body is worn out, his systems are shutting down."

Margaret let out a small squeak and Lauren felt her wobble. "Here, Mom, sit." She guided her to the chair next to Joshua's stroller.

Her mom's chin twitched. "There—" Margaret's voice took on a pleading childlike pitch. "There must be something you can do, Doctor. Remember Maya, you thought her a hopeless case and look at her now."

He softened his voice. "I remember, and I'm delighted Maya had such a full recovery. But it was an… anomaly. To expect the same for Joshua is unreasonable."

"You have to help my brother, Doctor Pavan."

The three of them turned to Maya, who stood stock-still, back rigid, arms by her sides, fists clenched. The tiny all-in-pink girl focused laser eyes on the doctor.

Pavan combed a hand through his hair. His mouth opened and then closed again. Lauren registered his discomfort but didn't bail him out. Let him answer. Maybe Maya could change his mind, make him think of an alternative.

Finally, he found his voice. "Maya, I'm doing all I can for your brother, but he doesn't seem to be getting well."

Maya smiled at the doctor. "So long as you're trying your best. That's what Grandma says. Always try your best." She looked across at her grandma, who forced a smile.

The dust cloud of awkwardness that had filled the room was complicating the consultation, and Lauren needed specifics. She turned to her mother. "Why don't you wait in the outer office with Maya while I speak with Doctor Pavan? I'll bring Joshua along in a few minutes."

Eyes blank and locked on Joshua's stroller, her mom nodded. Lauren held the door and Maya and her grandma left.

Once they were alone, Lauren touched the doctor's arm and lowered her voice. "How long does he have?"

Pavan stroked his chin. He took a deep contemplative breath. "Impossible to say. It may be months, or it could be a matter of days. Although the episodes are less frequent, multiple grand mal seizures have placed a tremendous strain on his heart. Ms. Doolan, if I thought there was any positive prognosis, or a viable treatment regime, believe me, I—"

Lauren held up her hand, unable to listen to more.

"I'm sorry," he said.

From a throat crammed with cotton, Lauren choked out a thank you and released the doctor. Maya had been the twin destined for death. Yet it now seemed Joshua was destined to suffer most from his father's violence. Not that Cliff cared a damn about his children. Five months after Patsy's death, he was caught on video surveillance robbing a 7-Eleven at gunpoint in Macon, Georgia. An assistant DA had called Lauren to confirm that the twins had lived. Cliff's alibi—that he had left town the day before Patsy's beating—convinced no one. Without witnesses, a capital murder conviction was impossible, but the state prosecutor made a voluntary manslaughter charge stick. That, coupled with the armed robbery, had sent Cliff to the penitentiary for twenty-four years. If there was any justice, Cliff would have suffered the same fate as Patsy. Yet her sister was dead, and Cliff lived. And now, five years later, his brutality was slowly stealing her son's life—a crime for which his father would never pay.

When Lauren entered the outer waiting room, Maya was on her grandmother's lap, hugging her neck, stroking her hair—taking responsibility, doing the comforting. Lauren cleared her throat. Her mom looked up, met Lauren's eyes, and burst into tears. Lauren took her mom's arm and helped her up. "Come on," Lauren said. "Let's get out of here."

On the way home, Maya sat in the back of the car, headphones on, enjoying cartoons on Lauren's iPad. Joshua slept, his head lolling, exhausted from the hospital visit. Friday afternoon traffic choked the roads, and the sixty-minute drive took ninety; the silence in the vehicle was stifling, but what could Lauren say? Her mom had devoted her life to raising Joshua. Such a thankless task—after five years, her grandson barely recognized her. The improvement Margaret had conjured from the changing pattern of her grandson's seizures was instead a sign of his decline. Lauren owed it to her mom to share Pavan's prognosis.

But how?

As they turned into their subdivision, Margaret broke the silence. "Lauren, I have something to say, and I know it'll annoy you, but I want you to hear me out. Let me finish before you argue. Okay?"

Lauren checked the driver's mirror. Maya was engrossed in SpongeBob. Her mom's hand trembled as she wiped at her eyes; her neck was blotched red. What was coming? "I promise," she whispered.

Her mom balled her fists and twisted them into her thighs. She took a deep breath and spoke on exhale, gabbling out the words. "I want to take the twins to New Beginnings Church on Sunday so Reverend Morgan can lay hands on Joshua."

Anger flared inside Lauren, but she choked it down. Her mom was at her wits' end. The only respite she received from a full-time job as caregiver to her unresponsive, mentally deficient grandson came at the weekly Sunday service. Without reservation, the woman believed the claims made by the church. And a large part of that belief was based on the miracle of her granddaughter's recovery, which Margaret attributed to Reverend Freddie Morgan. Lauren had never confessed the truth of Maya's cure, and she never could—not even to her mother.

If it helped her mom accept the inevitability of Joshua's death, who was she to stand in the way if she wanted to take him to New Beginnings Church? How different was this request from Lauren's Hail Mary to save her daughter? That had been a hopeless long shot as well. Sadly, that cure had died along with Doctor Arrunsen. But, just like Maya in the NICU, Joshua had nothing to lose.

"Why does Maya have to go?"

"I don't think I can cope on my own with Joshua. I'll need you there in case he, you know, goes off on me."

Lauren's voice lifted an octave. "Me?" She pulled into their driveway, stopped the car, and turned off the ignition. Silence wove a wall between them, penetrated only by tinny sounds from Maya's earphones.

Her mother stared at her lap. In a soft whisper, vibrating with emotion, she said, "Please, Lauren. Do this for Joshua."

Reaching across, Lauren squeezed her mom's shoulder. "Of course. And I promise to be on my best behavior. I'll even wear my Sunday frock."

On Sunday morning, the Doolan family piled into the car and headed to New Beginnings Church. Lauren was dreading the experience. Maya, on the other hand, was as excited as her grandmother and peppered the woman with questions.

"Who is God?"

"How will he help Joshua?"

"If Reverend Morgan isn't a doctor how does he heal sick people?"

"Why doesn't Doctor Pavan lay hands on Joshua?"

Lauren, with a slight smile on her face, listened as her mom struggled through a catalog of dubious answers—out of the mouths of babes...

At ten thirty, they parked in front of the church. Margaret had insisted on arriving early so she could speak to the preacher about Joshua. Lauren knew her mother would also have to grease his palm. How much money had this couple wrung from her mom over the years?

A tacky, hand-painted sign hung over the repurposed big-box storefront—how fitting.

Inside the converted Kmart, rows of white plastic lawn chairs filled the huge arena, radiating out from a central raised platform—room enough for thousands. At the back of the stage, an empty row of bleachers faced the auditorium. According to her mother that was where Joshua would sit if he were well enough to stay on his own. How manipulative and how stressful for the children to be exploited like trophies in full view of the crowd; what were their parents thinking?

Once they had seats, Margaret left Lauren with the twins and made her way down the aisle toward the stage. Maya stood on her chair, head on a pivot, taking it all in. Joshua slept in his stroller—since Friday's visit to Pavan's office, he had spent more time sleeping than awake—as though he were privy to the doctor's prognosis. A shawl of sadness draped Lauren as she stared at her adopted son's face, peaceful, at rest—so similar in features to Maya except for Joshua's brown eyes. Yet Maya's vibrancy, her every action, made them different as dark and light.

Her mom disappeared through a curtain at the left side of the stage and returned five minutes later, face flushed. She sat next to Lauren, and in an excited whisper said, "The reverend has agreed to come down from the stage to lay hands on Joshua."

Lauren bit back the half-dozen sarcastic comments that sprang to mind. On the drive over, Margaret had filled Maya's head with belief in the Reverend Freddie Morgan's ability to help her brother. To insult the preacher or contradict her mother might upset her daughter, and based on Dr. Pavan's prognosis for Joshua, she would suffer enough distress in the near future. So Lauren suppressed her disdain. Maya was an intelligent child, the most intelligent child Lauren had ever known. When she lost Joshua, explaining the failure of the blessing at New Beginnings Church would be the least of Lauren's challenges.

By the time the service started, Lauren estimated the congregation at seven or eight hundred people—the number surprised her. How could so many be so easily fooled? Or was it possible that their belief did help with healing. Placebos could cure. So why not faith? She looked over at Joshua, fast asleep, face slack, and her throat tightened. If God existed, why would he treat her son this way? Perhaps faith might work for a common cold or a sore finger, but Joshua needed a miracle.

The service started and Reverend Morgan led them in prayer, and then the organ struck up and they sang hymns. Lauren's focus remained on Maya, sensitive to any confusion on her daughter's face, but the child appeared to soak up the atmosphere. She shared her grandmother's hymnal and sang along as though she were a regular. Each time Maya caught Lauren sneaking a peek, she delivered a broad grin. Perhaps she had been wrong to stop her daughter from accompanying Margaret each Sunday. What harm could come of attending church with her grandmother? Maybe she was the one who needed to revisit her religious biases. Maya was smart enough to make up her own mind what to believe.

When the last organ note died, the preacher moved front and center on the stage and said, "Today is a healing Day."

Folk applauded, and a few shouted, "Praise the Lord."

As a series of images flashed on two screens suspended above Freddie Morgan's head, the preacher read from a list of names—these were pictures of children he claimed to have cured. Lauren's cheeks burned when the final picture was displayed on the left screen—an image of Maya taken in the NICU when she was destined for death. Lauren glared at her mom, who kept her eyes fixed on the screen.

"Maya Doolan," the reverend said. Maya's head jerked up, and she focused intently on the man in the blue and white robe with his arms spread.

She tugged Lauren's sleeve and pointed at the screen. "That's me," she whispered.

Lauren nodded but before she could speak, Reverend Morgan said, "I believe Maya is with us today." He gave a hand signal. "Can you lift the house lights, please?" The room brightened. "Is Maya with us today?"

If she'd been close enough, Lauren would have punched the man. He knew good and well Maya was here; her mother had been backstage to tell him. Margaret Doolan shot to her feet, raised her arms, and waved like a game-show contestant who'd won a prize.

"Ah. There's Maya's grandmother." He pointed, and hundreds of people craned their necks, focusing on Lauren's family.

Maya, seated between Lauren and her mother, jumped up and shouted, "I'm here too! I'm Maya Doolan."

Laughter rippled around the hall. Lauren wanted the ground to open and swallow her. She leaned behind Maya's back and whispered in her mom's ear. "Did you set this up?"

Her mom frowned and shook her head. "He just wants to see her—to say hello."

For her daughter's sake, Lauren gritted her teeth.

Reverend Morgan left the stage. Microphone in hand, he strode down the aisle toward them. His voice boomed from the speakers, "By the grace of the Almighty, Maya Doolan was saved from certain death. But, brothers and sisters, today it is her brother who needs your prayers. Joshua's doctors have given up hope." The preacher reached them. After a glance at Lauren, fleeting, but long enough to receive her dagger-glare, he addressed Maya, still standing. "Hi, Maya." He spoke into the mic then held it close to her face so the congregation would hear her answer.

Maya's voice rang out. "Hello, Reverend Morgan."

Chuckles and comments murmured through the crowd.

"May I pick you up and hold you high so all the people can see how pretty you are?"

Maya looked to Lauren and raised one eyebrow in question. What Lauren wanted to do was tell this man to get the hell away from her daughter, but she couldn't, not without mortifying her mother and frightening Maya. She gave a nod of approval and Maya reached out her arms to the preacher, who lifted her high in the air and turned a slow circle. The camera operator zoomed to the action, and Maya's smiling face appeared on the right screen— presenting a dramatic contrast with the image of baby Maya surrounded by IVs and encased in a plastic isolator.

Applause exploded from the congregation. Maya grinned and giggled, basking in the attention. If Lauren had known this was the price she had to pay to help her mother, she wouldn't have come. After two rotations, the preacher stood Maya on her chair. "And how do you feel now, Maya?"

"I've very well, thank you. How are you today, Reverend Morgan?"

The audience laughed, Maya grinned, and so did Reverend Morgan.

"What a polite granddaughter you have, Mrs. Doolan… I'm in good spirits, Maya, thank you for asking. But how is your brother?"

Lauren put an arm around her daughter's shoulders and glared at the preacher. "That's enough," she snapped. The mic picked up her words, which triggered a hushed silence. Lauren whispered in Maya's ear, "Sit down, sweetie." Maya sat, and Lauren focused on the reverend, who shifted his attention to her mother.

Freddie Morgan spoke into the mic, sounding his words in a measured preacher's cadence. "Because of Margaret Doolan's belief in the healing power of God… Because of Margaret Doolan's unerring faith in the strength of the prayers of the congregation of New Beginnings Church, her granddaughter was saved from death and grew into the beautiful child you see before you today. But Margaret has more to ask of you. More to ask of God!" He allowed the final word to echo and die in the silent hall. "Will you join me in prayer as I lay hands on Joshua Doolan?"

A few answered, "We will."

He lifted his voice, increasing the urgency. "Will you call on the healing power of the Almighty and save this young boy so he may take his place beside his sister?"

"We will," came the reply, stronger now.

Reverend Morgan bent and lifted Joshua from the stroller. The child's brown eyes sprang open; he sucked in a breath and let out a piercing scream.

As Lauren moved toward him, her mother took one step to the side and blocked her way. "You promised," she hissed.

Lauren backed off, but the need to protect her son from this stranger tore at her heart and clenched her fists.

The preacher held Joshua, screaming and wriggling, high in the air. "In the name of the Almighty Healer, I cast out the demons that cripple this young body." Then he babbled indecipherable words that sounded to Lauren like a childish made-up language and ended by shouting "Amen!"

And the congregation responded, "Amen."

He lowered Joshua and handed him to his grandmother, who hugged him to her breast. With one hand spanning the boy's head and the other holding the microphone, raised high, the preacher faced the heavens, screwed his eyes tight shut, and shouted out the prayer.

"In the name of the Almighty Healer. I cast out the demons that cripple this young body."

Reverend Morgan paused for five seconds, frozen in his pose, then blinked his eyes theatrically as though he had just woken from a deep sleep. He smiled at Margaret, brought the mic to his lips, and whispered, "It's in the Lord's hands, now. Have faith, Margaret." He glared at Lauren before whisking away down the aisle, silky blue and white robes billowing behind him.

As he returned to the stage, an overweight woman appeared from the side curtain.

"That's his wife, Deacon Nina," Margaret said.

Dressed in a long purple robe, she was followed by a half-dozen teens in white slacks and blue shirts. They passed out collection bags.

"Please," Reverend Morgan said, "give generously so we can continue to spread God's message of healing in the community." The image of infant Maya remained on one screen. A freeze-frame of five-year-old Maya smiling into the camera beamed out of the other.

A shiver snaked down Lauren's back as she exited the church. The reverend and his wife—in fact the whole New Beginnings experience—left her feeling defiled, as though thieves had broken into her home and rifled through her drawers. On the drive back, she gripped the steering wheel, struggling to restrain the fury seething inside her like an overheating pressure cooker waiting to blow. That man had taken credit for healing Maya, and now he had used Joshua to squeeze money from her mom and from others in today's congregation.

But nothing positive could come of venting her anger. And based on the questions Maya was firing at her grandmother, Lauren had plenty of work ahead of her to repair her daughter's moral compass. Yes, she was smart, but she was a child for goodness' sake. What was her mom thinking? Exposing a young, impressionable mind to the theatrical hocus pocus and misdirection Reverend Morgan presented as faith healing? If it were humanly possible, steaming geysers would be spurting from Lauren's ears.

Yet, contrary to all that Lauren had observed in the church, Margaret seemed happier now than she'd been in weeks. At home, before she climbed from the car, her mom said, "Thank you for coming today. I know you don't believe, but it meant a lot that you witnessed the reverend's laying on of hands."

"Do you really think that man helped Joshua?" Lauren snapped.

Ignoring or failing to notice Lauren's sarcastic tone, her mother replied in a soft, reverent voice, "It's no longer up to Reverend Morgan. Joshua is in God's hands now."

Lauren spun away and headed for her room. She needed to put distance between her and her mother. "I have reading to catch up on for work tomorrow. Can you fix Maya a snack?"

"Of course."

As she reached her bedroom door, Lauren heard Maya ask her grandmother, "Did Reverend Morgan make Joshua better?" With one hand on the doorknob, Lauren paused, and listened.

"Well, now," Margaret said, "it's not that simple. You see. It's not the reverend who heals. Only God can heal. But God is in heaven, which is far away, so he uses Reverend Morgan's hands to connect with Joshua. If God wills it, the healing will flow through the reverend and into Joshua to make him well."

Lauren waited to see how Maya received that pile of horse poop, but the child made no reply. Lauren closed her bedroom door. She knew her daughter's forehead would be wrinkled in a deep concentration as she tried to process her grandmother's latest pearl of confusing wisdom. Maya was intelligent, but no one could make sense of the ridiculous. Lauren decided she'd probe a little after tonight's bedtime story, try to gauge the damage today's excursion had wrought.

After dinner, Lauren organized Maya's bath and fifteen minutes later brought her back to the living room—bright-eyed and sweet-smelling. After Maya gave her grandmother a hug and a goodnight kiss, Lauren said, "Why don't you go to your room and pick a book. I'll be along shortly to read the story."

"Princess and the Pea?"

"Anything you like," Lauren said, and Maya ran full pelt down the hallway to her room.

Margaret returned from settling Joshua in his bed and sank into the sofa. Dark rings under her eyes revealed the strain she was shouldering. Lauren decided not to mention New Beginnings Church. Nothing could persuade her mother that Freddie Morgan wasn't genuine, and what was wrong with having hope? "How about a cup of tea?" Lauren asked.

Her mother sighed and mustered a wan smile. "That would be nice. I'm exhausted. But what about Maya? You promised her a story."

"She can look at the pictures for a few minutes."

Lauren made her mom a drink and took it to her in the living room. "You relax. I'll settle Maya."

"Okay, dear." Her mother looked all in. Lauren would send her to bed as soon as she finished with her daughter.

When Lauren opened Maya's bedroom door. The storybook was on the top cover, unopened. Her daughter wasn't there. Based on the neatness of the bedclothes, she hadn't even climbed onto the bed. That was unusual behavior. Maya loved story time. "Maya?" She headed toward the bathroom, but as she passed her mom's room, Lauren heard Maya's voice. She peeked in.

Because he needed constant attention, Joshua still slept in a crib beside his grandmother's bed. Maya was standing over him, one hand on her brother's head, the other raised high. The hairs on Lauren's arms prickled to attention when she heard Maya say, "In the name of the Almighty Healer. I cast out the demons that cripple this young body." The words, delivered with an uncanny similarity to Freddie Morgan's cadence, tied a wet knot in her stomach.

Lauren cleared her throat. "Maya? What are you doing?"

Her daughter turned. Face serious, voice firm, she said, "I'm making Joshua better."

Maya stared at her, waiting. Lauren struggled for breath. She needed to say something. But what? How much damage had been done to this child's psyche today? When Joshua's illness snatched away his life in the next weeks or months, would Maya now blame herself for failing to heal him? Lauren rubbed an invisible itch on her cheek, buying a few precious seconds. Guarding her tone, she whispered, "That's sweet of you, honey. I'm sure your brother wants everyone's help to get better."

"Yes," Maya said. "He'll be better soon, and then we can play together."

Lauren turned away to hide the tremble in her bottom lip. She should never have exposed this innocent child to New Beginnings Church. "Come on, now. Let Joshua rest… story time, remember."

"Coming, Mommy."

Lauren fluffed Maya's pillow, tucked the covers around her daughter, and sat beside her on the bed. This wasn't the time to discuss God or magical healing.

At the end of the tale, as the princess showed herself to be a worthy wife for her prince, Lauren's mom tapped on the doorframe. "Lauren. Can you come?"

"Almost finished, Mom."

Margaret made an urgent hand gesture and hissed, "It's Joshua. I need you now!"

The fear in her mom's voice sent an ant army skittering across Lauren's scalp. Could this be his time? Why now? Why so soon? She stroked Maya's hair and forced unfelt softness into her words. "Look at the pictures for a few minutes, sweetie. I'll be right back. Grandma needs me." Lauren slid off the bed and followed her mother, hardly able to breath. As she entered Josh's room, her mom stood over the crib. Lying on his back, Joshua's body jerked and trembled; his face was screwed into a grimace. White drool foamed at his mouth, which opened and closed like a gasping fish.

"Lauren, I'm scared." Her mom's voice shook.

She moved to her mother's side and placed an arm around her shoulders. Wracked with guilt, Lauren stared at her son. Today's outing had been too much for both children. If this was a full-blown grand mal seizure, as weak as he was, could he survive? Was she watching her son's death throes? Finally, Joshua snatched a deep breath, wheezed it out, and after a final shudder his face relaxed. Like an electronic toy running low on batteries, the spasms slowed and then stopped. His breathing took on an even rhythm as he fell back to sleep. Relief washed through Lauren.

Not now. Not yet.

"Is he all right?" her mother asked.

Lauren leaned over the crib and felt for a fever; his forehead was warm but not hot. "He's exhausted," Lauren whispered, "but he's sleeping now. Come on." She guided her mom from the room. "Let him rest."

Outside the bedroom, Margaret gripped Lauren's arm and stopped her. The look on her mother's face left Lauren in no doubt that she didn't believe Joshua would be fine any more than Lauren believed in the Reverend Freddie Morgan. "What did Doctor Pavan tell you?" she asked.

Lauren squeezed her mom's shoulder. It felt thin, and frail. The woman had lost weight. Lauren had insisted that she visit their GP next week for a checkup. "We'll talk later, okay. Maya's waiting. Let me finish her story, and I'll see you in a few minutes." Her mom shuffled away.

As Lauren entered Maya's room, violet eyes locked on hers. "Is Joshua better?" she asked.

"I—" Where did that come from? "He had a bad dream is all."

Maya's face dropped. "Oh," she said, and the word was laden with more sadness and disappointment than any five-year-old should be asked to bear.

Lauren finished the fairy tale and tucked Maya in. She closed the bedroom door.

Before rejoining her mother, she looked in on Joshua again. The boy was sleeping. She placed a hand on his forehead. Normal.

Joshua flinched. He moaned and stretched. Then his eyelids sprang open. And he stared up at her with vivid violet eyes that were filled with intelligence and life.

"Hello, Momma," he said. "Is it time to get up?"

Lauren's knees jellied. She gripped the side of the crib for support. Invisible monster hands spanned her chest and squeezed. She gulped in a breath, then another, and gazed at her son.

What have I done?

CHAPTER 12

One Week Later...

Riley Brown sat in his car and peered through sheeting rain at the front doors of New Beginnings Church. When he graduated from The Atlanta School of Journalism nine months earlier, Riley had been so thrilled to land the job as a reporter for News Channel 13 that he'd bought a keg and thrown a party. He hadn't expected to be given a prime-time story right away, but he had hoped for something better than interviewing a bogus faith healer. And, sadly, this was far from the weakest lead he'd chased down. New Beginnings Church beat out last week's unconfirmed downtown black-bear sighting, and before that, the crazy couple who swore they'd seen a UFO (their camera's battery was dead, so they didn't have pictures).

After six months of cat-up-a-tree stories, he had complained and drawn a lecture from his boss about gaining experience, putting in his time. So far, his pieces hadn't even made the thirty-second feel-good slot at the end of the six o'clock news program; the job was getting old—fast.

He checked his watch—five of eleven. Nina Morgan, or Deacon Morgan as she called herself, had contacted the News Channel claiming that her husband, Reverend Freddie Morgan, had cured dozens of sick children. In particular, twins who had been hours from death. Riley was to attend a service and then interview the preacher.

The previous day, while researching story angles online, he'd found a dozen examples of faith healing churches exposed as a fraud. But if the healings were bogus, why invite a journalist? It seemed a risky strategy. Maybe the deacon assumed that any publicity was good publicity. In a couple hours, he should know the answer.

He'd waited ten minutes for the rain to ease, but still it hammered on the car roof. Riley considered skipping the service and taking a nap in his car until it was time for his face-to-face, but that wouldn't be professional, and journalism was his chosen profession. Ever since he watched a rerun of All The President's Men as a teenager, investigative reporting was all he'd wanted to do in life.

He sighed, grabbed his umbrella, and made a dash for the doors—only two hundred feet, but the parking lot was old, the concrete uneven, and the surface water plenty deep enough to soak his socks.

As he squelched into the lobby, a young woman dressed in blue slacks and a white blouse, her blond hair pulled back in a ponytail and tied with a blue ribbon, stepped toward him and offered a flyer. The name tag above her left breast identified her as Joanna—Junior Healer.

"Welcome to New Beginnings Church," she said in a sweet Georgia accent.

"I'm Riley Brown of News Channel 13. Deacon Morgan told me to give my name when I arrived."

Pretty without a trace of makeup, Joanna blushed and beamed a smile that lifted Riley's spirits. "We were expecting you, Mr. Brown. Follow me. The reverend has reserved a seat close to the front."

She led him down an aisle bordered by hundreds of plastic lawn chairs. He estimated six or seven hundred were seated, waiting for the service to begin; hardly enough attendees to justify such a large auditorium. Perhaps the weather caused the poor turnout and the rows of empty seats were normally filled.

The Junior Healer led him to a chair, front and center, with a VIP card taped to the seat. Riley thanked her. After she left, he stood and did a slow scan of the auditorium. What struck him most was the scale. He'd been in Kmart stores before, but never one without shelves crammed with product. This building could house three or four football fields. Counting rows, he came up with two thousand chairs and space enough for five times that number. The available space dwarfed the seated congregation clustered near the front—fleas on an elephant's back.

Those present—the faithful, he assumed, given the foul weather—were younger than he expected for churchgoers. Mostly middle-aged family groups with quite a few children. About eighty percent were African American, which fitted the demographic in this part of Atlanta. A few stragglers still filtered through the doors, shaking their umbrellas and stripping off their coats.

He took his seat and faced the stage: a five-foot-high wooden platform. Blue and white cloth draped the front edge, matching the colors of the Junior Healer's uniforms and the gaudy sign over the entrance. New Beginnings Church was at least making an effort at branding.

Three young children, two boys and a girl, sat at the center of the stage to the rear on the lowest tier of a row of bleachers. They seemed uneasy, not speaking, just staring with hands clasped on their laps—hardly surprising, as they were the focal point for the congregation. Gregorian chants played from speakers hung from beams above the stage between two large suspended flat screens.

Riley made a rough-cut cost estimate and arrived at $50K for the technology alone. The Junior Healers were probably volunteers, but accounting for chairs and the stage, this added up to a large capital outlay for a church service attended by six hundred believers. Either Reverend Morgan was confident of growing his market or else he was heading for bankruptcy. Many questions and not too many answers buzzed through Riley's mind. He might at last have a reportable story. Riley switched on his digital recorder and clipped it to his shirt.

The music changed to a single soprano singing "How Great Thou Art." The number of singers on the track increased along with the volume as the hymn progressed. Riley stood with the congregation, who sang along enthusiastically. Stirred by the rousing music, the expectation level in the hall rose as the arrival of the preacher grew near.

In the hush that followed the last organ note, from the blue curtain stage left a tall black man emerged. From his Internet research, Riley recognized Reverend Morgan. His caramel skin and strong jaw reminded Riley of Denzel Washington. Good looks never hurt, and they would play well if Riley's post-service interview triggered any follow-up video footage. He wore a white robe trimmed with blue and made of material light enough to billow behind him as he strode to the front of the platform, where he stopped and faced the congregation. Arms held high, a broad smile lit his face. The screens above filled with close-ups of the handsome preacher and his striking chocolate-brown eyes.

"Today," he said. The speaker volume had been cranked up and his voice, deep and resonant, boomed forth and filled the hall. "Today… is a healing day."

Choruses of "Amen" and "Hallelujah" and "Praise the Lord" rippled through the congregation.

"Thank you all for fighting through the devil's weather to get here. You are battle tested, true believers one and all. The Lord recognizes your sacrifice. And these poor children behind me," he spun and waved a hand toward the kids on the bleachers, who shrank from the increased attention, "these ailing souls also thank you for lending the power of your prayers to their healing. The Holy Spirit blesses you because the Holy Spirit is with us today! Can you feel it?"

He waited for the initial weak response before repeating himself, more of a chant this time. "Can… You… Feel… The… Spirit?"

"Yes!" they yelled.

And the preacher nodded, and smiled, and scanned the seats. When he caught Riley's eye, his gaze dwelt there for two heartbeats and Riley's pulse quickened.

Choir music fired up once again, and the reverend used it as a background to heighten the impact of his words. "I feel the Holy Spirit in this room. Though we are few, I feel his strength here with us. A strength swollen with pride that so many would neglect their own well-being, forsake their own comforts, to help these three unfortunate children. Your fortitude and belief outweighs your numbers a thousandfold! Let us pray."

Reverend Morgan led the congregation through thirty minutes of prayer and song. Recording the service freed the reporter to observe the preacher's performance. There was an undeniable charisma about the man. But the sequence of music and prayer followed time-worn techniques of psychological manipulation; even some of the hymns were the same as those used by the bogus churches he'd researched. What seemed unusual about Reverend Morgan's church was the focus on healing children. Unusual because, according to Riley's research, children were less susceptible to the pseudo-hypnotic suggestion pioneered by TV evangelists and the Bible-thumping tent revivalists who preceded them. Convincing children they were cured was more challenging than persuading adults who were already locked into a faith-based belief mechanism.

At the end of the prayers, as Morgan moved to the center of the stage, six Junior Healers, three boys and three girls, approached the children sitting on the bleachers. One by one, they were brought before the preacher, who entered a trancelike state as he laid one hand on the child's head and held his other hand high, palm out, as though receiving power from above. The reverend chanted a prayer pleading with God to heal the child and then maintained his stance for thirty seconds, speaking in tongues, before thrusting the child away as he simultaneously took a step backward. The move was synchronized with the Junior Healers, who also took a half step back so the child swooned backward and almost struck the floor before being caught.

After the children returned to their parents in the auditorium, Morgan listed off the illnesses he'd cast out: a leaking heart valve from the girl, and cystic fibrosis from the two boys who looked similar enough to be twins. How could faith possibly heal CF?

After asking the congregation to give generously, "How Great Thou Art" again boomed from the speakers and Reverend Morgan exited through the side curtains to an energetic round of applause, and Riley joined in. The man was a terrific showman.

Deacon Nina, a short, overweight black woman whose purple robe made her look larger still, replaced the preacher on the platform and distributed blue cloth bags to the Junior Healers, who descended on the congregation and took a collection. Riley dropped in five dollars and passed the bag to the next person in his row. Questions filled his mind. The most pressing one being how long could this church continue with so few in attendance?

After the collection, the congregation filtered from the hall. Joanna, the Junior Healer who had helped him to his seat, signaled him from the aisle. Riley made his way forward, and she led him onto the stage and through the side curtain. At the end of a dimly lit hallway, she opened the door to a room and waved him through. "Please wait here. The reverend and deacon will join you shortly." He thanked her. She left and closed the door behind her.

Based on the dozens of desk-high marks scraped on the walls and the large number of power outlets, this appeared to have once been the Kmart's administrative office. Hundreds of plastic chairs were stacked against the far wall. A small, round conference table sat in the center of the room with three chairs arranged around it. Riley assumed that was where they would meet, so he sat.

Ten minutes later, Deacon Nina Morgan entered and held the door for her husband. Both still wore their robes.

Riley stood, and they all shook hands. Bags puffed under the preacher's eyes, and thin red veins webbed the whites of his eyes. "Please, take a seat, Mr. Brown. I appreciate you coming." The man's voice was raspy; he looked and sounded exhausted. Maybe the performance took that much out of him. He'd held the stage for an hour—that was quite a show. Or perhaps he used stage makeup, and this was the real Freddie Morgan.

Riley tapped the digital recorder attached to his breast pocket. "I'd like to tape the interview if that's okay."

"Of course. We have no secrets at New Beginnings Church." The preacher's mouthwash failed to disguise the smell of alcohol. Dutch courage for the performance, or something else? Hardly a good sign for a man of God.

The deacon's chair creaked as it took her weight. Riley judged her to be significantly younger than her husband. The reverend waited for Riley to seat himself before he joined them at the table. "And please, Mr. Brown, call me Freddie, and this is Nina." The woman nodded toward Riley, although her quick glance at Freddie and her pursed mouth indicated she didn't approve of the informality.

"Thanks. I'm Riley. I enjoyed the service. You have powerful stage presence."

Freddie's smile showed teeth but failed to lift the weariness from his eyes. "Thank you, but I hope you understand that you witnessed far more than a theatrical performance."

"Great," Riley said. "Let's start there. What exactly do you believe happened with the three children on the stage?"

Freddie eased back in his chair. Puzzlement filled his face. "Why, they were healed of course." He turned to his wife. "What were the ailments today, my dear?"

In a clipped voice, she said, "The Booker twins have cystic fibrosis, and Shanice Mosely suffers from a leaky heart valve."

Riley didn't need to be much of a reporter to detect the tension between these two.

"Why don't you tell us what you think happened, Riley?" she asked.

"Oh! I meant no offense. My opinion isn't important. My job is to hear the story from its source and report the facts."

The reverend nodded. "Then, we are alike, you and I. You act as a conduit, receiving information and focusing it into a story. I too am a messenger, through which the Holy Spirit passes its healing power."

"An interesting metaphor."

The reverend sighed. "I trust your work is not as taxing as mine, Riley."

Riley smiled. "I wanted to ask about that. You look all in."

"Channeling the healing power drains me. I—"

Nina put a hand on Freddie's arm and squeezed. His mouth clamped shut, and she took over. "Today's congregation was small due to the weather. Some Sundays, Freddie has twice as many children to heal. He can hardly walk through the curtain after the strain of such a large healing." As she stared at the side of her husband's face, Riley was reminded of Nancy Reagan at her husband's first inauguration. But he couldn't shake the feeling that he was observing a performance.

"That was another question I had. How long have you occupied these premises?"

"Five years," Nina said.

"I imagine the upkeep is expensive. The hall has space for many more people than I saw in attendance today."

Freddie opened his mouth to speak, but Nina's fingers again pressed on his arm, and he stayed quiet. Freddie was the stage presence, but his wife seemed to handle everything else. "Every week is a struggle, Riley. When our previous prayer hall became too small to accommodate the congregation, we prayed for guidance and God told Freddie to expand. We trust that over time Freddie's flock will grow to fill the space."

Freddie patted her hand. "It will, my dear; have faith. God moves on a celestial timetable."

She nodded along with his words. "As Freddie says. But for the kindness of strangers we wouldn't be able to continue. That's why I contacted News Channel 13. Every Sunday, Freddie performs the miracle of healing. If more people knew of us, his reach could expand. Many more children are in need of his healing touch. I hope you will help spread the word."

Riley smiled. "So you could kill two birds with one stone: increase your income and heal more children."

The deacon attempted a smile, but her pinched expression reminded Riley of someone biting a lime. "Perhaps you could have chosen a nicer metaphor, but the sentiment is correct. Freddie's mission is to heal. The collection and tithes are a necessary evil. Like everyone, we have to pay our bills."

Riley pretended to make a few notes. He had his angle. Unfortunately, it was a similar angle to the other exposés he'd read. The Morgans preyed on desperate peoples' vulnerability, and they hoped to leverage publicity to expand their reach. But unlike the other faith healing churches he'd researched, New Beginnings Church targeted the basest human emotion—extracting money because someone feared for the health of his or her child, and that was newsworthy. If Nina Morgan had the hubris to call in a journalist, she and her husband deserved everything they got.

After a few more seconds of scribbling, Riley looked up and focused on Reverend Freddie. "Tell me about the Doolan twins." Nina Morgan had mentioned the twins by name more than once, so Riley expected their story to be a powerful endorsement of the reverend's healing powers. But two swallows did not make a summer. He suspected there were many other healed children whose stories wouldn't play so well. To build an exposé, he needed access to those children. But first he needed to convince the Morgans that he intended to report what they wanted the public to hear. It appeared that Freddie believed from the tips of his slick black hair to the bottoms of his shiny shoes that he was healing kids every Sunday. Riley surmised that Nina had a more practical handle on the church's business model. And it was she who answered his question.

"Such a tragedy," she said, her chubby face cast with an instant mask of sorrow. "Five years ago, the twins' mother, Patsy

Doolan—not much more than a child herself—was beaten to death. She was in her third trimester carrying twins, a boy and a girl. Margaret, Patsy's mother, is a long-time member of our church. She told us her granddaughter, Maya, was going to die. Freddie offered to visit the child at the hospital, but she was in a plastic bubble in the NICU. So he arranged a prayer offering— that's when the whole congregation focuses on healing one individual. The Holy Spirit responded to our pleas and saved Maya Doolan."

"So you never met Maya? Never laid hands on her?"

"Not until last week. Her mother—who was her aunt, she adopted the children after her sister's death—is a nonbeliever, but Margaret kept us informed."

"I see. But, and pardon me if this seems a naïve question, how do you know Freddie was responsible for her cure?"

Freddie smiled, spread both hands on the table and stared into Riley's eyes. "Faith," he said. "It was the faith of her grandmother and the congregation that called down the power of the Holy Spirit. You see, Riley, He… is everywhere."

Nina jumped in. She seemed to have little confidence in Freddie's ability to convey what she wanted Riley to hear. "Even the doctors described the child's recovery as a miracle. They had given up hope. Maya's life support machines were scheduled to be turned off the day after Freddie led the healing service."

"I see. That is a remarkable story. And the other twin?"

"Was healed last Sunday," Nina said, her voice stronger now as she got into the stride of her story. "Although he was the stronger baby, poor Joshua suffered from hydrocephalus; his heart was weak, and he was mentally… limited. The doctors operated three times to balance the pressure in his brain. Two weeks ago, they told Joshua's mother they could do no more, and she brought him to see Freddie." She softened her voice as though sharing a secret. "Riley, even a nonbeliever will trust in God when all else has failed. There is faith inside us all."

"So, Freddie laid hands on Joshua and healed him?" Riley strained to keep skepticism out of his tone.

"Yes. The fluid in his brain is in balance. His heart is strong. The boy is well. His grandmother tells me he's healthier than at any time in his life. The Doolans are twice blessed."

"Wow. That is extraordinary. This should make a compelling human-interest story. If more people hear about your abilities, I'm sure you'll fill a few of those empty chairs."

Nina Morgan puffed up with pride, and her husband delivered a knowing smile.

While they were busy being pleased with themselves, Riley went after the real data. "And the children you healed today. What were their names again? I'd like to follow up with them."

Nina's flinch was almost imperceptible—a slight easing away from the table, a twitch of her left eye. "Is that necessary?"

"Oh, yes. My story will have a far greater impact if the parents of those you healed at the service I attended corroborate the success." Riley waited, pen poised over his notebook.

"Go ahead, dear," Freddie said.

If looks were knives, the glare his wife threw him would have lacerated Freddie's face. She turned to Riley and managed a grim smile. "I have their details in the church's database," she said. "I'll email you their contact information this afternoon. You already have contact information for the Doolans, right?"

"Thank you, yes. You sent that earlier." Today's children and their families might have been stooges set up by the Morgans to feed him false information, but he didn't think so. On stage, the children had been terrified, and Freddie had totally committed during the healing ceremony. Riley stood and shook hands with the Morgans. "I have everything I need. Give me a few days to do my follow-ups, and then I'll get back with you." Riley didn't know how useful the twins' supposed miraculous cures were. The girl had gotten well five years ago, apparently using prayer telepathy, but two boys with cystic fibrosis and a teenager with a leaky heart valve—if Freddie had fixed those ailments that would truly be a miracle.

"Must you?" Nina's sharp tone of voice halted his pour.

Freddie put down the bourbon bottle, and like a scolded child he took a pull of liquor from his half-filled glass. "I thought a celebration was in order."

The pleading in his voice turned her stomach. "As though you need an excuse."

He narrowed his eyes. "You got what you wanted, didn't you—a television spot."

What was the point? One or two more drinks and he'd try to convince her the interview went well. "Why the hell did you offer him contact information for today's children."

"He asked."

"If he asked you to jump from a ledge, would you? I told you to keep him focused on the twins. Their story's rock solid. The twins are healthy, Margaret Doolan is a true believer, and her daughter is a skeptic who will have to admit she doesn't know how they recovered."

"When he witnesses the new healings, he'll be even more convinced."

She turned away. Couldn't bear to look at him. After six years of pretending and begging and cajoling, she had finally gotten a chance to promote the church, a chance for some powerful public relations, and his blind belief and big mouth had screwed it up in ten minutes.

"Nina, I'm beginning to think you have less faith than Riley Brown," he said.

"What?" Freddie was preaching. Preaching at her! She spun around and marched across their living room until she was in his face. He took a step back. "Riley Brown hasn't had to spin-doctor your healings for six years. And now, thanks to you, he won't have to. He'll just call up the parents of those three kids, and they'll tell him everything he needs to know about the supposed faith healing he watched today."

Freddie straightened and lifted his chin. "Not every healing is successful. You know that, Nina. The parents need to have faith. They need to believe."

She glared into his face, into the face of the man she once adored. And felt nothing but disgust. She'd turned into an apologist for his ineptitude. And now he was quoting the excuses she made to disgruntled parents back at her as though they were true. In six years, his successes numbered in the low dozens. And those could equally be attributed to luck. Children got sick, and then they got well again. Sometimes, the timing worked in Freddie's favor. That was all it was. That was all it had ever been.

"I'm done," she said, and left the room before he started pleading again in his whiny voice. She went into their bathroom, swilled her face, and studied her reflection in the mirror. Gone was the slim girl who'd rushed to marry the preacher before someone else snatched him away from her. Freddie leaned on the bottle, and she buried her disappointment in carbohydrates. But she could get back in shape. Freddie would always be a drunk. She leaned close to the mirror. How many times had she had this bathroom conversation with herself? She had to leave, get out while she was still young enough to start over. But with what? A twenty-six-year-old black woman with no education who had never held a steady job, how would she survive? McDonalds' wages wouldn't even cover rent on a place of her own. She could go home. Ask her mom's forgiveness. She shuddered. No. Staying with Freddie was better than that path. If only the idiot had kept his mouth shut. The reporter was primed and ready to run with the Doolan story.

She patted her face dry. Maybe he'd use the twins anyway.

"If not," she said to her reflection. "It's time to go. And to hell with the consequences."

CHAPTER 13

The following morning, Riley called in to work and explained he was doing follow-up interviews. The Doolans lived twenty minutes from his apartment, so he went there first. He could have called ahead, but face-to-face surprise visits usually delivered better results.

Another storm front had swept into town. Rain hammered on his car's roof. After double-checking the address—no point in getting wet for nothing—he pulled an umbrella from the passenger seat, climbed out, and stepped in a puddle. The water was deep enough to top his shoe and soak his sock. *Damn it.*

On his laptop, Riley had copies of the images of Maya Doolan emailed to him by Nina Morgan. But after his interview with the deacon and reverend of New Beginnings Church, he didn't trust a single pixel of the evidence they'd presented.

Twins Miraculously Cured or *Faith Healer Exposed.* Either story would work although the second option wasn't new and seemed unlikely to get an enthusiastic response from his editor. Even so, his pulse quickened when he rang the Doolan's doorbell. Chasing down facts, piecing together a story. This was what he'd studied for. This was what he loved. As he saw a shadow approaching through the front door's glass panel, Riley folded the umbrella and leaned it against the wall, out of sight. He hunched his shoulders and raised his collar before pulling out his plastic-covered press card and holding it next to his face.

A worn-looking woman, early fifties, answered the door. "Yes?"

"Riley Brown, News Channel 13." He handed her his ID. "Reverend Morgan of New Beginnings Church sent me. He said you could tell me about the twins' faith healing."

"Oh, dear. The reverend didn't mention… I mean—"

Riley pointed to the sky. "Any chance I can come in out of the rain?"

"Who is it, Grandma?" A young boy, five or six years old, stepped into the hallway behind the woman, followed by a girl. Their faces were remarkably similar; both had unusual eye coloration, clearly they were brother and sister. So the twins existed, and based on a cursory glance both seemed healthy. Interesting—according to the media coverage of Patsy Doolan's death, the babies had suffered severe damage at the end of their father's boots.

The woman stepped back. "Just for a few minutes then. You do look very wet."

"Thank you, ma'am. Much appreciated. I don't think it's ever going to stop raining." He smiled and offered his hand. She shook it. "I'm Riley."

"Margaret."

He peered past her. "Are those the twins?"

The woman turned. "You two. Go back into the living room and watch TV."

The boy disappeared, but the girl lingered for a few seconds, intently focused on Riley. Her eyes were deep violet, striking. And there was something about her, a presence; the intensity of her stare made Riley's scalp prickle.

"Go on now, Maya," their grandmother said. The girl dragged her feet after her brother but held Riley's gaze until the doorway interrupted the contact.

Riley pulled a notepad from his inside pocket and made a performance of leafing through to find the information he sought before looking up again. "I attended yesterday's service at New Beginnings Church."

"I was there."

"So you saw the three children on the stage. Do you believe Reverend Morgan cured them?"

"If they have faith."

"After the service, I spent time with the reverend and the deacon. They told me a prayer service held at their church cured"—he glanced at his notes, although he didn't need to—"Maya when she was in critical condition in the NICU."

"That's correct."

"And Joshua's healing occurred just last Sunday. Is that right?"

"The Lord works in mysterious ways."

"Indeed. But did Reverend Morgan of New Beginnings Church cure your grandchildren? Or would you categorize their improved health as heavenly intervention unconnected with the church?" Riley felt sure he knew the answer. Five minutes with Nina Morgan convinced him that she was manipulating whatever had happened to the twins to gain publicity for her church and money for her collection plate.

Margaret frowned, hesitating for a few seconds before answering. "I believe that God works through the ministry of Reverend Morgan, yes. And through that ministry, God took pity on my grandchildren and saved them."

Her words were carefully chosen and deliberately articulated. Damn it. Why did she have to speak in mystical riddles? "So to be clear, you think God cured the twins, and to do so he used the reverend as a... vehicle?"

Face serious, she nodded. "Precisely."

"And what ailments did he cure?" Riley heard a tinge of cynicism in his words. Perhaps she wouldn't notice.

But she did, because her tone changed. "I'm sorry, Riley. I don't feel comfortable discussing this further with you. Why don't you come back when their mother is home."

He took another unnecessary glance at his notes. "That would be Lauren Doolan, their adoptive mother?"

"Yes. She's at work just now. Wait one moment. I'll get her number for you."

Margaret left him. As soon as she disappeared into the kitchen, Riley moved along the hall until he reached the living room. He looked in. The boy sat in front of the TV, watching cartoons. The girl stood statue-still in the center of the room with her back to the screen, staring at the open door as though she'd been waiting for him to appear. Again they locked eyes. The stare was mesmerizing, unnerving. His stomach clenched. He struggled to swallow, but couldn't look away.

As a child, Riley had once stood with his nose pressed against the thick glass of the tiger enclosure at Zoo Atlanta. A big cat had rushed forward. Stopping inches from his face, it fixed him with a hungry, penetrating glare that speared terror into Riley's heart. Rooted to the spot, his legs had turned to string. The animal sensed his vulnerability, and the fear-memory had never left him. As he stared into Maya's eyes, he experienced that feeling again—defenseless prey facing an overwhelming opponent. And yet he felt a powerful urge to move toward her, to enter the living room even though that would upset Mrs. Doolan and ruin his chance at further information.

"Should you be standing there, Mr. Brown?" Maya's tone was clipped and carried an authority far beyond her years.

Margaret Doolan came out of the kitchen holding out a scrap of paper. "Here you are, Riley… Oh!" She peered into the living room and her granddaughter spun around so she faced the TV alongside her brother. And when she broke eye contact, Riley took an involuntary half step back, as though he'd been straining against a rope that suddenly went slack.

His heart rattled his ribs; his brain flooded with a primal flight response. Only when Margaret Doolan tapped his arm did he drag his eyes from the girl's back. "Ah. Sorry. I'd best be going." He strode along the hallway and opened the door.

"Don't you want this?" she asked.

He stared past her, expecting to see the girl again, relieved when she wasn't there. "Huh? Oh, yes. Sorry." He accepted the paper with Lauren's phone number handwritten on the top and slipped it between the pages of his notebook.

"Thank you so much, Margaret. I appreciate the time you've given me." He tripped on the doormat on his way out. Got halfway down the path before he remembered his umbrella. When he returned for it, Mrs. Doolan stood at the door with a puzzled look on her face. He forced a smile, grabbed his umbrella, and marched toward the garden gate. Pulse pounding, Riley quickstepped to his car as though that tiger had smashed through its glass cage and was hot on his heels and ready to pounce.

CHAPTER 14

Lauren dropped onto the sofa, sank into the cushions, and took a few seconds to steady herself. "What did he want?" she asked. Her mother, in a casual how-was-your-day voice, had just informed her of the reporter's morning house call.

"He interviewed Reverend Morgan at the church after yesterday's service and the reverend told him about Joshua and Maya's *healing*."

She held up her hand. "Why was he at New Beginnings Church?"

"Oh!" Her mom put a finger to her chin. "I didn't think to ask. That's why I gave him your number. I told him you'd be better—"

"You did what?"

"Gave him your number."

Lauren took a couple deep breaths. She patted the sofa beside her. "Sit, Mom. Start from the beginning."

"You're angry. I knew you would be. His visit caught me off guard, but he's a very nice man."

Lauren shook her head, forced a smile, and kept her voice calm despite the anxious tingling in her stomach. The last thing she needed was a reporter investigating how the twins got well. "I'm not angry. I just want to understand what you told Mr. Brown so I'm prepared if he calls me."

Her mom narrowed her eyes and stared at Lauren for a few seconds before her face softened. "Okay." She sat on the couch and squeezed her daughter's thigh. "Actually, it's quite exciting. Maybe the twins will become famous."

The anxiety crested into a wave of nausea that flipped Lauren's stomach and she swallowed, hard.

Later that night, Lauren sat in bed with her laptop and pulled up Riley Brown's LinkedIn profile to confirm that he *was* a reporter for News Channel 13 and not an imposter. She still couldn't believe her mom had invited a stranger into her home because he was getting rained on! Twenty-five-year-old Riley was fresh out of journalism school. If the news network thought they were onto a big story, surely they would send a more experienced reporter. That logic gave her hope. But reporters were paid to snoop, and if he discovered the truth about how Maya had recovered, Lauren was in big trouble: federal-prison-type trouble.

She got out of bed and paced.

If the reporter contacted her, she needed a strategy. Perhaps she could turn adversity into opportunity. Perhaps Riley Brown offered a way out, a way to deflect unwanted attention from her children. When Lauren first joined Pharmacon, Dr. Arrunsen only trusted her with simple tasks. Maybe News Channel 13 sending a rookie to check up on New Beginnings Church was the journalistic equivalent of test-tube sterilization, or slide cataloging—a simple job with little need for expertise and difficult to screw up.

Much as she disliked Reverend Morgan, her mom was convinced that God had worked through the man to cure Maya and Joshua. That's what her mother had told the reporter, so Lauren would stick to the same story. Then Riley Brown could focus on the church and its faith healing, not on her children.

On Wednesday morning, her phone woke her. She fumbled, found the device on her nightstand, and pulled it under the covers to answer.

"Hello?"

"Is this Lauren Doolan?" a man asked.

"Huh?" She checked the bedside clock—six thirty.

"Who wants to know?" She stifled a yawn.

"Riley Brown, News Channel 13. Your mother, Margaret Doolan—"

"I know my mother's name." Lauren sat up in bed.

"I apologize. Is there a more convenient time? I can call back later this morning, or drop by if that works better for you."

This rookie was pushy. "No. This is fine. You woke me is all. My mother told me about your visit. What can I do for you?" Lauren was wide-awake now. Nervous energy prickled her cheeks. She had to get this right. For the twins' sakes. For everyone's sake.

Riley cleared his throat. "If I may, I'd like to ask a few questions about the twins in relation to New Beginnings Church. Would you mind if I taped this conversation, that way I won't have to make notes as I go."

"Uh, fine. Go ahead."

"Thank you. Last Sunday, I attended a service at New Beginnings Church. I watched as Reverend Morgan laid hands on three children. Afterward, I spent an hour with the reverend and his wife."

Poor you.

"The reverend showed me two photos, which he claimed were images of your daughter, one before she was *healed*, and one after."

"Go on."

"He told me your mother supplied the pictures, and that they represented the successful results of the faith healing services he holds on Sunday mornings."

Lauren itched to ask if the reverend had supplied before and after images of any other children, but she remained quiet. She needed to make a believer of Mr. Brown.

"Are you still there, Ms. Doolan?"

"Yes. What do you want to know?"

"Oh." His voice was less sure. Maybe he had expected her to sing the praises of New Beginnings Church. But Lauren didn't trust herself to maintain a pretense of belief in Freddie Morgan—that was her mother's role. "I met the twins yesterday when I visited your home. You have two beautiful children."

"Thank you."

"And they did seem healthy. *Was* Reverend Morgan responsible for their recovery?"

This was important. Riley was reporting his story from the church's perspective; and that was where she wanted him to stay. "My mother has been a church member for many years. She explains the *healings* like this—only God can heal, but he uses earthly vehicles to transmit his power. For the twins that power came through Reverend Morgan at New Beginnings Church. Does that help, Mr. Brown?"

"Please, call me Riley."

A smile crept across Lauren's lips. She seemed to have gained his confidence, now if she could just nudge him in the right direction, any direction so long as it was away from the twins. "So tell me, Riley. If Reverend Morgan explained how he *healed* the children why call me? Don't you believe him?"

"I have to validate my sources."

"I see. Look, Riley, my daughter was very ill. Her mother died in childbirth." Lauren swallowed. Talking about Patsy's death still clogged her throat.

"Please accept my condolences."

"Thank you. My mother petitioned the church to pray, and Maya recovered. I'm just grateful to have my daughter home and healthy. When Joshua's hydrocephalus worsened, we took him to a church service. One week later, he was much better. I can't explain the cause and effect, but I'm forever indebted to *whatever* power was responsible for making my babies well again."

"So you do believe in the case of your twins that Reverend Morgan wielded that power?"

"I don't think my beliefs are important. I'm just happy my twins are healthy."

"I see," he said, but his tone implied otherwise.

A four-heartbeat silence became uncomfortable for Lauren. "Will you be interviewing other church families?" she asked.

Riley sighed. "Therein lies my problem, I'm afraid. Yesterday I visited the families of the three children I saw at church last Sunday. Reverend Morgan laid hands on them at the service. But unlike Maya and Joshua, they haven't been cured. The children's mothers are very upset. They feel they've been duped."

Damn it.

"Ms. Doolan, your mother is a member of New Beginnings Church, but you aren't. Correct?"

"Yes. She's attended the church ever since they operated out of a derelict wooden hut. Frankly, I'm glad they moved. I was never comfortable with her traveling there."

Riley laughed. "I understand. I visited the original building to pick up background shots. I wouldn't like *my* mother going there either. No. The reason I asked was so I don't offend your beliefs with what I'm about to say. You see, I can't see how to validate the church's claims of faith healing. Between you and me, it isn't unusual to discover that the miraculous healings claimed by churches such as Reverend Morgan's don't stand up to investigation. But your twins are an exception. Their recovery seems remarkable. Somehow I have to reconcile the facts to form a coherent story."

"I see."

"Could there have been another cause for the twins' recovery?"

Cornered, Lauren's heart skipped and bumped in her chest and she hunted an escape. After a couple steadying breaths, she answered in what she hoped was an offhand manner, "I can't think what. I'm sorry. As I said, I'm just delighted to have my babies home safe and sound."

"Of course. Thank you for your time. May I call again if something else comes up during my research?"

"Sure. But not at six thirty a.m."

He laughed. "Agreed. Oh. Just one more question. May I use the images Reverend Morgan provided of Maya? The before and after shots."

Lauren slammed her fist into the mattress. "Absolutely not!" Her voice came out sharper than she intended. That damned preacher shouldn't have displayed them on the screens at church. Lauren hadn't complained at the time because that ship had sailed, and she didn't want to hurt her mom's feelings. But the last thing she needed was Maya's or Joshua's face on TV. "I don't want the twins used in your story at all."

"I don't really have a story otherwise."

"I'm sorry about that, but the pictures the pastor gave you are *not* public record. You do not have my permission to use them. My children are minors, and if I hear their names or see their likenesses used on TV, I assure you I will sue."

The line went silent. Blood thrummed in Lauren's ears. She eased the mouthpiece away from her face in case he picked up the sound. Had she gone too far, inadvertently raised his suspicions that something else was at the root of the twins' recovery?

"I understand, Ms. Doolan. That's why I asked."

Lauren let out the breath she'd been holding. "I'm sorry for snapping at you."

"Not at all. You're protecting your children. Thank you for your time, and I'm sorry I woke you."

She hung up, leaned back against her headboard, and flexed her arm a few times to ease a cramp in her elbow caused by gripping the phone so tightly. Clearly, Riley Brown had as low an opinion of New Beginnings Church as she did. But he couldn't run an exposé trashing the church's claims because two cures *had* happened; so his story didn't work. Tough. Mr. Brown would just need to find something else to fill his newscast.

When she heard no more from Riley Brown, Lauren assumed he'd abandoned the New Beginnings Church story and moved on to more fruitful pastures. Driving home from work on Thursday, her phone rang. She answered hands free. "Hello?"

"Lauren? Is that you?"

It was a woman's voice, one she recognized but couldn't place. "Yes. Who's this?"

"It's Dorothy."

The hospital's patient advocate—Dorothy had been a saint during those terrible weeks when Maya was confined to her isolator. Lauren always made a point of dropping by and saying hi to the woman when they visited Dr. Pavan. "What a lovely surprise. How are you?"

"Fine. I'm not interrupting am I?"

"Hardly. I'm crawling through rush hour traffic. I'm glad of the company. What's up?"

"Probably nothing, but I wanted to give you a heads-up. A journalist from News Channel 13 was at the hospital today. He told me he needed background about our NICU for a story he was working on. I gave him the CliffsNotes tour, but the longer he stayed, the clearer it became that he was more interested in asking questions about Maya and Joshua. Of course, I told him all patient

MAYA

information was private and protected. Good gracious, he's a reporter, he should know that."

I'm sure he does.

"Obviously, I didn't tell him anything about the twins. But his questions struck me as odd—as though he didn't believe they'd ever been ill. Anyway, you know me, overprotective of my babies. I just thought you should know in case he contacts you."

So much for Riley Brown abandoning his story. Instead, it seemed he was focusing on the twins. Why else would he visit the hospital? Lauren sucked in a deep breath and spoke in a voice far calmer than she felt. "Well, that is odd. Thank you for letting me know."

"As I said, it's probably nothing."

"But forewarned is forearmed, right? How are you anyway?" They made small talk for a few minutes. "And how is Joshua?" Dorothy asked.

"Oh, you know," Lauren feigned a tired voice, deflecting the question.

"Ha! I thought as much," Dorothy said.

"Excuse me?"

"That reporter told me he had interviewed your mom, and Joshua was at home and seemed perfectly healthy. Honestly, these journalists will say anything to get a story."

"Seems that way. Thanks again, Dorothy. Look after yourself."

"You too. Say hi to your mom for me."

"Sure thing." Lauren hung up.

The grizzly commute flashed by for a change, and by the time she arrived home, Lauren had figured two possible courses of action. She could own up to stealing an experimental drug from the laboratory and administering it to a premature infant and suffer the consequences, or she must shift Riley Brown's focus back to New Beginnings Church and away from the twins. The first option didn't appeal on any level. She would be in deep trouble, but what really scared her was the possibility that Maya would be taken from her.

And anyway, if she owned up to using Dr. Arrunsen's serum on Maya, that only solved half the problem—what about Joshua. How could she explain his recovery? *She* didn't even understand that. It was as though Maya had infected him with the same

104

retrovirus that had cured her as a baby. But if Maya was contagious why was no one else affected?

To increase his focus on New Beginnings Church, Riley Brown needed more success stories to report.

After dinner, while her mom dealt with Joshua's bath, Lauren took Maya into the kitchen. They sat at the table, and her daughter fixed her with penetrating eyes.

"Yes, Mommy?"

"Last Sunday, when you were in Joshua's room and you told me you were making him better, what did you mean?"

Maya's eyebrows lowered. "I just made what's inside of me go into him."

Lauren smiled, keeping it light. "So you transferred something into Joshua. Is that it?"

Maya clapped her hands and grinned, obviously relieved that her mother understood. "Yes."

Lauren leaned back and took a deep breath. "How did you know what to send?"

Again the eyebrows knitted. Maya shook her head, opened her mouth and went to speak, but stopped herself. She was struggling, but Lauren couldn't fathom how to help.

"Well," Maya said. "It's hard to describe. It's like when I breathe in and out. I know how to do it, but I can't explain it to you."

Her five-year-old daughter was using a metaphor to explain the subconscious mind! A wave of anxiety clenched Lauren's stomach. Who, she wondered, was the real child at this kitchen table? "That's called an autonomic function—like making your heart beat or digesting food. No one knows how to do those things. We just do them."

Maya nodded a few times. "Passing the *healing* into Joshua was the same. But I never knew to do it until I watched Reverend Morgan at the church."

"What makes you so sure that the reverend didn't pass a *healing* into Joshua?"

"He doesn't know how." Blurted out, her answer was filled with certainty.

"How can you tell?"

She smiled. "I just can," she said.

Lauren moved on to the million-dollar question. "Could you do it to anyone? I mean, could you pass a *healing* on to me, or is there something special about Joshua, maybe because he's your twin?"

Her daughter grinned. "You're not sick, silly."

"But if I were?"

Maya's focus drifted to the ceiling, far away, thinking deeply. The sound of the kitchen clock filled the silence between them.

Tick.

Lauren waited, her jaw locked with tension.

Tick.

The plug was pulled on the bath. Joshua and her mom would be back soon.

Tick.

Water gurgled in the drain.

Tick.

When Maya returned her gaze to Lauren's face, tears welled in her eyes. Her daughter's fingers trembled as she reached across the table and laid her tiny hand on Lauren's bare arm. "I can't. You're too formed." Tears tumbled down her daughter's cheeks. "Don't get sick, Mommy. If you get sick, I can't heal you."

A boulder of guilt lodged in Lauren's throat. She opened her arms. "Come here, you!"

Her little girl slipped off her chair. Head bowed, she shuffled around the table. Lauren picked her up and enfolded her in a big, soft hug. She squeezed and rocked and breathed in her daughter's fresh smell then peppered her cheek with kisses until she forced a giggle. "I'm not planning to get sick. I'm sorry if my questions frightened you." She stood, shifting Maya onto her hip. "Come on, I hear Joshua and Grandma coming. Bath time for you."

After she had finished bathing Maya, while her daughter was enjoying ten minutes of water play, Lauren fired off her last question. She hated to do it, hated that she might upset Maya again. But the stakes were high, and she had to know. "One more question. At last Sunday's New Beginnings service, Grandma told me Reverend Brown *healed* three other children."

Maya locked eyes with her. This time there were no worry lines on her forehead; her answer was matter-of-fact. "Reverend Morgan didn't *heal* them. He thinks he did, but he didn't."

"I see. That's a shame for the children. Tell me, if you laid hands on them like you did with Joshua, could you make them well?" Lauren asked.

Maya plunged her plastic duck under the water, let go, and squealed as it broke the surface with a plop. "Of course I could," she said, and drowned the toy again. "As long as they're *children* like Joshua and me."

Lauren lay awake until the small hours, lights off, staring at the ceiling, listening to the sounds of her sleeping family: soft snoring from her mom's room, the occasional cough or snuffle from her children. She couldn't lose them. But if Riley Brown discovered she had stolen the serum from the lab, she'd lose not only her children but her job and, most likely, her freedom. Each month was a struggle to make ends meet. Without Lauren's paycheck, how would her mom manage?

And what of Maya and Joshua? They'd be harangued by the media and studied by medical experts; they'd effectively lose their right to a life that their father's brutality had almost stolen from them once before. A right she'd promised to protect.

But to pull off this act of misdirection, she'd be asking her daughter to deceive others, to perpetrate a lie even to her grandmother, because Margaret's faith in New Beginnings Church was key.

Riley Brown didn't believe Reverend Freddie Morgan possessed a healing ability. Otherwise, the reporter wouldn't be poking around in her life, trying to build a story about Maya's and Joshua's cures. Lauren could never lie convincingly about Freddie Morgan's abilities, but her mom believed without question that the man channeled a curative power that came from on high.

And in a roundabout way, the twins' survival *was* the work of God. A god who had chosen Dr. Maya Arrunsen's science as a vehicle through which to deliver a cure rather than a phony church run by a bogus pastor.

Five years earlier while Patsy lay lifeless and cold in the morgue and the twins fought for life in the NICU, her mom had said, "Family looks after family." Riley Brown's snooping had forced her to decide between the truth, and the safety of her family.

She chose family.

CHAPTER 15

"See you this evening," Lauren said in a casual voice as she was leaving for work on Friday morning.

"Have a nice day," her mom said.

Lauren paused at the kitchen door. "By the way, Riley Brown called me yesterday."

"Oh?"

"He told me the three children *healed* at last Sunday's service had failed to improve."

"That's a shame. But those parents need to be patient. The reverend tells us some healings take time to work. They need to have faith."

"Unfortunately, Riley Brown *has* no faith and News Channel 13 has no patience. I'm pretty sure he's preparing to expose Reverend Morgan and New Beginnings Church as fakes. True or not, the publicity will be very damaging."

"Oh, dear." A frown creased her mom's forehead.

"I was thinking," Lauren said, "after all the church has done for the twins, I'd hate to see Reverend Freddie lose his congregation and have to close his doors."

Her mom's eyes widened. "Do you really think—?"

Lauren put up her hand. "I was wondering," she said, "if the parents of those children met Maya and heard her story, heard how she'd gotten better, mightn't that strengthen their faith in the church's ability to help their children?"

"I'm sure it would."

She squeezed her mom's shoulder. "Look, I have to run, but I have no plans this weekend. Why don't you ask Reverend Freddie where the children live, and tomorrow I'll take Maya along and pay them a visit—help them to believe."

Her mom beamed. "Thank you, Lauren. That's very considerate. I'm sure the reverend will be grateful."

I'll bet.

Lauren pulled out of the driveway, ready to face the Friday morning rush hour. Selling the lie to her mom was easy. Margaret operated on blind faith, which didn't require logical explanations. But how the hell would she explain her plan to Maya?

On Saturday morning, Joshua threw a tantrum when he realized Lauren was taking Maya for a drive without him. But this project was complicated, and Lauren needed alone time with Maya to finesse a cover story.

The children *healed* by Freddie Morgan belonged to one extended family who lived near the church's original location in Smyrna. For ten minutes, she and Maya rode in silence. Snug in her car seat in the rear, her little girl gazed out of the side window, absorbed in the shops and streets on this unfamiliar route. Once they hit the I285 loop, Lauren took a deep breath and broached the subject. "Maya?"

Her daughter made eye contact in the driver's mirror. "Yes, Mommy."

"Remember how you told me you can heal children the same way Reverend Morgan does?"

"Reverend Morgan can't heal children. He only thinks he can."

"Right. Well, last week at the Sunday service, he brought three children onto the stage at church and tried to heal them. Those children are sick, and unless someone helps them, they might—" Lauren's voice failed her. She swallowed and recalibrated. This was tricky; she should go slower.

"They might die?" Maya said.

Lauren glanced at her daughter, but her face was worry free. The statement had been just that, an unemotional declaration of fact. "Right. That would be horrible for the children and their families."

Maya nodded along.

"So I asked Grandma to get the address where the children lived. That's where we're going."

"And you want me to heal them?"

And there it was. All the guilt-filled hours lying awake last night worrying how this might affect Maya, blown away by one simple statement spoken with the innocent voice of a five-year-old. She smiled at her daughter. "Yes, that's what I was thinking."

"You're kind to care so much for someone else's children."

Lauren cleared her throat and paused a few seconds to steady her voice. "Is it difficult for you to heal someone?"

Maya's brow knitted, and she took a few seconds to consider the question. "It's not hard. I just have to hold them and think about passing some of me to them. Why?"

"Why? Hmm. Let me see. Well, *I* can't heal sick children, so I don't know what it's like. And I don't want you to do it if it harms you in any way. Your wellbeing is more important."

"Okay."

"One last thing." Lauren took a deep breath. "We need to keep this a secret."

The frown returned. "A secret?"

"Yes. From everyone. From Grandma, from Joshua, even from these children and their families. Can you do that for me?"

"But when they get well won't they guess?"

"No. They won't, because if we don't tell them it was you who cured them, they'll think that Reverend Morgan's *healing* worked."

Maya nodded along with the words, but the frown remained. "I can't keep the secret from Joshua."

"Oh. Why not?"

"We can't have secrets."

Lauren hadn't expected that plot twist. "Okay. Can you ask him to keep the secret, too?"

"Oh, yes. Joshua's good at keeping secrets."

What the hell does that mean?

The GPS told Lauren to take the next exit. "We'll be there soon. I'm very proud of you for doing this."

Maya grinned.

Lauren turned on the A/C. She grabbed a Kleenex and dabbed at her brow. With each step she took down this path, her feelings of uncertainty grew, and her options for backing out diminished. But she'd labored over the approach last night and couldn't see a better way to deflect Riley Brown.

As she turned onto the street where the Booker family lived, her gut churned. Rows of old single-story clapboard homes crowded together on tiny lots that lined both sides of the road. Overgrown gardens, filthy windows, broken or missing fences— every third home appeared to be abandoned. A group of six youths standing near a power pole turned as one and focused on her car. As she passed, their sullen, hooded eyes glowered. If the Booker's house was located near this gang, she would hit the gas and figure out an alternative arrangement. No way would she risk her daughter in this neighborhood.

Number 2514 was three blocks east of the youths. She checked her mirror. They hadn't followed. A rusted Ford pickup parked in the home's driveway had duct tape holding together its rear window. Lauren pulled in behind the vehicle and glanced back toward the power pole. The boys hadn't moved. She pivoted in her seat and scanned the street and the houses opposite. No one had watched their arrival. She took a deep breath, eased it out, turned, and smiled at Maya. "You ready, sweetie?"

Maya undid the buckle on her safety restraints and clambered from the car seat. Lauren opened the back door, helped her daughter out, then locked the car. "Reverend Freddie has called ahead, so the Bookers are expecting us, but they don't know what you will do."

"I understand, Mommy. It's our secret." Maya reached up and took Lauren's hand. Two of these children suffered from cystic fibrosis. How could those tiny, soft fingers heal cystic fibrosis? Doubt flooded her mind and stopped her in the driveway.

"Don't worry, Mommy. I can do it." The sureness in Maya's voice and the touch of her hand calmed Lauren. Maya gave Lauren's fingers a squeeze and smiled up at her. She should have faith in her daughter.

They walked up a pathway of cracked concrete and weeds. The front door inched open. An African American woman peered through the gap then pushed the door closed again and slid off a safety chain before opening up.

"Mrs. Booker?" Lauren asked.

"I'm her sister, Kiara. Imani's inside with the children."

Kiara let them in then poked her head out the doorway and glanced left and right along the street. She closed the door, threw a deadbolt, and secured the safety chain. Lauren glanced at her daughter, whose eyes were wide, taking in everything. One overhead light with a single uncovered low-wattage bulb lit the way. The carpet was threadbare, and the drab walls needed a fresh coat of paint. The home felt cold, unwelcoming. This was very different from any environment Maya had experienced. But no finger-squeeze of uncertainty came from her daughter.

They followed the woman down the hall and through a door on the left into a small living room—maybe fourteen foot by twelve—smaller than Lauren's bedroom. Two boys with a jigsaw puzzle spread out between them sat on the floor at the feet of a grim-faced African American woman who wore a loose-fitting dress patterned in orange, gold, and black. Her matching head square was shaped into a turban. Next to this ample woman sat a thin girl with rounded shoulders. Kiara pointed to her. "That's my daughter Shanice." She waved a hand at the boys. "And these are my sister's twins."

As if on cue, one of the boys bent forward and coughed then wheezed in a short, rattling breath and coughed again, and again. His chest sounded heavy with mucus that his meager wind was insufficient to clear.

Shanice eased closer to her aunt on the sofa as though trying to disappear into the woman's folds. The girl turned away from Lauren's smile and focused on the boys, who stared up at Maya, eyes wide and full of mistrust. Lauren felt like an underprepared job interviewee. She hadn't thought this through. When she introduced herself, her voice sounded disconnected from her, far away, and too high-pitched. "I'm Lauren Doolan, and this is my daughter, Maya."

After a quick, raking appraisal of Lauren's tight jeans and stylish blouse, Imani fixed her with a fierce stare and did not conceal the sarcasm in her voice. "That reverend from New Beginnings Church tol' me you got somethin' to say 'bout my kids."

Lauren swallowed, opened her mouthed, but before she could reply, Maya detached herself, stepped forward, and sat between the boys on the floor. Thankfully, the coughing bout had ended. Maya pointed at the puzzle, partially completed on the carpet. "Can I play?" Turning to the sofa, Maya lit the women up with a dazzling smile. As though her daughter had flipped a switch, the tension dissipated.

I don't know how she did that, but I'm glad she did.

One boy said, "We're stuck."

Maya narrowed her eyes and studied the jumbled pieces that lay next to the puzzle.

"They're not dumb," Imani said to the top of Maya's head, "just sick. Both got CF. Turns out me and their baby-daddy was both carriers. I have to pummel their chests every day to help loosen the phlegm, otherwise they can't breath right."

"The puzzle's for a twelve-year-old is why it's hard," Shanice said.

Lauren sensed their defensiveness. Was it because she was white? Was it her clothes? It never crossed her mind to dress down. Her jeans had cost one hundred dollars; there were no hundred-dollar jeans in this house. She and her mom were far from rich, but everything about this home and these people screamed poverty.

Maya's cheerful voice broke the tension again. "I'm a twin, too," she said to the boy on her left. "Here, Terrell," Maya picked up a puzzle piece, lifted the boy's hand, and placed the piece in his palm. "I think this goes with the red part near the hood of the car." She pointed with her free hand, keeping a grip on the boy's wrist. "See? Right there." Maya indicated the place, and the boy followed her finger and fitted the piece into the puzzle. "Good job," Maya said with the voice of a teacher praising him for completing an assignment.

Everyone stared at Maya, transfixed by her. Like the only light in a darkened room. "Tyrone," Maya said to the other boy.

He nodded, still staring at the puzzle. Maya released Terrell and lifted Tyrone's hand from his knee. "Here," she said, and moved his hand toward the jumble of pieces. "That blue one fits in the cloud at the top corner."

The boy picked up the piece and allowed Maya to guide his fingers. "Thanks," he said, and slotted the piece into its place.

Maya selected five more pieces from among the jumble on the floor and assembled them in her palm. "Here's a flower." She turned to face Shanice, still pressed against her aunt on the sofa. "Will you help?" Maya tilted her head in question.

"Shanice has a bad heart. She don't have no energy for puzzles," Imani said.

But Maya smiled and nodded, and the girl slipped off the sofa and onto her knees beside her cousins as though Maya had caught her on an imaginary fishing line and reeled her in. She took the girl's arm, turned over her hand and placed the flower in her palm. Shanice's fingers trembled as she accepted the assembled section. A grin split the girl's face as she clicked the large piece in place.

"There now," Maya said, and it was as though she had snapped her fingers and woken the occupants of the room from a trance.

Lauren hadn't thought to ask how long Maya needed to duplicate whatever she'd done to Joshua. How could she tell whether her daughter had completed the attempt to cure these sick children? They should have agreed on a signal. She wrenched her gaze from the children and focused on the question Imani had posed when they first entered. How much time had passed since the woman had asked? "It wasn't Reverend Morgan's idea. I volunteered to come and see you."

Kiara stepped across the room, momentarily blocking her sister's hostile stare before lowering herself into the place on the sofa vacated by her daughter. Her eyes held less malice than Imani's, but clearly, neither of them felt comfortable having Lauren in the house.

Lauren cleared her throat as the nervous tension returned. "I know it's hard to believe, but as a baby, Maya was twenty-four hours from death." The women both widened their eyes, and the family resemblance became more pronounced. "My mother has been a member of New Beginnings Church for many years, and she petitioned the reverend to dedicate a *healing* to Maya. As you can see, she recovered."

"I'm glad for you," Kiara said. "She's beautiful."

"Thank you. Then last week I took Maya's brother, Joshua, to the church. He received a *healing*, and he's much better now. I know you also asked Reverend Morgan for a *healing*. I thought if you heard my family's story and met Maya, saw what was possible, it might help you to believe."

"How much did you pay him?" Imani's voice blistered with anger.

"Uh. Sorry. I don't... I mean. Mom arranged—"

"Well good for you, but we don't have no rich momma. Nine hundred dollars we gave. Three hundred each." She pointed to the kids in turn. "The family took up a collection. That's a lot of money for *us*," Imani spat the final word like bullet.

The shot struck its target. Lauren took a half a step backward. Her mouth dropped open. Kiara nodded, and then broke eye contact, perhaps sensing Lauren's embarrassment at Imani's aggressive tone. And who could blame Imani for being angry? Lauren knew the Morgans were charlatans, but to think they would extort nine hundred dollars from these poor people who had already suffered so much with their children. How much had the reverend extracted from her mom, she wondered?

Maya sprang to her feet. "We have to go now. I'm glad I met you, and I hope the reverend's *healing* works for you like it did for me and my brother." The three kids stared up at her, and the montage reminded Lauren of an oil painting she'd once admired in a Catholic church. The scene depicted the Virgin Mary, a halo surrounding her head, arms slightly spread from her sides as she smiled down on a group of children who stared adoringly at the icon with upturned, innocent eyes.

"Yes," Lauren said. "We must be going." She expected no argument, and she received none. Kiara showed her out. When Lauren stepped through the front door, she was relieved to find her car where she'd left it, and with all four tires intact.

"Thank you for coming," Kiara said. "Don't mind Imani. She's a good person. Just bitter about the money… well you know."

"Yes. I do." Lauren shook the woman's hand. And followed Maya to the car.

The neighborhood gang stood at their lamppost. Lauren drove by and their hostile stares did nothing to ease the stress she felt after the uncomfortable visit. She took the ramp onto the outer loop. "Are you okay?" she asked Maya.

"Yes."

"Were you able to help the children?"

"I did what I did to Joshua."

"Thank you." Keeping her voice light, matter-of-fact, Lauren said, "By the way, how did you know the boys' names?"

"They told me."

Lauren took a few seconds to replay the visit then shook her head. "I don't remember."

Maya smiled. "Silly Mommy," she said, "You couldn't hear them."

"Oh." The children must have exchanged names while she was reeling from the news that the church had extorted money from this family. Although Lauren hadn't expected to be welcomed as an angel of mercy, and news of the financial transaction had added tension to an already difficult visit. Nine hundred dollars. No wonder they were angry. The reverend had ripped them off just as he ripped off her mother every Sunday. And what really creamed her corn—if Maya *had* cured the children, his fee would seem a bargain, even to Imani and Kiara.

Lauren realized she was flying along the outer lane of the freeway, white knuckles gripping the steering wheel. She glanced at the speedometer—eighty-five, and she was too close to the vehicle in front. She eased back on the gas and slid into the slow lane, but her pounding pulse wouldn't subside.

Maya said, "It's okay, Mommy. We did a nice thing. Stop worrying."

Like oil poured on rippling water, a calmness descended on Lauren, and she saw the visit through Maya's lens. Saw it for what it was—a well-meaning and kind gesture. Compared to her family, these people lived in poverty, their children's illnesses must be a constant drain on their finances and their hopes. If Maya *had* helped, then her gift would be the greatest they could have received. And if not, then nothing they had done today could make matters worse. Out of the mouths of babes… her daughter was right. There was no need to be uptight.

"That's better." Maya's violet eyes smiled at Lauren from the driver's mirror.

"Thank you, sweetie," she said and smiled back.

When they arrived home, Lauren let Maya in and Joshua ran into the hallway to greet them. He stopped in front of his sister. Cheeks flushed, arms rigidly at his sides with fists balled, he glared at her. Maya returned the favor, and they faced off, inches apart, reminding Lauren of two ants meeting each other and touching antennae. After a few seconds, Joshua turned to Lauren. Eyes blazing, he shouted, "You should have taken me!"

"Stop!" Maya's voice bounced off the walls and flooded the hallway. The sound swamped Lauren's mind, set her heart slamming and emptied her lungs of air. Joshua's head yanked around as though jerked with a rope, forcing him to break eye contact with Lauren.

"Go—a—way!" Maya said, and each syllable hammered Lauren's body like a percussive wave.

Joshua clapped hands over his ears and screamed, "I hate you!" He ran into the kitchen.

Lauren stared at her daughter. "What?"

In a honeyed voice she said, "It's okay, Mommy. Joshua's just jealous." Maya smiled up at her. That was the first serious argument she remembered the twins having, and something about it niggled in the distant recesses of her mind. But she struggled to grasp what was bothering her, what was out of place? Her mother appeared from the kitchen, drying her hands on a towel. Her gaze darted from Maya to Lauren and back. "What's happening?"

"I—" Lauren tried to focus through the foggy confusion clouding her mind.

Maya reached out and took Lauren's hand. The touch of her tiny fingers dispelled any lingering doubts. When she looked into her daughter's smiling face, contentment and pride tingled Lauren's cheeks—such a beautiful, loving child. Why had she been so concerned? Siblings had arguments all the time. She shook her head. "Oh, nothing, Mom. We just got back."

"What's wrong with Joshua?"

Maya stretched out her free hand and stroked her grandmother's arm.

Margaret smiled. "Thank you, sweetie. How was the visit, Lauren?"

"The visit?" It took Lauren a few seconds to connect with the question. "Oh, it went well. Such a lovely family. I think we helped them."

"That's good. If they have faith, God will help their children"

Maya pulled on Lauren's hand. "Come on," she said, "Grandma's just brewed fresh coffee." Lauren smiled and let Maya lead her into the kitchen.

CHAPTER 16

When Riley Brown opened his boss's office door, Maxwell Priory was on the phone. He signaled Riley in and pointed to the chair across the desk from his. The reporter sat, and waited, but his eyes widened when he noticed the printout of his New Beginnings Church story treatment opened in front of his boss with comments scrawled in the margin.

Priory hung up the phone. "Now"—he locked eyes with Riley—"tell me more about these *miracles* at New Beginnings Church."

Riley launched into an overview of the teaser he'd written about the church's faith healing successes. Ten seconds into his precise of the story that sat on his boss's desk, an impatient scowl formed on Maxwell Priory's face. He held up a hand and cut Riley off in mid-sentence.

"I know all that. I've read your outline." He picked up the papers and slapped them with the back of his hand. "What about interview potential?"

"Ah. Right. The Bookers and the Moselys will speak, but they want a fee."

"They have twins with CF and the girl with the heart murmur, right?"

"Yes. Actually, both the Doolans and the Booker families have twins."

"Is that significant?"

"Doesn't seem to be."

"Hmph." Maxwell glared at him, lips pursed, and shook his head. "What about the Doolans?"

"According to the mother, absolutely no interviews or access to her children."

"Who else can we speak to?"

"The grandmother is a possibility. She's committed to the church and devoted to Reverend Morgan."

Maxwell stood, turned his back on Riley, and moved toward the window. His gray slacks bagged at his skinny butt. A misshapen cardigan hung from stooped shoulders. The bottom of the garment bowed up at his waist and the wool was threadbare in the center where his spine rubbed against his office chair. He reminded Riley of a stick insect. "Can *she* provide access to the children?"

"I don't think so."

Maxwell spun and glared at Riley. "I don't care what you think. Can she or can't she?"

"No. Her daughter is adamant we not use the Doolan twins. She can't stop us mentioning them in general terms of course. If we use their images she's threatened to sue. But we have enough without her. I spoke to Imani Booker this morning, and she's convinced that her twin boys are cured of cystic fibrosis."

"I thought CF was incurable."

Riley grinned. "It is."

"Hmph." Maxwell turned back to the window. "What about the Mosely girl."

"Shanice was born with leaking heart valves. Her mother says they don't leak anymore."

Maxwell pirouetted on his heel and narrowed his eyes at Riley. "Are you telling me you believe this faith healer is for *real?*"

"Here's what I know. The first time I visited Imani Booker, she would have hung Reverend Morgan from a tree if I'd supplied the rope. He charged three hundred dollars each to *heal* her sons and her niece, and she saw no improvement."

"No surprise there."

"Quite. And their story is more current and accessible than the Doolan twins', who recovered from serious injuries, but at separate times. The boy, Joshua, did attend a church service but not the daughter. Her only connection with the faith healer was through her grandmother, who paid the pastor and the church members to pray for her. Margaret Doolan believes Reverend

Freddie's prayers cured her granddaughter, but she and the reverend are the only ones who do."

"Not even their mother?"

"Especially not their mother."

"Okay, so we can use the Doolan kids as referential support. How do we prove the other *miracles* happened?"

"Imani Booker and Kiara Mosely will give permission for a medical examination of their children."

"Good work." Maxwell stroked his chin.

"But first," Riley said softly, "they want three thousand dollars."

The chin stroking stopped, and laser eyes locked on Riley's. "What will the doctor find?"

Excitement tingled Riley's stomach. The editor hated spending money, but he was intrigued; Riley sensed it. *Play it cool.* "Obviously, I'm not medically qualified, but both mothers insist that their kids are healthier than they've ever been."

"You haven't seen them?"

"Not since my first visit when they were three of the sickest kids I'd ever laid eyes on. But Imani Booker called me, and I don't think she would have unless she felt certain something had changed. Like I said, they were all about helping me hang the church out to dry the first time we met."

"Where did they come up with the idea we'd pay them three thousand dollars?"

"Not sure."

"I hope you weren't too excited when you heard news of their miracles on the phone."

Riley's cheeks heated. He'd been like a kid in a candy store. "No, sir."

"Sure you weren't." Maxwell's voice oozed sarcasm. "Chalk that down to experience, young man. Never show them what you think. It colors their story, and it costs me money. Okay. Damage done. Let's move on. What'll the doctor charge?"

"Fifteen hundred for all three kids to have a thorough checkup including blood work."

Maxwell moved back to his desk. He stood behind his chair and leaned forward, placing both hands on the desktop. The stick insect had become a praying mantis—the female, about to eat its mate. He glowered at Riley. "Will we get our money's worth?"

His heart was pumping so hard he was sure the editor-in-chief would hear the beat. This was his moment. Months of man-bites-dog trivia was over. He was going to get his first story. "Yes, sir. I'm sure of it."

"You'd better be. Okay, set it up with the doctor. Don't tell him *why* he's doing the physical. I don't want his judgment colored. Also, when you speak to the kids' mothers make sure they don't go blabbing to anyone before we have the proof. Get legal to draw up contracts. We must have exclusive rights to the story or no deal. Clear?"

"Yes, sir."

"The reverend charged them nine hundred dollars, right?" He didn't wait for an answer. "Okay, we'll pay nine hundred when they sign and the rest if the kids' health checks out. Got it?"

"Yes, sir!"

"Well?" He straightened and made a shooing motion with his hand. "Jump to it."

Riley sprang to his feet. "Thank you, sir."

As Riley opened the door, Maxwell said, "Good work, Riley. But the devil's in the details. Don't screw this up."

"I won't." He closed the door and punched the air. Behind him he heard, "One more thing."

He turned, cracked the door, and peered into the office. "Yes, sir."

"Don't give up on the Doolans."

"Huh?"

"Do you like the mother? Is she attractive?"

"I—"

"Shame. That won't work then. What about the father?"

"He's served five of a twenty-four-year sentence for voluntary manslaughter. A family court removed his parental rights and approved Lauren Doolan's adoption. The children are hers, and she's determined to keep them off the TV."

"In that case, work through the grandmother."

"The grandmother?"

"She wants everyone to believe in *her* reverend. Let her help you make that happen."

"Oh… okay?" Riley closed the door, quietly. Maxwell Priory sure knew how to kill a buzz.

With contracts in hand, Riley drove to Smyrna. He'd called ahead, and Imani Booker opened the front door before he knocked—must have been waiting for him to arrive; three thousand dollars will do that. She greeted him with a wide grin. Her enthusiasm put him on guard.

"Come in. Kiara's in the living room with the kids," she said.

She led him into a tidy kitchen that felt warm and smelled of baking. She pointed to a chair near the table. "Wait here. I'll get my sister." Imani's demeanor was strikingly different from his first visit. That day, she'd been so angry that he wondered if she planned to tackle Reverend Morgan herself and demand a refund. She was a woman to be reckoned with. Riley didn't rate the reverend's chances of besting a determined Imani Booker.

Both women joined him at the table, and he pulled two contracts from his briefcase. "Okay. Once you sign these, I'm authorized to arrange a doctor to give the children a checkup."

"They're on Medicaid. They already have a doctor," Kiara said.

Riley's nagging doubts bloomed again. Perhaps his boss's suspicions were on point and these women planned to string him and the corporation along just to make money? God knows, they could do with the extra cash. "It's better if they see a GP who doesn't know their medical history. That'll give us an unequivocal baseline." The women looked at each other. Either they didn't understand, or their ruse was about to be exposed.

"It's normal practice," Riley said. "Their own doctor will focus on what's changed, maybe get excited by the improvements. Whereas an independent examiner will approach the checkup without preconceived notions."

"When do we get the money?" Imani asked.

"Sign the contract and you'll receive nine hundred now. That makes you whole for the cash you gave the church. If the doc gives them clean bill of health we'll release the remaining funds." He pointed to the contract. "You can read the fine print if you want to, but basically you are granting News Channel 13 exclusive rights to tell the story of how your children were *healed*. Once our doctor has examined the children, we'll want them to see their regular physician. He or she can offer an opinion on how much improvement they have made. We'll want to interview him or her for the story."

"What do you think, Imani," Kiara asked.

Imani fixed Riley with a hard stare. "Three thousand, right?"

He nodded. "Nine hundred now and the rest to come so long as the children are cured. But only if you don't speak to anyone else before we air the story."

Imani turned to her sister. "Seems fair enough. Can't expect them to pay if the kids are still sick." She unclipped a pen from the top pocket of her blouse. "Where?" she asked, and Riley showed her. Once they'd both signed, he returned the papers to his case, handed over a cashier's check for $900, and pulled out a business card. "Here's the doctor's address. He's expecting you tomorrow morning at ten. Can you make that?"

Kiara glanced at the address. "Downtown. Yeah, we'll be there. That's all paid, right."

"His fee is taken care of. He'll deliver results in a couple days. If everything checks out with the children, and based on what you told me over the phone, I'm sure it will, then I'll come by with the balance, and we'll get into details about how we plan to shoot the news story." He leaned back in his chair and smiled. "Either of you ladies ever been on television before?"

Kiara blushed and stared at him with deer-in-the-headlight eyes. Imani slapped her sister on the shoulder and let out a huge guffaw. Big and loud and larger than life, Imani would play well on camera.

"You'll be fine. Our team will guide you."

"Will we get our hair done and makeup and all?" Kiara asked.

Riley grinned. "Yup. You'll be treated like movie stars."

Both women were beaming, money forgotten—amazing how the possibility of five minutes of TV fame changed people.

He closed his briefcase and placed it on the floor beside him. "Now. Can I see the children?" He'd already decided if the kids showed no signs of improvement today, he'd head back to the office and resurrect his previous story, exposing the church as a scam. He could still use the doctors' reports and interview the mothers. It would work. Not as effectively as a miracle cure but perhaps good enough to appease Maxwell Priory. Riley hoped he wouldn't have to have *that* meeting with his boss.

Imani shouted, "Terrell, Tyrone, Shanice. Come into the kitchen and say hello to Mr. Brown."

The girl was first to appear. She stopped in the doorway. The boys came right behind and bumped into her. Giggling, they pushing her toward Riley, and his jaw dropped. The women noticed his reaction and laughed.

"I don't think Mr. Brown believed us, Kiara," Imani said.

"Reckon not. He looks even whiter—anyone'd think he'd seen a ghost."

The kids giggled and blushed.

The boys looked, well, normal. On his previous visit, they'd been playing in their bedroom, and he'd only seen them briefly when they were called in to say hello. But the girl had transformed from a haggard, nervous, bent-up bag of bones who had sat on the sofa next to her mother too shy to even look at him. Her face, her hair… the girl glowed. Then she locked eyes with him and her smile lit up the room. "Nice to see you again, Mr. Brown," she said and flexed one leg to make a tiny curtsey.

"Wow! You look terrific, Shanice."

She covered her mouth and blushed.

Imani tapped his arm. "Well? What do you think now, Mr. TV Newsman? Do you have a story?"

The kids stood in a line. He studied each of them in turn, and they met his gaze. They stood with straight backs and mischievous grins, no hint of a wheeze or a cough. The twins and their cousin looked to be in great shape.

And that was when he noticed.

They all had violet eyes.

"Oh. I definitely have a story."

CHAPTER 17

On Tuesday afternoon, Riley rang Lauren Doolan's front doorbell. Margaret opened the door and eyed him over the safety chain.

"Mrs. Doolan. How nice to see you again." He smiled at the narrow slice of face visible through the crack. "I wondered if I could ask a few more questions about New Beginnings Church. News Channel 13 is—"

"I'm sorry, Mr. Brown. I have nothing to say."

"I understand. It's just that we're preparing a news item on the church. I've spoken to the two families whose children were *healed* at last week's service, and they've agreed to appear on TV to share with everyone in Atlanta the miraculous work Reverend Morgan is doing. I'd love to feature your twins as well."

She shook her head. "We're a private family. We don't want our children bothered by this."

He leaned a hand on the door as she eased it closed. "Not even to help the church?"

"You need to go now!"

"Mrs. Doolan. One more question. Did the twins always have violet eyes?"

She increased the pressure on the door, and it clicked shut in his face. *Damn it, I should have asked that first.* Disappointed, but not surprised, he turned heel and drove to his next appointment, where he had no chance of being rejected at the door. When Nina

Morgan learned he was planning to run a story about the church, she had invited him to visit her and her husband at home.

The Morgans lived in a modest two-bedroom ranch near Marietta, in the north of Atlanta. Riley pulled into their driveway and parked behind a weathered-looking blue Camry. The deacon, dressed in jeans and a blouse for once instead of a purple robe, led him to their family room.

He accepted their offer of iced tea, and the three of them sat around a coffee table.

"I visited Shanice Mosely and the Booker twins."

Freddie nodded and smiled, but his wife snapped out, "I told the Booker woman she needs to have faith and be patient."

Seems like Imani Booker's not the only one who needs to have faith.

Still smiling, the reverend asked, "How are the children?"

"I'm no doctor, but they sure looked well to me."

The deacon leaned back into the sofa cushions. The panic of a few seconds earlier sloughed off, and her frown melted. "Praise the Lord," she said.

"I want to bring a camera crew to next Sunday's service."

The Morgans received the news with wide grins and enthusiastic head nods.

"We'll put on a great show for you. Won't we, Freddie?"

Freddie finger-drew an imaginary stage on the tabletop. "I move around a lot to position each child close to where his or her family is sitting." He jabbed with a manicured fingernail to illustrate his point. "For the cameras, perhaps it'd be better if I stayed center stage throughout."

"Well, the most important thing is to heal the children, right?" Riley said.

"Of course," Nina said. "Freddie's just trying to help with the optics."

Riley leaned forward, hands on his knees, and lowered his voice—becoming their confidant. "There is one thing you might help with. It would significantly strengthen the piece."

Nina leaned in—they were a team, now. In an urgent whisper, she said, "Name it."

"The Doolans are refusing to cooperate. Maybe you could persuade them. The story would be so much more impactful if we had five successes to trumpet instead of three."

"Freddie will talk to Margaret Doolan, won't you, Freddie?" She answered so quickly her words ran together and took her husband by surprise.

"I—"

"Great." Riley clapped his hands together then pulled out his notepad. Pen poised, he asked, "I want to deliver the strongest story possible. Perhaps you can suggest other families with *healed* children I might contact?"

Nina straightened and adopted a thoughtful expression. She remained silent for ten seconds as though she were searching through a mental list of potential candidates. Finally, she frowned and shook her head. "That would cause delay. I'm sure Freddie can persuade Margaret Doolan to help. But if not, the three children you have will convey a powerful message. Don't you agree? After all, their diseases were incurable, and they are *healed*, right?"

The deacon's answer confirmed Riley's suspicions. New Beginnings Church *had* no other success stories that stood scrutiny. In fact, Nina Morgan sounded surprised to learn of the successful cures in Smyrna. Regardless, he needed to tie New Beginnings Church to a confidentiality agreement before he could pursue his first breaking-news story.

After the Morgans had inked a contract granting News Channel 13 exclusivity to the story, they walked him out. On the front doorstep, as they all shook hands, he said, "There is one thing I don't understand."

They both tilted their heads, waiting. Their synchronized movement so reminded Riley of prairie dogs that he was forced to pause and compose himself before asking, "How do you explain the children's unusual eye coloration?"

If he'd taken a photo of Freddie and Nina Morgan at that instant, he would have captioned it "Baffled and Bemused."

Freddie recovered first. "I'm sorry?"

"The children," Riley said, "Terrell, Tyrone, Shanice, Maya, and Joshua, all have violet eyes."

Freddie nodded, knowingly. "Except that you see signs and wonders, you will not believe."

"So God changed their eye color as proof of his miracle?"

Freddie delivered a condescending smile. "Mr. Brown. You are a good man but a nonbeliever. I hope by the time this project is complete you may see the light. I—" Nina Morgan wrapped both hands around her husband's arm and squeezed until her knuckles turned white. He closed his mouth.

Riley smiled and nodded. "I'll work on that, Reverend. I'll be in touch to coordinate the camera crew for next Sunday's service. Remember. Don't speak of our plans. If someone else reports the story before us, my boss will pull out. Exclusivity is essential."

As he backed his car out of the drive, Freddie and Nina Morgan stood on the doorstep grinning and waving like proud parents seeing their only son off to college. His five-minute documentary about their church would make this couple famous, locally at least; it would generate much-needed money for Imani and Kiara, and provide a leg up the career ladder for Riley Brown. So why second-guess himself?

Why? Because of Nina Morgan's reaction when he told her about Shanice Mosely and the Booker twins, that was why. There was no doubt in his mind the deacon had not expected to hear that those children had been cured. But the camera crew was scheduled. Riley had completed the storyboards, and Maxwell had approved them; he'd even complimented the rookie on a fine job. If he raised these concerns, his boss would take him off the story, and he'd be back to chasing UFOs, or worse—out of work. If something didn't quite fit in the Morgans' story, so what? His college advisor had been fond of warning Riley never to let the perfect ruin the good.

Nevertheless, on his way to the office, he punched the speed dial for Imani Booker. She answered immediately. "Riley Brown! What can I do for my favorite TV newsman?"

"Just checking that you're ready for the big day." Next week he would take a camera crew to their home and interview Imani, Kiara, and the children.

"We're all excited."

"Great. I was wondering about something. Maybe you can help?"

"Ask and you shall receive."

"Cute. Okay, when we first met, you were furious with Freddie Morgan. You called him a fraud, and a few other unpleasant names."

Imani liberated one of her big-woman guffaws. It roared from the speakers and filled his car. "Among many other *far* worse names," she said.

Riley laughed along. "So when did you change your opinion? When did you start to believe the children would recover, and you hadn't been conned?"

"I was angry, right enough—angry with Reverend Morgan for taking my money. But after Miss Lauren visited with her daughter and gave testament about how the church had helped her kids— well, me and Kiara decided maybe we should wait some, seeing as how the reverend had *healed* her twins so good. She was a pretty thing, the daughter I mean, smart as a whip, too."

The driver in the vehicle behind laid on his horn. Riley glanced down. He'd slowed to thirty. He waved an apology and stepped on the gas. "Miss Lauren? You mean Lauren Doolan called on you?"

"At first I thought the preacher had sent her. You know, to shut us up. But that woman is a true believer because she came on her own dime to show us how healthy her daughter was after her healing."

"That was thoughtful of her. Did you know the Doolans from church?"

"Nope. Never laid eyes on them before. Hey! You should have them on the show too. 'Cause the preacher's black and we're black. Folk need to understand that God cures white kids as well." Her laugh boomed out again.

Riley pulled to the side of the road and put on his emergency flashers. "And it was after Lauren Doolan's visit that the children recovered?"

"Yup. That night. Pretty soon after Miss Lauren left, they started jiggled about as if someone had fed 'em too much Pepsi. Took us forever to get them settled down. And the next morning, they was cured, like you seen them. I guess we didn't wait long enough for the preacher's *healing* to work."

"I guess. Anyway, I'll see you next week for the interview."

"We're excited!"

"Me too."

He hung up and pulled back into traffic.

He didn't know Lauren Doolan, but she was a million miles from being a "believer," and she was no fan of New Beginnings Church. So why go to so much trouble to help Freddie Morgan?

CHAPTER 18

Lauren accepted the gravy boat and splashed a healthy portion on her potatoes. "Thanks, Mom. How was your Tuesday?"

"Well, Riley Brown came by this afternoon."

Lauren's hand froze halfway to her mouth. She lowered a fork full of food and waited.

Her mom lifted her chin. "Don't worry," she said in a firm voice, "I didn't even take the safety chain off the front door."

Why couldn't he leave her family alone? "What did he want?"

"He said he'd just returned from Smyrna and those three children had gotten well. They will be on the television news next week. He wanted the twins to appear as well."

Panic knotted Lauren's stomach. "What did you tell him?"

"I told him we're a private family." Her mother gave a firm nod of her head.

"And he accepted that?"

"I didn't give him a choice."

Lauren reached across the table and patted her mother's arm. "Thanks."

Margaret smiled. "Riley's visit got me thinking, though."

Now what?

"What harm would there be in people hearing Maya and Joshua's story?"

Through narrowed eyes, Lauren studied Margaret's face—open, hope filled, innocent. It was a fair question. Perhaps it was time to trust her, time to share the burden she had been bearing alone. Keeping the truth from her mother got more difficult every day. If she confessed about the lab and about Maya's remarkable gift, it would break the chain of lies that was tangling her life. She opened her mouth to speak, to blurt out the truth and stop this crazy charade, when her mom said, "Testifying about the twins' cures on TV would let lots more families with sick children know that Reverend Morgan is performing miracles at New Beginnings Church."

Lauren swallowed her words. Even if she explained about Dr. Arrunsen and confessed what she'd done to Maya in the hospital and what Maya had done to Joshua (whatever that was) her mother wouldn't believe her. Lauren's head felt like a balloon, overinflated and about to pop. She dropped her silverware on the table with a clatter, pushed her chair back, stormed out of the kitchen into her room, and slammed the bedroom door.

Sitting at her dresser, like her teenage self when her mom had frustrated her, Lauren spoke to her reflection. "The woman is incorrigible. How can she believe a self-proclaimed reverend waving his hands and uttering gibberish had cured those three children? How can she think that prayers sent across the ether from his pulpit to a hospital located twenty miles away had lifted a death sentence from Maya?"

But that's what you want everyone to believe.

With Riley's latest visit, the flaw in her plan to divert attention from Maya and Joshua, to hide her theft of the serum, had widened into a yawning chasm. Taking her daughter to Smyrna and providing Riley with proof that the incurable could be cured had worsened the situation. Now that the twins weren't the only *healed* children, he expected her to relent and give him access. If she didn't, would that make him probe more?

"If we hadn't gone to Smryna, Shanice, Terrell, and Tyrone would be condemned to live life as cripples."

But what right did she have to force Maya to use her ability to cure others? Who was *she* to pick who got *healed* and who remained ill? Wasn't she as immoral as Reverend Morgan? Lauren rubbed at the tension in her brow. Her daughter had almost lost her life once before when Patsy decided she knew best. Patsy wasn't here to make this decision and Maya was five—too young to cope with such complexity. Lauren was her mother now. And a mother's job was to protect her child.

"The plan will still work. Provided I keep Maya and Joshua out of the spotlight. Riley Brown is a newsman and newsmen need stories. To get this story, he will have to focus on the other children."

Calmer after her mirror-conversation, she returned to the kitchen. Her mom was stacking the dishwasher. Lauren came up from behind, leaned against her back, and hugged her. "I'm sorry for losing my temper."

Margaret put down a dish and squeezed Lauren's arm. "It's okay. You're a mother, and a good mother at that. That's what moms do. They protect their own. You're right. Maya and Joshua have had more than their fair share of crises. After Patsy died, those reporters called and called, pestering me to find out about Cliff, pretending to be concerned, but they didn't give a good damn about Patsy; all they cared about was the story. Riley seems like a nice young man, but he's the same as the rest of them."

"Thanks for understanding, Momma."

Riley reached over the video editor's shoulder and stabbed a finger into the computer screen. "Why not cut to a head nod right here, and then fade back to the tears spilling down Kiara's cheek as her daughter hugs her and says, I love you, Mommy?"

The tech clicked a mouse, typed a few commands, and reran the sequence. "Yeah. Nice. That plays."

Grinning, Riley said, "Let's run the piece through once more before we move to the doctor interview?"

Riley's interview with Imani Booker, Kiara Mosely, and their children had been chopped into dozens of cutaway sections. He was in the editing room helping to merge those pieces into a five-minute report that flipped between the Smyrna interview, the MD's office, and footage of last week's church service—five minutes to tell the story of the miraculous cures dispensed by Freddie Morgan. Riley's cheeks burned and his knee vibrated. This was why he'd studied; this was what he aspired to.

His interview with Dr. Christenson, the children's MD, had provided dynamite footage. The doctor was happy to confirm that the children were well. But his obvious embarrassment at being unable to explain *how* reinforced Riley's piece—if a medical professional with intimate knowledge of the children couldn't explain what had *healed* them, there was only one conclusion to draw. Riley had punched this point home: "Doctor Christenson, in the absence of a medical explanation, would you classify these cures as miracles?"

Mouth open, the doctor paused for four seconds—Riley counted them in his head, loving every beat. He kept the dead air in and cut away before the doctor answered, "Yes. I suppose so." Sometimes, less was more.

The reverend and his wife had put on quite a show for the cameras at the Sunday service. Freddie Morgan had flung himself around the stage as he passed his healing on to five children suffering from ailments ranging from what sounded like a case of the flu to a peanut allergy. Unlike the previous week, none of the illnesses were serious—the Morgans were hedging their bets. These children might recover or they might not, but Riley couldn't use them to prove or disprove the church's claims. Unlike Shanice, Tyrone, and Terrell, there could be no certainty about the cures.

Freddie Morgan was a good showman, but editing Sunday's over-the-top stagecraft so he came across as more than a sideshow barker ended up being the most challenging part of the project. And therein lay Riley's personal dilemma—reconciling a tacky pseudo-religious service in a repurposed Kmart with the proof of his own eyes that these children had been cured.

Perhaps if he hadn't studied so many bogus faith healers as he researched this story. Perhaps if he hadn't spent so much time with Nina Morgan, or if her husband had offered additional successful healings other than the Doolan twins, whose mother refused to take part. Perhaps if Deacon Morgan hadn't been so clearly surprised by the Smyrna children's cures. Perhaps then he wouldn't be suffering from so much doubt. Doubt that had solidified into a journalistic itch that he couldn't scratch because of the rock-solid medical evidence he'd gathered.

But why, after thousands of faith healing ceremonies, could Freddie Morgan only point to these five children?

When he spotted Margaret Doolan at the Sunday service, he had approached her, recorder in hand, but she raised her palms and walked away from him.

Without the Doolan twins, Riley had no other angle from which to tell the story. So it had to run as: *"Three miracles at New Beginnings Church."* Delighted with the piece, his boss upped the ante, promoting Riley's segment as a News Channel 13 Special Report and scheduling it as the final item in Friday's thirty-minute evening news. To build excitement, Priory ran thirty-second teaser commercials before and after the regular news slot Monday through Thursday.

By Friday afternoon Riley was so jumpy, he had to leave the office and take a long walk. Although the report was "in the can," he reran it in his head, over and over, searching for any flaw that could derail the story and destroy his nascent journalism career before it cleared the starting blocks.

Dinner, baths, and story time were over before Lauren and her mom settled in front of the television to watch the recording they'd made of the evening news segment. Margaret grinned as the story opened with a shot of Riley, wearing pressed pants, white shirt, and a red power tie. He stood outside the church. The hand-painted New Beginnings sign dominated the top third of the screen.

Riley spoke into his microphone in a serious *60 Minutes* voice. "When I heard of the extraordinary assertions being made by Reverend Freddie Morgan, pastor of New Beginnings Church, I was skeptical. Eight-year-old twin boys cured of cystic fibrosis—an incurable disease. And a ten-year-old girl whose misaligned heart valves had sapped her strength and left her a virtual invalid. After visiting Reverend Morgan, these three children were suddenly able to run and play and live a normal life. These claims and others seemed far-fetched. And because they involved children—cruel and cynical. Yet, the deeper News Channel 13 probed the facts, the more remarkable the story became."

The camera cut to the interview with Imani Booker. Her jet-black hair, braided and shiny, was piled on top of her head and tied off with a bright yellow ribbon. She spoke about her boys, how weak they were, how drugs could ease the symptoms of their cystic fibrosis but there was no cure. She told the camera how her twins spent a week in the hospital every few months receiving mega doses of antibiotics to clear out their lungs. Tears formed in her eyes as she confessed that her children would suffer all their lives and probably die before they reached thirty.

Next, Riley introduced the twins' doctor—a sixty-something man with silver hair, wire-rimmed glasses, and a hang-dog expression. The MD sat in an examination room dressed in his white lab coat with a stethoscope draped around his neck and answered Riley's questions. He confirmed that the Booker boys had suffered from CF. Although he confirmed they were now free of the disease, the man was clearly uncomfortable with his inability to explain how they had recovered.

A similar sequence followed for Shanice Mosely, whose mother had apparently visited the same hairdresser as Imani. Once the doctor had reiterated his delight and amazement, the camera cut to the three children. Lauren recognized the sofa they sat on. It was in Imani Booker's living room. The boys were dressed alike in gray shorts and white short-sleeved shirts. Shanice had on a colorful print dress, and her hair had been straightened and bobbed. All three beamed at Riley as he spoke to them.

But Lauren didn't hear the questions the reporter asked the children, nor did she hear their answers. Her ears buzzed. She gripped the arms of her chair to steady herself and sucked in a series of deep breaths. Cold waves of shock and fear quivered down her neck, through her chest, across her stomach, and down her legs.

Her mom's face swam into view, concern etched on her brow. "Are you all right, Lauren? You're pale as a sheet."

Lauren shook her head, but continued to stare at the screen. Not daring to blink. Hoping she had been mistaken.

But she hadn't been, because Shanice, Terrell, and Tyrone stared back at her.

And all three had violet eyes.

CHAPTER 19

Riley's phone woke him at seven thirty the next morning. "Hello?"

"Riley?" His boss. Calling on Saturday morning! "You awake?"

I am now. "Yes, sir."

"Get your ass over to the church stat."

"Church?"

"New Beginnings. There's a crowd building. Get interviews. I want a follow-up story ready for today's lunchtime news. Mark's on his way. He'll pick you up in the van."

Riley was sitting up in bed now—wide-awake. "What's going on?"

"Some of our Southern affiliates picked up your New Beginnings story last night, and CBS will run it on tonight's national feed." CBS was their parent company. No wonder Priory sounded so enthusiastic. "It's a hell of a story. But tell me. How are they doing it?"

"Doing it?"

"Curing these kids—what's the catch?"

"Honestly, sir, all I know is the three children were sick and now they're well. Those are facts. The how?" He sighed. "I wish I had a better answer than faith healing, but I don't. New Beginnings Church is the only external factor that connects the children and their cures."

"Damndest thing," Maxwell said. "Anyway, spend an hour with the crowd and then come into the office. Oh, and good work."

"Thank y—" In the background, Riley heard someone shouting Maxwell's name.

"Gotta run." The line went dead.

He'd lied to his boss—a lie of omission. The church *was* connected with the children and with the cures, but it wasn't the *only* link. Lauren Doolan had visited the three children in Smyrna, *and* she was the adoptive mother of the two other successful miracle cures. But he'd made his bed. Reverend Morgan's faith healing was the core of his story. Backtracking because he had a hunch would cast doubts on his fundamental premise, and he wanted that even less than Maxwell Priory did.

"Damn! Just look at them." Parked in the Kmart lot, Riley peered out the side window of the news van at a line of people that began at the closed front doors of New Beginnings Church and snaked across the concrete. It was eight o'clock, Saturday morning. Apparently, people had started arriving soon after the Friday evening broadcast—thirty-six hours before the next service.

Mark, News Channel 13's videographer, gripped the steering wheel and stared at the crowd. Woken early by Maxwell Priory's call, Mark's hair stuck up like Woody Woodpecker's. He screwed up his pudgy face in disgust. "I don't like this, Riley. I mean, we don't know what's wrong with those kids."

Mark was right. Those waiting, many in wheelchairs, represented a different proposition from Riley's meetings with the Booker twins and Shanice, whose ailments were known and not contagious. Why would these families sleep in a parking lot unless their children desperately needed a miracle? Riley speed-dialed his boss. "We're here. I'm guessing two or three hundred people waiting," he said.

"Terrific. There are bound to be heart-rending stories in that line. Go get 'em, Riley."

"Listen, Mr. Priory, can Mark and I wear surgical masks? I mean, we don't know what these kids have." A furious curse screamed from the phone. Riley held the device at arm's length and turned on the speaker so Mark could share in the boss's high-pitched lecture on journalistic integrity.

"Okay, boss. I understand. Mark and I just wanted to check."

"Well, never check again."

"Yes, sir. I'm on it." He ended the call and tossed his phone on the dashboard. "Damn Nazi."

"No masks then?"

"Very funny." Riley rolled his eyes. "Let's concentrate on the kids in wheelchairs; maybe they're only disabled and not afflicted with something infectious."

Mark climbed out of the van and opened the rear doors to gather his equipment. Riley stood to the side of the vehicle, facing the church fifty yards across the parking lot. Despite his personal health concerns, his cheeks burned and his pulse pounded. His story had legs. Riley made a frame with his fingers and squinted through, selecting a backdrop for his introductory pitch.

Mark shouldered the camera. "Ready."

"We'll open with a talking-head shot, my back to the building," Riley said. "Make sure the church's sign is in the frame. When I finish the intro, I'll turn. You follow, and zoom past my shoulder to a slow pan along the crowd. Then we'll move to interviews."

Mark nodded.

"Okay, on me in three—two—one. This is Riley Brown following up the exclusive News Channel 13 report on the strange, some say miraculous, events occurring at New Beginnings Church. Last night, we brought you the remarkable story of ten-year-old Shanice Mosely, whose leaky heart valves made it difficult for her to walk the length of her street, and her cousins Terrell and Tyrone Booker who suffered from cystic fibrosis—an incurable condition that limited them physically and threatened to curtail their lives before they reached middle-age."

Riley stared grim-faced into the lens and took a silent ten-count in his head. Later, they could edit in heart-wrenching pictures of the children from Smyrna. He loved being in front of the camera. He was living his dream, even if it was predicated on the misfortune of others. That was business as usual for an investigative journalist.

He counted himself in again. "Two weeks ago, in the church building behind me, Reverend Freddie Morgan laid hands on those three children and called on the Holy Spirit to heal them. When we interviewed their parents last week, they told us Shanice, Terrell, and Tyrone were no longer ill. Doctor Christenson, the family's physician, confirmed the cures." Again he paused, leaving a space where they could reuse Shanice's I-love-you-Mommy footage.

"Last night, we asked, 'Are miracles happening in Atlanta?' Well, the families you see behind me believe they know the answer to that question. Let's find out why these people have come and what they think about the healings."

Riley turned and walked toward the crowd. Mark followed five paces behind, camera rolling. On closer inspection, the jumble of humanity resolved into a series of groups, each with two or three adults. Most of those waiting had a child with them. Ten feet from the head of the line, he held up a hand to stop Mark. He took a couple more paces then faced the camera again.

"The next *healing* service takes place at eleven a.m., Sunday— over twenty-four hours from now." He shuffled backward for the few remaining steps until he reached an African American woman sitting in a camping chair close to the head of the line and bent his knees to bring the microphone level with her lined face. "What's your name, ma'am?"

"Destiny Farack."

"Where did you travel from, Destiny?"

"We"—she signaled to two more black women of a similar age who sat in the chairs next to her—"left Durham, North Carolina last night after we saw you on the TV news. Got here early this mornin'."

"And who's this with you?" He pointed to a small girl; her thin body was twisted to the side so she doubled over in the center of an old, worn wheelchair. The chair was for an adult, and it accentuated her tiny, frail form. The framing would play beautifully on camera.

"This is my first grandbaby, Mellisa."

Mark zoomed in on the child, who was in profile because her head lolled to the side as though she were striving to look skyward but couldn't turn her neck to achieve the task. A tremor shook her body, and a long string of spittle hanging from the corner of her mouth trembled and glistened in the light. The shoulder of her white blouse showed dark where saliva had soaked through.

Riley softened his voice, becoming the grandmother's confidant. "Why are you here, Destiny?"

"We came to meet Reverend Morgan and ask him to lay hands on my Mellisa and make her well, same as he done to them other children."

He and Mark dipped into the line a few more times before closing out the piece with a talking-head shot.

"There you have it. These people have traveled to Atlanta with their sick children. Some drove hundreds of miles to spend the night camped out in a parking lot. Why? Because for most of them, Reverend Freddie Morgan is the last, best hope to cure their children. This is Riley Brown for News Channel 13, reporting to you live from New Beginnings Church. Now back to the studio."

He and Mark strode to the van. While the cameraman stowed his equipment, Riley opened his briefcase and retrieved a bottle of antibacterial hand sanitizer. He rolled up his sleeves, pumped hard, and scrubbed his fingers and arms. Looking back at the line of illness he'd just visited, a shiver ran through him.

Equipment stowed, Mark joined him. "Man, I hope this reverend can help those poor kids."

Riley dried his hands on a paper towel before passing the sanitizer to his videographer. "Me too, but whatever happens, they make for terrific TV." Riley's grin stayed fixed to his face as they headed back to the studio.

His piece aired during the Saturday lunchtime news slot, and again at five p.m., augmented with footage from the interview that Riley had shot with Shanice's baffled family doctor. New Beginnings Church was the local lead story, and the national network picked up the feed for their evening news spots. By seven p.m., shots of the church taken from News Channel 13's weather helicopter showed that the earlier line outside the front entrance had morphed into an unstructured crowd of thousands.

Vehicles with trailers, and even a few tents, filled the shopping center's parking lot that was now so crowded that police were directing traffic away from the backed-up access road, preventing more cars from entering.

Nina Morgan stood in the doorway of her living room, watching her husband. Freddie, standing five feet from the television with the remote in his hand, replayed, again, the recording he'd made from the evening newscast of the crowds outside New Beginnings Church. He'd thrown up twice since dinner. She had tried but couldn't get him to eat.

"How will we make it through the crowd and into the church if the police aren't letting anyone pass?" He'd asked the same question repeatedly, chanting the words like a mantra.

"Freddie, for heaven's sake, I've spoken to the police. They will escort us in. They're trained to handle crowds. Anyway, all those people are wasting their time if you don't show up to heal them."

"But there are so many. What if I can't do it? What if I can't heal them all?"

After years of struggling, years of covering up for his religious delusions, this was her chance to milk some serious money from the church. All those people waiting, and the ones the reporter had interviewed, would pay anything to buy their children what Terrell, Tyrone, and Shanice had received. But Freddie had to perform. He was close to cracking, and she needed to calm him down. She softened her voice. "It doesn't matter, honey. They *believe*. That's all we need. No one's offering a guarantee. All they want is a chance. They've run out of options. We're a last resort. If you cure even one child..." She moved beside him and rubbed a hand up and down his back. "Relax. You're on record as healing two kids with CF and one with a flaky heart in the last two weeks. You can do this."

He crossed to the liquor cabinet and poured another shot of bourbon.

"Anyway," Nina said, "you *aren't* going to heal them all." Freddie spun around and stared at her like a startled deer. Sometimes he was so unconnected with the real world. A blind belief in his healing abilities enabled him to do what he did every Sunday, but this was different. This opportunity had to be managed. "What's the maximum number of kids you've ever handled on stage?"

He looked skyward as he sifted his memory. "Eight, we once did eight—one Junior Healer handled each sick child."

"Okay. So that's a minimum. What's the most you can cope with?"

Freddie rubbed his chin and sipped his liquor with a faraway look in his eyes. He took five paces, turned around, then repeated, wearing a groove in the carpet. "Well," he said, "we have ten Junior Healers. If they each take two children… twenty. I can restructure the service and handle them in two batches of ten. Any more and the stage'll be too crowded."

"Twenty it is, then."

"But how will we choose? The people waiting in line are strangers. You heard the TV news; they've traveled hundreds of miles."

"Only church members are eligible for a healing."

He stopped pacing and froze, his glass halfway to his lips. "We can't turn them all away, Nina. Those people have come for a *healing*. They need my help."

"They can make a one-time payment—fill out the application, pay one year's tithe, and their membership will be retroactive."

Freddie stared at her, eyebrows raised, eyes wide. "New Beginnings Church is a house of *God*, not some department store selling cures."

She moved closer and put a hand on his arm. Every time she got them ahead, Freddie would set them back again. He took the Kmart lease before they were ready. They struggled for three years to make the monthly payments until her web site and promotional efforts lifted the tithes enough to get their heads above water. And just when they were finally solvent, he bought a new BMW. Two years and one bankruptcy later, the car was gone, and they were still scrambling for every penny. This time, she would control the finances. She had made this opportunity happen. She had called in Riley Brown. She had pitched the story of the Doolan twins. And it had paid off. The kids from Smyrna were an unexpected bonus. But they could relapsed. She had to move fast. This was her chance at the brass ring. And she intended to grasp it in both fists and make enough money to get out from under Freddie Morgan's shadow. Nina softened her voice and sprinkled in a hint of pleading. "It isn't fair to our current members to let these strangers skip the line."

Her husband hung his head, eyes focused on the floor. She wrapped her arm around his waist, pulled him close, and kissed his cheek. "Freddie, these people are desperate. But there are too many. We can't cope. This way we give them hope for a future healing. And create breathing space for us. Otherwise, they might become angry. Don't you see?"

"But how will we even get in?"

Nina took a deep breath and let it out in a long sigh. "Leave that to me. Think about it this way, Freddie. When God told you to move to a larger building, he knew this would happen. This is his plan for us. We can finally use those chairs we have stacked in the back room. Look. No one foresaw this happening so fast. Tomorrow, we'll do the best we can. Next week we can put on an extra service. But you'll need more help. So we need to hire more staff. And to pay them, we need more tithes."

In a plaintive voice, he said, "But what happens if the healings don't work? A year of back tithes is four or five thousand dollars for a typical family. We'll be sued. It's extortion—"

She shook her head. "I believe in you, Freddie, and so does your congregation. You can do this. Let me handle the business side."

Freddie lifted his head and stared, childlike, into her eyes. Nina moved closer until she stood in front of him with one hand on each of his shoulders. In a firm voice she said, "Freddie, God has given you a gift. Not all the children *will* be *healed*; we know that; they never are. Without faith the cures don't work. But look at Imani Booker's kids, and young Shanice, not to mention Margaret Doolan's grandkids, and dozens of others over the years. You're doing important work, here, Freddie. God's work." She cupped his cheeks, stared into his face, and smiled. "Now come on. It's after midnight. We've got a big day ahead of us tomorrow. You need to rest. You can bring your drink." He nodded. Nina took her husband's hand and led him, like he was a four year old, to the bedroom.

CHAPTER 20

Lauren glanced down at the twins, walking on either side of her and holding her hands. They were on the way to kindergarten orientation, where they'd get a first look at their classroom and meet their teacher. Two middle-school students standing behind a small table greeted them when they entered the school atrium.

"Which classroom are you looking for?" one girl asked.

"Ms. Hollinsworth's."

"Name?"

"Lauren Doolan." The second girl leafed through a box of name badges. "Oh, sorry. That's my name… Joshua and Maya Doolan are the children. The students." Lauren's cheeks flooded with heat. The girl started again from the front of the box.

"Here we are."

Lauren took the name tags and handed them to the twins, who hung them around their necks.

"Straight down the corridor, the last door on the left. There are signs in case you get lost." The girl smiled at Lauren again. She'd clearly decided she was dealing with a moron.

"Thank you."

Their footsteps echoed in the empty corridor. The twins had been chattering non-stop in the car, but now they were quiet, maybe sensing the anxiety churning Lauren's stomach. In the classroom, a dozen children sat at low tables. At the front, a cluster of parents surrounded a tall brown-haired woman whom Lauren recognized from the school's web site as the twins' teacher.

Eyes wide, the twins remained silent, absorbing the scene. The class size was small—sixteen children—which Lauren liked. After a few stragglers had arrived, Hollinsworth welcomed everyone and passed out information packets. She encouraged the children to explore the classroom. Leaning on ten years of experience teaching kindergarten, Teresa Hollinsworth put the children and their parents at ease. Joshua and Maya, who was the tallest in the class by two or three inches, checked out the wall art while Lauren sat in a chair that was too small for her butt and fretted until the teacher was free.

She wanted to speak to Hollinsworth alone, worried that her words might be misinterpreted if overheard by other parents. She didn't want to seem like one of *those* parents who thought their children above the rest (although she did). When the opportunity arose, she strode across the room and shook the teacher's hand. Hollinsworth's grip was firm, her smile genuine. "So nice to meet you," the teacher said. "And how lovely to have twins in my class." She lowered her voice and leaned in. "Thank heavens they're different sexes. I had twin girls a couple years ago, and I got so confused that I had to ask their mom to always put a ribbon in Fiona's hair so I could tell her apart from her sister."

Lauren smiled. "I can see how that might be challenging."

"And the rascals weren't above trying to trick me, either."

"Cute. I'm sure Joshua and Maya would do the same given the opportunity." Lauren cleared her throat and glanced around. She still had the teacher to herself. "I have one concern to share."

"That's why we're here. How may I help?"

Lauren had tried to think of some way to say this without sounding like a pushy parent. *Here goes nothing.* "I wanted to make you aware that Maya is intellectually very advanced."

Teresa Hollinsworth nodded her head and gave Lauren a smile that was, to the woman's credit, devoid of condescension. "The school prides itself in offering equal education to all our children. But not all children learn at the same rate. That's why the small class size is so beneficial. It gives me time to tailor the curriculum so everyone can reach the required level of competence, but at their own pace."

"Thank you. That's very reassuring. I'm sure every parent thinks their child is special, as they should, but I did want to give

you a heads-up. I'm sure Joshua and Maya will enjoy your class."
Well, she'd put it out there. Nothing more she could do.

Lauren had grown accustomed to how forward her daughter
was—in speech, reading, logic, physique—everything—not to
mention her special ability to cure. Joshua was smart, but Maya was
unique, and after observing her with her classmates, the difference
became a yawning chasm. When Lauren had read through the
kindergarten curriculum, she wondered how on earth Hollinsworth
would cope—Maya was a force of nature. Whether that was Dr.
Arrunsen's doing or not, Lauren didn't know—although it seemed
likely. Schoolwork had been a struggle for Lauren. Patsy had been
clever, but no A-student, and the limited contact Lauren had with
the twins' father left her in no doubt that her twin apples had fallen
a long way from that tree. At least she'd broached the subject. That
might make it easier for their teacher—forewarned was forearmed.

Lauren took the twins to their first day of school the next
morning. Her throat stung at the sight of them walking hand-in-
hand down the hallway with brand new book bags on their backs,
swamped by the tall ceilings and institutional-green walls. She stood
in the atrium, and she wasn't the only mother with tear-filled eyes.
Maya grabbed Joshua's arm just before they entered their
classroom, and they both turned and waved. Lauren forced a smile
and waved back. *They'll be fine.*

That final image stayed with her all day. Margaret collected the
twins that afternoon, and when Lauren arrived home, Maya and
Joshua gabbled on for ten minutes about what a fun day they'd
had. It seemed Lauren's fears had been unfounded—until Friday
evening, when Maya handed Lauren a note from their teacher:
"Dear Ms. Doolan. I wonder if you could spare me thirty minutes
this weekend. There is a matter I'd like to discuss with you."

The hairs on her neck prickled to attention. She forced
calmness into her voice. "Did you two have fun at school today?"

The twins exchanged a glance before Joshua answered. "Oh,
yes. We learned French." He turned to Maya. "N'est pas, Maya?"

"Oui, Joshua, mon frère," she replied. And the twins giggled.

Nothing wrong there. So why did their teacher want to meet, and
on a weekend? Once the kids were in bed, Lauren called the
woman's home number. Hollinsworth wasn't forthcoming about

the reason for the note. "I'd prefer to discuss the matter face-to-face, but please be assured that the twins haven't done anything wrong." They arranged to meet for coffee Saturday morning.

Lauren was in line at the coffee shop counter when the twins' teacher tapped her on the shoulder. They shook hands. "Ms. Hollinsworth. Would you like a coffee?"

"Thanks. Regular, and call me Teresa."

"Hi, Teresa."

They smiled at each other, but an awkward silence descended while they waited for the drinks. Lauren moved to the sugar station, while Teresa found them a corner table.

Sitting opposite Lauren at a two-top, Hollinsworth sipped her coffee, put her mug down, and took a deep breath. Apparently, this meeting was also difficult for the teacher. "Thank you for coming," Teresa said. "First, I owe you an apology."

"An apology?"

"At the orientation, you tried to tell me about Maya being advanced, and I delivered a stock answer—one I'd used many times before." She gave a shrug of the shoulders and pursed her mouth.

"Nothing to apologize for. Frankly, I expected you to roll your eyes, but you listened, and you were very polite."

Teresa spread both hands on the table and studied her nails, as though she might find inspiration there. "Well, I'm glad you received my response as it was intended, but, clearly, my answer was insufficient."

Lauren waited. She didn't know what was coming, and with every silent second her stress level soared. Hollinsworth had assured her this was nothing negative, told her not to worry. So why was the teacher struggling to frame her words?

"My sister's oldest boy, Adam, is a high achiever." Teresa looked up from the table, face flat and serious. "He struggled for three years in kindergarten before my sister found a solution."

"How could he struggle if he was a high achiever?"

"Kids with high IQs like Adam—he tested out at over one hundred sixty—don't always become model students. In fact, the opposite is often true because our curriculum is constructed to be age-appropriate for an average child. Adam's intellectual age is considerably greater than his physical age."

"You mean he got bored."

"Yes. But also, a child with a higher-functioning brain may approach problem-solving in a different way than an average child. The teaching tools we have in the classroom instill one way of working—designed to guide children, to provide them with the most appropriate problem-solving tools. Adam had his own way of reaching the correct solution, so his teachers assumed he was struggling to grasp the fundamentals. That wasn't the case. Because Adam intuitively solves problems, he simply bypassed the fundamentals; he didn't need the tools we taught."

Lauren nodded but remained silent, waiting for Teresa to get to her point, the point that triggered this meeting.

"Which brings me to Maya." Teresa smiled. "By the way, who taught her French?"

"I thought you did."

The teacher tipped her head back and laughed. "After only two days? I *wish* I were that proficient an educator. I've taught French to high-schoolers, and I love the language. In my twenties, I lived in Paris for two wonderful years." Her eyes took on a faraway look. "Maya's fluency brought back fond memories."

"Oh?" *Is that why we're here?*

Teresa waved her hand, dismissing the topic. "No matter. I asked to meet because I don't want Maya to struggle like Adam did."

"You think she's higher-functioning. Like Adam?"

"When my sister asked for help with my nephew, I researched higher-IQ children. Adam is extremely bright. His IQ score placed him in the ninety-ninth percentile. Joshua is also an intelligent boy, but Maya embodies a phenomenon about which I've only read."

An icy trickle dribbled down Lauren's spine. "Meaning?"

"It didn't take me long in class to understand that, *as* you had warned"—she raised her eyebrows in acknowledgement—"your daughter is very advanced. Because of my experience with Adam, I thought it useful to understand what I was dealing with. I let the twins take the Stanford-Binet IQ test." She delivered a reassuring smile. "It's not as painful as it sounds. They enjoyed the process. But let me preface what I'm about to say—IQ is but one measure of intelligence, and it is most useful in the ranges closer to normal—between ninety and one-twenty with one hundred being the standard for an average person. Joshua scored one-twenty, which puts him in the ninetieth percentile—a very high score."

"Oh." Lauren eased back in her chair. Something more was coming. The teacher's stiff body language conveyed an uneasy feeling.

Hollinsworth gave a tight smile. "However, Maya scored the test's maximum—two hundred twenty-five." The teacher looked Lauren in the eye. "That's well beyond the point in the bell curve where the measurement is a useful guide to intelligence."

The news that her twins were high-functioning should have pleased her, but something in the teacher's tone told her this wasn't necessarily positive news. "I told you she was intelligent. Isn't it a good thing to have a high IQ?"

"Yes and no. On my recommendation, my sister pulled Adam out of public school. I helped her set up a homeschooling program for him. Adam is seventeen now. He's a freshman at Caltech, studying mathematics."

"Wow. And you think Maya might be similar."

Teresa shook her head. "Adam's test scores were high. For example, the physicist Stephen Hawking's IQ is in a similar range. But people with IQ scores over two hundred are described as *unmeasurable geniuses* because the tests can't provide useful data at those rarified levels." Teresa stared directly into Lauren's eyes. Her face was as serious as her voice when she said, "Lauren, only a handful of people alive today can match Maya's score. Possibly, no one can. Maya finished the test with plenty of time to spare, and she didn't skip a single question. Coupled with her score, I think that may be unprecedented."

A tourniquet tightened around Lauren's chest. Ever since she'd been in the womb, life had thrown curve balls at her baby. "I'm sorry to ask a stupid question, but what does it mean? What must I do?"

"That's a million miles from being a stupid question. I've been pondering the same thing for two days." Hollinsworth leaned back. Staring into the distance, she rubbed an itch on her cheek. After a deep breath and a long sigh, her gaze again met Laurens. "This is above my pay grade, Lauren. I've never come across anyone with an IQ as high as Maya's, and I know of no one who has. But I can tell you that my nephew sees the world through a different lens from normal folk like us. What Maya is capable of, I can't imagine."

"This is a lot to take in." With one hand on her chest, Lauren snatched a few quick breaths to steady her voice. "What do you recommend?"

"That's why I asked to meet. I'm duty-bound to teach Maya, and I will to the best of my ability. But the classroom I work in isn't equipped to help her. By Georgia state law, you are obligated to either send her to school, or provide a certified homeschooling equivalent. If you can work it out in time, I suggest you find an alternative method to teach your daughter. A method that will avoid the problems Adam faced; a method that will allow her to learn and develop in lock-step with her mental acuity rather than Georgia's ideas of what a five-year-old should and shouldn't be capable of."

Lauren sat back in her chair and stared past Teresa Hollinsworth with unfocused eyes. Homeschooling. Her income only just covered the bills they had. She had to work. Her mother had left school at fourteen without her GED. She couldn't teach a prodigy. Where would the money for homeschooling come from?

Hollinsworth cleared her throat. "I'd be happy to refer you to the tutors my sister used." The twins' teacher reached across and touched Lauren's hand. "Are you okay?"

The contact brought Lauren back. "I'm sorry. This has come as a shock."

"I hate to drop it on you so suddenly, but the state's deadline is firm. You must submit a declaration of intent to homeschool by September first."

"I understand, and I'll be grateful for any help you can provide. I want to do the best by Maya and Joshua."

Hollinsworth nodded. "This *will be* for the best. Trust me. Once my sister removed Adam from the school environment, he flourished."

Lauren tightened her gut, straightened in her chair, and focused on the teacher, meeting her gaze. "Where do I start?"

Hollinsworth pulled a folder from her purse. "This is the program Adam used. The structure complies with state requirements. There are also two state application forms in there, and I've listed the tutors my sister used. Although the twins' education shouldn't be governed by finances, you understand this must be privately funded. The state offers no assistance."

"We'll work something out." Lauren reached across the table and squeezed the teacher's arm. "Teresa. Thank you so much for taking the time to explain this and for thinking of my children's wellbeing."

Hollinsworth leaned back in her seat, wiped the back of her hand theatrically across her brow. "Phew. That's a relief. Thanks for taking this in the way I intended. I had concerns about... well, I thought you might think I didn't want your children in my class, and that couldn't be farther from reality." She stood and gathered her things. "I'll make myself available if you need further guidance. I just want Maya to fulfill her potential. A mind like hers must be capable of extraordinary things."

CHAPTER 21

Morning sunlight streamed through the kitchen window blinds, painting bright stripes across the papers strewn over the table. Lauren shook her head and took in a faltering breath. Tears were close. Teresa Hollinsworth had been kind to provide the information about homeschooling and private tutors, but Lauren would need triple her salary to afford them. Low giggles came from the living room, where Maya and Josh played with Legos. Maya was happy for now, but how long would that last if she were condemned to spend every school day bored and frustrated? Margaret had offered to return to work, but a cashier's pay barely covered the cost of textbooks.

The front door opened and closed, and her mom came in.

Lauren broke from her reading, looked up. "I thought you were going to the eleven o'clock service."

"So did I, but I couldn't get near the building. The police have the access road closed. I told one of the traffic cops I was a church member. He told me the parking lot was crammed like a tailgate party. They even had a hot dog vendor. He said to go home and watch on Channel 13."

"They're televising the service?" Lauren's voice rose an octave.

"Apparently."

"This I have to see." Lauren followed her mom into the living room. After skirting the twins' construction area in the middle of the floor, she turned on the TV. A rerun of Riley Brown's newscast from the previous evening was playing. A banner at the bottom of the screen ticked away the seconds to the upcoming eleven o'clock service, which had been delayed thirty minutes.

The programming switched to a live feed from inside the church's lobby. Riley Brown's face filled the screen. In hushed tones, he whispered into a hand-held mic: "Momentarily, we'll take you inside the church for live exclusive coverage of Reverend Morgan's faith healing service. Thirty minutes ago, the first twenty families in line, including many of the children we featured on yesterday's News Channel 13 exclusive broadcast, were invited into the church and given the opportunity to pay one year's back tithe to become instant church members so they would be eligible for a *healing.*"

"Wow!" Lauren said. "What's the tithe, Mom? Ten percent?"

Her mom straightened and jutted her chin. "It's perfectly fair. Those people can't just cut the line."

Riley continued, "We believe the Reverend Morgan will *heal* these children at today's service."

"So that's at least twenty times, what, four or five thousand dollars? Eighty thousand, minimum. Not bad for one hour's work," Lauren said.

Lips pursed, her mother tsk-tsked, her stern face signaling disapproval. Even after this blatant display of avarice, the woman refused to see the Morgans for what they were.

The camera tracked Riley into the church.

"Oh, dear!" Her mother's hand went to her mouth. The camera slow-panned across a sea of heads. Extra chairs had been set out and filled. Where the chairs ended, people stood shoulder to shoulder. Impossible to estimate, but thousands more than at the service Lauren attended.

"So many," her mother said.

The organ played the opening bars of *"How Great Thou Art,"* and Freddie Morgan strode across the stage. He attempted to lead the congregation in song, but this wasn't his usual congregation, and the hymn fell flat. The cameraman roamed down the center aisle and panned the pews. No one was smiling. Faces were stern, some angry. Even through the television screen, Lauren sensed high tension in the church. Which made sense. Apart from the twenty children chosen for today's healing, hundreds of others must have felt they'd wasted their time traveling to Atlanta and camping overnight in a Kmart parking lot, in many cases accompanied by children who were too ill for an impromptu camping trip.

Freddie Morgan wasn't his usual assured self. He stumbled over his words as he welcomed the congregation. The children seated on the bleachers behind the pastor outnumbered the Junior Healers.

Each child was brought forward, and Freddie went through his performance—laying on hands, and mumbling incomprehensible words.

"He's channeling the Holy Spirit," her mother whispered, "talking in tongues."

Right.

When the last child was prayed over and then flung backwards into the waiting arms of a terrified-looking female Junior Healer, Lauren became aware of Maya leaning against her leg. Joshua had moved beside his grandma, who was stroking her grandson's head. They stood as a family, transfixed by the screen.

"Mommy?" Maya's voice sounded shaky, uncertain. Lauren bent her knees and sank to her daughter's level.

"Yes, sweetie?"

Tears glazed Maya's eyes. "Those children are very sick."

"I know."

"But what will happen to them?"

"I—"

"The reverend will heal them," Margaret said, her voice confident and swollen with pride.

Tears spilled down Maya's face. Her neck and cheeks were blotched red. Her little girl understood the folly in her grandmother's words. Lauren's heart splintered. She started to speak, needing to comfort her baby. "Well, sweetie—"

Maya gave a small shake of her head and nodded toward her grandmother—so smart. But Lauren had to deal with the pain and confusion in her daughter's eyes. She had anticipated the arrival of this moment—when Maya would realize the power of her gift. The church service had accelerated the inevitable. But what was unfolding on the television was too complex for a five-year-old to handle, even for a five-year-old genius.

"Maya can cure them," Joshua's voice rang out, clear and certain.

His grandma graced him with a condescending smile and ruffled his hair. "Oh no, Joshua. Only someone like Reverend Morgan who is chosen by God as a vehicle for the healing spirit can make those children well."

Joshua opened his mouth, poised to argue. Maya reached across and tapped one finger on his arm. He clammed up, but frustration smoldered in his eyes.

"Mom," Lauren said, "why don't you finish watching the service while I fix the twins a drink?" She didn't wait for a reply. "Come on, kids." She led them into the kitchen and sat them at the table. "Joshua knows?" she asked Maya.

"Of course."

"Is this one of the secrets you mentioned after we visited Terrell and Tyrone?"

Maya smiled. "One of them."

The twins stared at her, faces open and innocent, waiting. Under her children's unblinking gaze, her scalp tingled. She gritted her teeth, searching for the right words. Lauren felt as though she were about to sit an exam for which she hadn't properly prepared. But first, she had to find out how much Joshua knew.

"So, Joshua, did Maya tell you what happened when we visited Smyrna?"

"She cured the twins and Shanice just like she cured me."

Maya touched his arm, and the twins locked eyes with each other. For two heartbeats, Lauren felt cut off from them, excluded.

Then Joshua returned his attention to Lauren. "Why not let Maya cure those children on TV?"

Lauren sighed and softened her voice. "Joshua, you aren't old enough to understand, but I don't want either of you exposed to the hoopla associated with New Beginnings Church. If people find out about Maya's gift, our front yard will soon look like that church's parking lot."

Maya laid her hand on Lauren's arm, and Lauren took a deep, calming breath and eased it out. She repeated the exercise, and her head felt clearer.

Maya said, "No one needs to know about Eureka."

Lauren's mind shrieked to high alert. Panic dried her mouth and clamped her throat. She covered her mouth and coughed, buying time.

155

Maya's tiny fingers pulsed and squeezed; a warm sensation flowed up Lauren's arm and spread across her chest. She took another deep breath and tried to hide her surprise when she said, "What do you mean, Eureka?"

"Doctor Arrunsen's mouse," Maya said.

"How do you know that name?" Lauren asked.

Joshua giggled. "You told her, silly."

A fog of confusion washed in, swamping her mind until, like an ebb tide, it was pushed back and calmed by the gentle stroking of her daughter's fingers. Joshua moved around the table. He laid his hand on Lauren's other arm. With the children either side of her, Lauren took another deep breath.

"We need money for the tutors," Joshua said.

Lauren looked into his eyes, wide, upturned, innocent. "How—?"

"Maya heard you and Grandma talking about it."

"We're fine."

"Mommy," Joshua whispered, "those families would give money to Maya if she *healed* their children. After all, they're paying Reverend Morgan, and he's just *pretending*."

"Lauren!" her mother called from the other room. "Come quickly."

Her mother's voice seemed to come from a faraway place. Lauren blinked a couple times to re-engage her brain. "Come on, you two," she said. "Let's see what Grandma wants." *And give me time to figure out what just happened.*

She and the twins moved into the living room. Her mom, standing at the center of the room, pointed to the screen. The service was over, but a semicircle of people, mostly men, clustered in the front row. On the stage above them, Deacon Nina, in her purple robes, was making *calm down* signals with her hands. The people were leaning against the stage, pointing, shouting, furious. Riley had made it to the stage and his mic picked up some of the comments: "How long before David will be well?" "Should I still take Michelle to chemo? When can my daughter get a *healing?*"

Nina Morgan's eyes darted back and forth between the people as they yelled questions and talked over each other. She looked trapped, confused, out of her depth. "You must have faith in the healing," she said. "Shanice Mosely's mother had faith, but it still took two weeks for her daughter to get well. It may take even

156

longer. The healing only works if you have faith in the Holy Spirit. There are no guarantees—"

A large man with a full ginger beard and buzzed hair, who could have been a retired NFL linebacker, muscled his way to the front of the crowd. His face was flushed, and he pointed a fat finger at the deacon. "I just wrote you a six-thousand-dollar check. That's faith enough for me!"

That comment elicited a chorus of agreement from the crowd.

When two police officers made their way across the stage, Nina stepped back from the edge. The relief on her face was impossible to mask. The deacon was rattled. But what did she expect? These people were desperate. They'd paid a lot of money. And they wanted results.

Maya took hold of Lauren's hand and looked up at her with eyes brimmed full of sympathy. *"I can help those people, Mommy. Why don't you talk to Deacon Nina tomorrow."*

Lauren nodded and smiled. "Okay, honey. I will."

Margaret turned to her. "You will what?" she asked.

"I—"

And that was when Lauren realized.

Maya hadn't spoken the words aloud.

CHAPTER 22

Nina watched her husband scoop ice into the dregs in his glass. Freddie splashed two fingers of bourbon over the cubes and raised the drink to her. "Sure you don't want one?"

Nina shook her head. "Haven't you had enough?"

"It'll calm your nerves," he said.

The aggression from the parents after this morning's service had taken them both by surprise. Freddie had been *calming* his nerves for the past hour. He rocked sideways and steadied himself on the liquor cabinet as he lifted the glass to his lips and took a pull. "Thank heavens the police were there. I thought we had a riot on our hands."

"We'll be better organized next week."

"I don't know, Nina." He shook his head and showed her hangdog eyes. "I don't know if I can go through that again."

Typical. Every time life looked difficult, her husband wimped out. *Not this time, mister.* He went to pick up his drink and she stepped forward and knocked his hand away before it reached its destination. "Listen to me, Freddie Morgan." She poked the words into his ribs. "We just need to manage their expectations better." His eyes widened, but he backed up a half step. Six months after they were married, Nina had figured out that Freddie wasn't really *God's chosen healer.* But Freddie didn't know that—Freddie never would—which was why he could do what he did. A girl like her, born without much, learned early in life how to think on her feet, how to make the best of a bad job. There were bills to pay,

158

promises to keep. So, before each service, she had started *selecting* the children for Freddie, stacking the odds in his favor. Often, the kids weren't seriously ill, or as with the Booker twins' cystic fibrosis and Shanice's heart problems, their symptoms fluctuated. She hammered home that the healing only worked if the family had faith, shifting the blame. No mother wanted to fail her child. Her system worked. But today's crowd had been too amorphous and too large. The illnesses had been too severe, the parents too insistent, and the money too tempting.

"I hope you're right," Freddie said.

"I am." Tonight, her husband was too fragile to hear the truth. But *that* conversation would happen tomorrow. There was no way she could *manage* expectations for today's twenty anxious families. The TV station would follow up and New Beginnings Church was certain to be exposed. She had to get ahead of that. This was her ticket out and no one, not Riley Brown, not News Channel 13, not CBS, and certainly not her drunkard husband was going steal it from her. "We collected a hundred thousand dollars today, so we can recruit security for next week's service."

He stared into his drink, didn't respond. Freddie was an artist, a performer, a convincer, a salesman without an iota of business instinct. He didn't see the opportunity. But she did. She saw a way out of a lease they couldn't afford and credit cards they couldn't pay and a marriage that no longer worked. But the opportunity was time-critical. Timing was everything and sometimes, as Kenny Rogers said, "You've got to know when to fold 'em."

Leveraging the TV exposure, she could enroll a hundred new members before next weekend. People were desperate, competing for a place on the stage, willing to pay extra for preferential treatment. She'd put on extra services—two on Saturday, two on Sunday, then, on Monday, she'd cash the checks and run. She looked over at Freddie and shook her head. He'd collected his glass and bottle and slumped into his recliner. He'd be okay. Heck, he could blame it all on her. She didn't care. And even if he wasn't okay, she still didn't care. After tolerating his bullshit for six years, this was Nina's time. She'd earned it. Freddie could do whatever he wanted. Except come with her. Like every action movie plot, Freddie had one last service to perform and then he could hang up his spurs. She smiled, enjoying the metaphor, picturing the hero riding off into the sunset. But the hero was her, and the sunset was on a Mexican beach.

The hall phone rang again. It had been ringing all afternoon. Messages were stacked up, dozens and dozens of voicemails from families desperate to pay their tithe, offering cash, offering a credit card number over the phone, offering anything to skip the line, to join the church, to get their golden ticket and save their sick child. She stood in the hall and listened to the phone's speaker as voicemail picked up:

"This is Lauren Doolan, Margaret Doolan's daughter, calling for Nina or Freddie Morgan. I know you didn't cure my daughter, Maya—" Nina held her breath and listened to dead air for six thumping heartbeats. A tingling started in her fingers and flowed up her arms, across her chest, around her neck, and flooded her face with heat. "—I know you didn't cure my son, Joshua. And I know you didn't cure Terrell and Tyrone Booker or Shanice Mosely. I saw the angry crowd at the end of this morning's service."

Creeping closer, jaw locked, Nina's ears strained for every word.

"Well, Deacon and Reverend Morgan, I *do* know how the children were cured, and I may be willing to tell you, but not on the phone. We need to meet face-to-face. Call me back. Today." She hung up.

Nina jumped forward and reached for the phone. Then stopped.

Wait.

This could be a setup. Riley Brown had visited the Doolans. After today's debacle, maybe he had turned against the church, decided to cut his losses, and was using Lauren Doolan to trick her into telling the truth. If Nina returned the call, the Doolan woman might tape the conversation. Recoiling from the handset as if it were covered with slime, she turned away, took a step toward the living room. Hesitated. Turned back.

But Freddie had never had successes like this before, and the Doolan twins had gotten well somehow. That was why she'd called in Channel 13. Maybe their mother knew how. If she did, maybe there'd be no need to cut and run.

Nina drifted back to the phone. Her fingers hovered over the device. She pinched her bottom lip between her teeth and glanced toward the living room doorway. No need to bother Freddie with this. Her husband believed in his healing powers every bit as much as his congregation, and no matter what Lauren Doolan did, she needed to keep him thinking that way. She needed Freddie's big finale performance. Nina dialed *69 and returned the call.

A woman's voice answered, "Hello?"

"Lauren Doolan?"

"Yes?"

"This is Deacon Morgan." The key was to give nothing away. She was simply calling back as a courtesy.

"There's a mall at Exit 88 on the I85. Do you know it?" Lauren's voice was clipped, businesslike.

"Yes."

"Meet me in the food court in one hour. Come alone."

The line went dead. Lauren Doolan was being cautious. She sounded nervous. Did she have the cure? Or did she smell the money?

When Nina returned to the living room, Freddie was snoring in his recliner—head back, mouth open, arms draped across his chest. Beside him on the floor, his glass had tipped on its side next to the empty liquor bottle. The spilled bourbon would stain unless she cleaned it up.

To hell with it. I'm done cleaning up Freddie's messes.

She left a note on the table, telling him she had gone to the store. Quietly, she closed the front door then climbed into their Toyota and backed out of the driveway. Her mind swirled, reliving the phone message, trying to guess Lauren Doolan's intentions, trying to prepare. For what? She gripped the wheel tightly. This meeting could be a defining moment.

Or it might be the start of a journey that ended in federal prison.

Lauren spotted Nina Morgan's large frame as soon as the woman turned into the hallway leading to the food court. She didn't signal. Nina scanned the atrium until their eyes met.

When the deacon reached the table, she offered her hand. Lauren ignored it and pointed to the chair opposite. "Sit."

For a second, Lauren thought the woman had winked at her, but the action repeated, and she realized it was an involuntary twitch in Nina's left eye. Good. "Are you recording this conversation?" Lauren asked.

Nina's head reared back and her mouth formed a perfect "O." "No. Are you?"

"Certainly not. If anyone asked, I'd insist none of what we're about to discuss ever transpired."

"Okay by me."

The deacon sat and Lauren allowed a silence to form. She had kept the twins out of Riley's broadcast, and the reporter had focused on New Beginnings Church as the source of the cures. That alone vindicated her actions with the Booker twins and Shanice. But the three-ring circus in the church today was a taste of what would happen if anyone discovered that her daughter *really had* the healing touch. She was here to fulfill her duty, and her duty was to protect Maya.

Nina's eyes hardened. "Well, Ms. Doolan. You called this meeting. What have you got to say?"

"Before I tell you, I need to be sure that certain assumptions I've made are correct."

"Assumptions?"

"I need you to acknowledge that your husband didn't heal any of the children at today's service."

The deacon swayed back as though she'd taken an uppercut to the chin. In an indignant voice she said, "As I told the children's parents, you must have faith, Ms. Doolan. The reverend—"

Lauren snapped out of her seat. Her chair screeched. The couple at the next table stared. "We're done here," she said, and picked up her purse.

Like a cobra strike, Nina's hand flashed forward and snagged Lauren's purse handles. "Wait."

Lauren glared at the woman. Nina Morgan had been telling the same lies for so long, it would take a crowbar to free the truth. But she had to be certain of the deacon's position. She planned a deal with the devil, but if that devil believed in Freddie Morgan, the deal wouldn't work. When New Beginnings Church was exposed, as they certainly would be after today's service, the cheated families would seek retribution. Who would their attorneys go after? The church? Sure. But they wouldn't stop there. News Channel 13's parent company, CBS, had deeper pockets. A major network wouldn't just roll over. Five of the cures they had reported were real and verifiable, so they'd need to discover *how* those children got well, and this time they wouldn't send a rookie to investigate.

"Please, Ms. Doolan. Sit. Give me time to explain."

Nina Morgan's eyes clouded with fear. Lauren held all the cards, and this woman needed to acknowledge that sooner rather than later. She sat, but placed the purse on the table between them and held the strap. "Go ahead," she said, "but lose the dogma."

The deacon winced. She took a deep breath as though the coming words needed extra air to propel them from her mouth. "Let's say that, due to unusual circumstances, the children Freddie *healed* at this Sunday's service didn't pass through my normal vetting process. Consequently, their recovery is in more doubt than usual."

"Uh huh. As I said on the phone, I don't believe you cured any of those children. If that's correct, I assume you are interested in hearing how the healings could be accomplished."

"How?"

Lauren sighed and pursed her lips. She leaned in and hissed, "Is. My. Assumption. Correct?" Nina Morgan was not stupid, but unless she could deny her husband's curative powers, Lauren needed a different solution.

"Yes." The deacon expelled the word as though she were spitting out a poison pill.

Still not satisfied, Lauren pressed. "Yes, the reverend *healed* none of the children?"

The deacon nodded. "As you say."

Lauren leaned back in her chair and placed her bag on the floor at her feet. She rolled her neck and let out a slow breath. The woman was a crook, not a fool.

"But, Ms. Doolan, is what *you* said true? Can you arrange for them to be *healed*?"

"Yes."

The deacon glanced at the people sitting at the next table, leaned in, and whispered, "All of them?" Her voice was edged with excitement.

"I believe so."

"How?"

"As to that, *you'll* have to have faith."

A low chuckle rumbled in the woman's throat. She adjusted her butt and her chair creaked. A smile squeezed dimples into her fat cheeks. In a voice heavy with sarcasm, she said, "Really?"

Lauren smiled. Now it was her turn to do the convincing. "Imani Booker and Kiara Mosely were angry because you charged nine hundred dollars for a cure that didn't work."

Nina shook her head. "But it did work."

"After I visited them it worked."

"You?" The deacon's mouth hung open.

"Call them and ask."

The deacon blinked rapidly as though roused from a deep sleep.

"Do you know why the cured children have violet eyes?" Lauren asked.

"Freddie says it's God's mark."

And *that* made Lauren wince. The doctrine was deeply embedded. "We've already established your husband doesn't have the healing touch. Unlike him, I *do* know why their eye color changed, and it will change in every child that gets cured. Apparently you've spun the color change to your advantage."

Nina narrowed her eyes. "If you have this miraculous power to heal the sick, why not announce it to the world? Why tell me?"

"Because I don't want to deal with the chaos I saw at your church this morning. I asked you here to make a business proposition."

The deacon tilted her head. "Go on."

"I'm interested in operating as a supplier of cures, but I'd like to use your church as my retail outlet."

"So. You don't want anyone to know that you're doing the healing? The ultimate Good Samaritan?" The woman's voice was laden with skepticism.

Lauren was sure this was the right decision. The only decision. This would protect Maya and Joshua and herself. It would provide for the twins education. And protect Maya until she reached an age where she could decide for herself what to do with her gift. "I want Freddie to continue with his performances. I want you to continue collecting tithes and handling the media and everything else that goes along with delivering miraculous cures to incurable diseases."

"And what do *you* want?"

"Total anonymity. And fifty percent of the tithes."

Nina's mouth yawned. Her eyes widened and her chin jutted forward, but no words arrived. Fifty percent of a lot was better that one hundred percent of nothing, which was what Nina would end up with once the parents of those children got through with her. The deacon's silence told Lauren that she had also done the math.

"How would it work?"

"I'd need a private room at the church. I'll have Maya and Joshua with me. Before each service, the sick children must meet with mine, who will increase their faith by giving testament to Freddie's healing abilities."

"How long does your treatment take?"

"A few seconds."

The deacon's eyebrows lifted. "Really? And what about your children. How will you explain this to them? What if they go blabbing about how the cure works?"

"They won't. Think this through, Nina. I'm risking as much as you. If the truth comes out, I'll be inundated with requests from the medical authorities. I want to help these children, but I also want a life. You've already chosen this path. What I'm offering will be worth money and prestige. And—if it's of any interest—you can actually *cure* the children."

Nina smoothed a hand through her hair. "We have to keep this arrangement between ourselves. Freddie can only perform because he believes he's channeling the Holy Spirit."

Lauren nodded. Freddie's enthusiasm and showmanship were key. If he believed now, then when the church showed foolproof results, his performances should really shine. "Agreed."

"Frankly, Ms. Doolan, this sounds too good to be true. How sure are you of the cure?"

Lauren shook her head. Unbelievable. This question came from someone who had for years sold a cure that *was* too good to be true. "Very sure. But let's start slowly. On TV, Riley Brown announced your plan to increase the number of children next week. Don't."

"If they'll all be *healed*, I won't need to."

"Good. And keep the price the same."

Nina's face contorted. As though leaving money on the table was painful to her. "But, this will be worth far more."

Lauren shook her head. "Actually, it should be worth the same as your previous healings, right?"

Nina pouted but remained silent.

"And I want to see the accounts every week."

Stillness settled over the deacon. Lauren could almost see synapses firing in the woman's brain. "When do we start?" Nina asked.

Lauren had gotten what she came for, but now she'd have to deliver, or rather, her daughter would. Her voice cracked as she said, "Next Sunday."

CHAPTER 23

"There's Mrs. Fitzthomas," Margaret said, pointing out the front windshield, "and the Jacksons." She rocked back in her seat. "This is more like the old church." Margaret got out of the car and headed for her friends, leaving Lauren with the twins, who sat in the rear. She kneeled up in her seat and faced them. "Are you sure you want to do this?"

"We're sure," Joshua answered.

"Maya?" Staring into her daughter's face, Lauren searched for signs of stress, but all she received was a warm, confident smile. "Of course, Mommy. Think how happy those children will be when I make them well."

Maya unclipped her seat and laid a hand on Lauren's arm. Warmth and reassurance flowed from the touch and enveloped Lauren, soothing her anxiety.

"Okay. Let's go." Lauren collected a small black leather bag from the trunk and guided the twins across the parking lot. Margaret joined them in the lobby where Karen, the Junior Healer who helped last time they visited the church, signaled them over and led them to a room down a hallway to the left of the stage. A half-dozen plastic chairs lined the wall, and a picnic table sat in the center.

After Karen left them, Lauren said, "Mom, why don't you wait in the church to make sure no one takes our seats?"

Her mom squeezed Lauren's shoulder. "Thank you for helping the reverend."

Lauren smiled. "Go on now. We'll join you before the service starts."

When she and the twins were alone, Lauren placed the black bag on the table.

At ten thirty, Deacon Morgan knocked on the door and entered. Already dressed in her purple robe, her gaze flitted around the room. When her eyes locked onto the medical case, tension lines around the woman's eyes softened.

In her teens, Lauren had read a biography of Houdini. He claimed the secret behind all illusions was the art of misdirection. The bag was sleight-of-hand, another way of diverting focus from Maya's magic.

The deacon yanked her gaze from the bag, threw a tight smile to the twins, and then focused on Lauren. "Everything ready?"

"Send the children in individually."

The deacon moved closer to Lauren, nodded toward the table, and whispered, "Is it safe?"

Really! This was the first time the deacon had considered the possibility that the children might be harmed. "Let's get moving, shall we?" Lauren snapped.

With a last, lingering look at the bag, Nina's robes swished as she spun away and opened the door. She pulled a sheet of notepaper from her pocket and read off a name. "Nathan Milor?"

A middle-aged woman appeared at the door pushing a cadaverous boy in a wheelchair. His sunken cheeks and the yellow tinge to his skin spoke to a deep-lying illness. Nina pulled the boy's chair into the room and went to close the door. In a clipped voice, Lauren said, "Deacon Morgan. You need to leave us."

Nina hesitated for a second, but backed down under Lauren's firm gaze. "Right—call me when you're done."

After she left, Joshua and Maya moved either side of the boy. Maya held one wrist, and Joshua put his hand on the boy's shoulder. "Hi, Nathan," Joshua said, "I know you're sick. Maya and I were sick once, but Reverend Freddie *healed* us. He can *heal* you, too."

From the medical bag, Lauren took a small tin containing white Tic Tacs. The bag also contained a couple sodas in case the twins got thirsty and a pack of Kleenex. But it said much more. To Nathan—whose eyes locked on the white pill—it said cure. Lauren told Nathan to open his mouth, and she dropped the candy on his tongue. "It tastes pretty good for medicine," she said. The boy stared up at her. His face was tight with fear, but his eyes glimmering with hope. Maya released his arm, and Lauren took that as her signal. "You can go back to your family now," she said. "Have faith in the reverend and you will get well."

Joshua tapped on the door, and Nina opened it. Her gaze darted around the room and landed on the pillbox in Lauren's hand. The deacon smiled. "Ready for the next one?"

"Yes," Lauren said.

When the tenth child had left, Nina waited in the doorway. Her foot tap, tap, tapped, and she rubbed her hands together. "Well?" she asked.

"All done," Lauren said.

"Are you sure?"

This came from a woman who had spent years peddling false cures. To stop herself from exploding, Lauren picked up the bag and focused on the twins. Nina Morgan was a hard person to like. "Come on, you guys," she said.

The deacon waited a few seconds for an answer. When she realized Lauren had no intention of gracing her with one, she said, "I have to get back to Freddie. He's been looking for me."

"What did you tell him about"—Lauren waved at the room—"this?"

"He thinks it's a terrific idea to instill confidence in the children. He asked me to pass on his thanks."

Lauren nodded. "We'll be out in a few minutes."

After Nina left, Lauren crouched low and signaled her children close. She hugged them both. "How do you feel?"

"Good," they spoke in unison, and that made them all laugh. Amazing. It was as though the extraordinary events of the past twenty minutes had been the most natural process in the world. As though miracles happened every day. But Maya's healing ability *was* natural to her. It was a lot to take in. "Are you tired?"

Maya shook her head and smiled. "Come on, Mommy. Grandma will be worried."

Pride pinged through Lauren's chest. Maya had passed her gift to ten more families, changed the lives of ten sick children. And soon there would be ten more children in the world with violet eyes, ten more reasons for Riley Brown to not single out her twins.

MAYA

As they came through the curtain at the side of the stage and descended the steps, her mother stood up in the fourth row and waved them over. Lauren looked at the auditorium—not as chaotic as last week, but still filled beyond capacity.

Riley Brown caught her eye from his position behind the control panel that handled the audio-visuals. He tapped his videographer on the arm and pointed. When the man swept his shouldered camera toward her, she shielded her face with one hand, dipped her head, and hurried the twins down the steps. But not before she registered the journalist's puzzled expression.

CHAPTER 24

"Yes. I hope so, too. Goodbye, Mrs. Yosling." The woman at the other end of the line choked back another sob, and the sound lingered in his mind after Riley returned his desk phone to its cradle. The reporter leaned back in his chair and emptied his lungs in a long sigh. He pulled a handkerchief from his pocket, blew his nose, and dabbed moisture from his eyes.

"Damn it!" He slapped both palms against the desk and sprang to his feet. He needed to get out of the office and breathe fresh air. Jackie Yosling's was the last name on his list of families from the previous Sunday's service. Twenty families whose hopes had been raised by Reverend Morgan only to be shattered against the rocks of reality every morning when their child's promised and paid for remission failed to materialize. Monday was half over, and Riley felt like an old rag that someone had wiped their soiled hands on and tossed in the garbage.

What Freddie and Nina Morgan had done to these families was unforgivable. And Riley was responsible because he had focused the media spotlight on the church.

Thirty minutes later, Riley sat in a café, toying with a tuna wrap and watching a young mother tidy the remnants of her son's sandwich before using a wet wipe to clean his ketchup-smeared mouth. Those twenty families ached for a simple moment like that. A normalcy so mundane it went unnoticed unless it had been stolen away. He cleared his trash and sloped back to the office on leaden legs.

The last thing he wanted this afternoon was to call the families of the children from yesterday's service, but it was his job. He'd stick to the same script as this morning. Share a few minutes of grief and sympathy with a broken-hearted mother or father. Pour a few socially required platitudes into the mouthpiece. Then hang up the phone feeling like crap. When he'd checked off all ten families, he'd dust off his original story outline—the one he'd prepared before he learned about the Doolan twins and the kids in Smyrna. He'd update it and then wrap it with words and images powerful enough to tear apart the Morgans, expose their shameless scheme, and stop them from breaking the spirits of decent folk like the Yoslings.

If, that was, he still had a job after he broke the news to Maxwell Priory, who had been reveling in the national attention and earning brownie points with his superiors at CBS.

He sat at his desk, put a check mark against the first name on his list, let out a long sigh, and dialed. A woman picked up. "This is Riley Brown from News Channel 13. I'd like to speak to Martina Anders, please."

"This is she. Mr. Riley, I'm so glad you called. I—" Her voice cracked.

For the twenty-first time that day, he waited for the anguish to play out. Her sobs stung his throat and misted his eyes. To hell with working on the new story outline. As soon as he'd called everybody, he was going home for a drink.

"I'm sorry," she said, her voice still trembling. She pulled in a breath and said on exhale, "You're the reporter who broke the story, right?"

"Yes." This would be another rough call. A few of the families had blamed him for reporting the story—he should have known the healings were bogus, should have warned them before giving their children false hope. "I'm following up after yesterday's service. I wondered if you could give me an update. How is"— Riley glanced at his list—"Braxton?"

"He's cured. I mean. I don't know. That is. Sorry. I'm waiting for the doctor to see him, but he's so much better. I can't thank you enough. If we hadn't seen your news report Braxton would—" He heard her sucking in quick, short breaths to regain control.

Riley blanked for a couple seconds. He'd heard the woman speak but couldn't be sure he'd comprehended the words.

"Hello? Are you still there, Mr. Riley?"

"Yes. Sorry. So you've seen an improvement?"

"Oh, yes. But more. It's difficult to describe to someone who didn't know him before, but—"

Riley waited while the woman gathered herself again, but these were tears of joy. One success out of twenty-one. Fantastic news for the Anders family, but what did this do to his story? Braxton's recovery could be coincidental. Was a five percent success rate good enough? Martina Anders would think so. But what kind of story did it leave Riley with?

"When is the doctor due?" he asked.

"Within the hour."

"Can I call back after his visit?"

"Of course. Anything we can do to help, just name it. We owe you more than you can know."

Wow!

The next child had shown significant signs of improvement and the next and the next and the next.

Ten of them.

Cured.

The word *miracle* was used more than once by a delighted parent. Particularly striking was a nine-year-old boy with pancreatic cancer whose tumor had failed to respond to chemotherapy. The doctors had given the boy weeks to live. Because of her son's sudden improvement in attitude and energy levels, his mother, Stephanie Powell, had demanded a new MRI, which had revealed a pancreas with ninety percent less malignancy. The hospital claimed the improvement as a delayed effect from his last chemo treatment. But that claim made no impression on the boy's mother, who was certain that Reverend Freddie Morgan was her son's savior. That Stephanie Powell was an agnostic and a trial lawyer who had only attended New Beginnings Church at the behest of her father as a last, desperate act of love, added further weight. As a storyline, it was a reporter's dream.

During the third call, the mother mentioned her daughter's violet eyes. Riley took note and started asking each time. The color change cemented the parents' belief that Reverend Morgan was channeling a mystical power. Riley called back to the first two families and confirmed that all ten children now had violet eyes.

Riley was giddy. He wouldn't have to present his boss with a story that contradicted News Channel 13's New Beginnings scoop. But why did the results of this Sunday's service differ from the week before? Reluctantly, he called back to three of the families from this morning's list. None of their children had experienced a change in eye color.

He phoned Nina Morgan and asked for an explanation.

"You saw the crowds," she said. "Freddie was blindsided last week. He tried his best, but he couldn't focus."

"I've spoken to all twenty families. They're very upset."

"We're going to arrange a second *healing* for them at a private service, with no distractions."

"I'd like to record the proceedings."

"I said without distractions, Mr. Brown."

The eye color wasn't the only thing that had changed. A week ago, Nina Morgan would have marched barefoot across glowing coals to get New Beginnings Church more media exposure. Suddenly, she was turning away free publicity.

The idea that Freddie Morgan could cure one day and not another left a bad taste in Riley's mouth, but he had to run with it. The reverend had apparently performed ten miracles yesterday, and Maxwell Priory was demanding an outline for the second-day story. Riley had until Thursday to complete a three-minute follow-up. If he failed to deliver, every journalist at the news station would trample over him to steal the story and make it their own.

Swept along by the euphoria of instant cures, the ten families offered Riley anything he needed. The story grew stronger by the hour: the medical evidence *was* remarkable; before and after optics provided by the families were superb; Ms. Powell's interview would give any nonbeliever cause to reconsider their faith.

His previous story had triggered a mob at the church. This piece was far stronger—without precedent. News of these new cures would bring thousands more parents begging for spiritual healing. These children—castoffs from the healthcare system, lost causes every one—were cured. With a few muttered words and a wave of his hand, the Reverend Freddie Morgan had made the USA's top medical professionals look impotent and inept.

The memory of his calls to the twenty families was too fresh for Riley to be fully convinced, but if Freddie Morgan cured them at a second service, well.

That wouldn't be news.

That would be a miracle.

⚛━⚛━⚛━⚛

Lauren answered her phone. A woman screamed, "It worked. They're all *healed*."

Recognition took a few seconds. The high-pitched voice and rapid-fire words didn't even sound like Nina Morgan.

"That's great news."

The deacon paused. That's it! Aren't you excited?"

"Of course." Confident in Maya, Lauren expected nothing less, but Deacon Morgan had never presided over a truly successful healing. Lauren glanced at the clock. It was after ten on Tuesday night. "Why are you calling so late?"

"I wanted to be certain, and I just got hold of the last family. Well, perhaps this'll excite you. After subtracting our overheads, Sunday's *healings* netted you eighteen thousand dollars, Ms. Doolan."

That was more than Lauren brought home in six months from her job at Pharmacon. And it was more than enough to pay for the homeschooling program.

"Are you still there?" Nina asked.

"Yes, sorry. What were you saying?"

"I've promised a new *healing* to the twenty families from the previous week. I'd like to coordinate that with you outside of the regular Sunday service."

"I work full time. Midweek is difficult." Also, Lauren didn't want to spend more time with Nina Morgan than necessary. Ten children each Sunday was enough.

"It's worth forty-two thousand dollars to you, Ms. Doolan, and we've already collected those tithes."

Lauren heard her own intake of breath in the earpiece of her phone. "Oh… I'll have to get back with you."

"Or, you could just give me the pills."

It took Lauren a couple seconds to make the connection—the Tic Tacs. "No!" Her response came out sharper than intended.

175

"Okay, okay, but these parents are desperate. They've heard about last Sunday's miracles."

Because you told them?

"Several families have a long way to travel. They want a date. They need to plan. Also, Riley Brown from News Channel 13 has been sniffing around, asking why last Sunday's kids were *healed* but not the other twenty. And he wanted to know why these children have violet eyes and not the others."

"What did you tell him?"

"That the sudden hoopla had disturbed Freddie's connection to the Holy Spirit. But Riley Brown's skeptical. I heard it in his voice. An anomaly like that will make him dig deeper."

An anomaly. That's how all this had started. A mouse that lived despite the odds. And now this process she'd constructed to protect her children and fund their education had taken on a life of its own. But the woman was right about Riley. A journalist would home in on the differences. "Okay. I'll take a sick day on Wednesday. Make sure everyone's there by three."

When Lauren arrived at the church, a group of people—the families from the failed *healing,* she assumed—crowded the front of the stage. Nina noticed Lauren and the twins and rushed from the stage, leaving her husband to handle the families. Voices were raised.

Flushed cheeks, darting eyes, the deacon marched toward Lauren and met her in the aisle. "You're late," she hissed. "The parents are angry." Then she glanced at the twins. "You didn't need to bring *them* along."

"They're here to bolster the children's faith. Remember?"

"Right." Nina's cynicism was thinly veiled. She glanced back at the stage where Freddie was fielding questions and looking flustered.

Maya reached up and took the woman's hand. "It's okay, Deacon Morgan. Reverend Freddie will *heal* the children."

Nina's face softened. She took a deep breath, let it ease out of her and her shoulders dropped an inch. She smiled. "Yes he will, my dear."

Nina returned her attention to Lauren, her voice calmer now. "I've set you up in the same room." With a nod to Lauren's medical bag, she said, "Do you have everything?"

Lauren glared at her. "Give me a couple minutes and then bring them through one at a time."

They climbed the steps at the side of the stage. Nina strode back to rejoin her husband, who was struggling under the weight of questions coming from parents whose faith in his ability was, for obvious reasons, in short supply.

As she led the twins through the curtain and along the hallway, Lauren heard the deacon addressing the parents, describing how close to death Maya and Joshua had been until Freddie channeled the Holy Spirit to *heal* them. "Ms. Doolan has offered to help today. Before your children receive their *healing* from the reverend, I want them to meet Maya and Joshua, to strengthen your child's faith."

Lauren let the twins into the office, placed her bag on the table, and got the Tic Tacs ready.

By the time the twentieth child walked through the door, Lauren's nerves were frayed like rope strained to its breaking point. For forty minutes, she'd passed out false-hope-mints and projected a positive demeanor despite the illness and misery she'd seen written on the childrens' faces as they shuffled, or were wheeled, into the room.

The skinny teenage girl with bloodshot eyes and hollow cheeks who now stood before them had on a multicolored woolen cap, covering her shaved head. At least Nina had arranged name badges for the children. "Hello, Katie," Lauren said. "I'd like you to meet Maya and Joshua."

The twins moved toward Katie, but as Joshua was about to begin his litany about being cured by Reverend Freddie, Maya took two fast steps to get ahead of him. She darted out an arm and yanked him away from the girl.

"No!"

Maya glared at her brother for the briefest of seconds. He stepped back, shying away from the teenager, or perhaps from Maya, whose face was flushed and fierce.

"Maya?" Lauren said, "What is it?"

Her daughter grabbed Lauren's hand, led her to the far corner of the room, and signaled for her to bend. She whispered in Lauren's ear, "Katie's too formed. I can't help her." Maya turned and glared at her brother, who had followed them. He avoided her gaze.

Lauren glanced at the sickly girl. The teenager stared back with wide, confused eyes. Katie didn't understand why she'd been brought to the room in the first place, and now…? Lauren chewed on her inner cheek. What should she say to the girl? Already, she'd grown accustomed to the fact that Maya could cure anything, anyone, but apparently not this girl. "Maya, stay here with Joshua." She moved toward the girl, took a deep breath, and continued with her normal patter: "As I was saying, Katie, Maya and Joshua were once very ill. Reverend Morgan *healed* them. You can see how healthy they are now. If you have faith, he can help you too." And with those easy words, Lauren stole Katie's cure from her.

The teenager turned her eyes to the floor. "I hope so," she said, and her tiny tentative voice scratched like a hangnail across Lauren's heart. How could Nina Morgan have done this all those years? How black was her soul? She reached out and stroked the girl's arm. "You can go back to your parents now, Katie."

The girl left, closed the door, and Maya burst into tears.

Lauren strode toward her little girl and enveloped her in a hug. What huge pressure she was putting her children under. It wasn't fair. She'd tell the Morgans this was the last time and figure out another way to protect her family. Perhaps they should leave Georgia. Settle in a new state. Start over far away from Riley Brown and News Channel 13.

Maya whispered, "No, Mommy. We can't. There are so many sick children we can help. Just make sure they aren't formed."

Lauren pulled back and looked Maya in the eye. "Formed?"

Joshua answered for his sister, "Past puberty."

Lauren searched his face to be sure he knew what he was saying. He did. Her cheeks grew warm; how could he even know the word never mind what it meant? And how could Maya know that Katie had started her periods?

Maya said, "I can't explain, Mommy, I just do." She focused on Joshua like a laser and pointed her finger at her brother. "And so did he!"

"What would happen if you tried to *heal* her?" Lauren asked.

"She would die. Like Maya Arrunsen," Joshua said. The careless edge in his voice lifted the hairs on Lauren's arms. She glanced at her son, and he was smiling.

Lauren released Maya and straightened. "Katie was the last. We're finished. How are you two feeling?"

They exchanged one of the looks she was so familiar with, then came to her and hugged her legs. Tears spilled unbidden from her eyes. If the twins wanted to continue, she'd allow it, but never again would she handle that many children in one session.

The twins' hug seeped up her legs—a soft, warm tingling that settled the panic in her mind and the nausea in her stomach. "You worry too much, Mommy," Maya said.

"Helping these children is a good thing," Joshua said, "and we need the money, right?"

Lauren smiled. They were correct about that. *Healing* ten children each week would provide more than enough to buy the twins the best education in America, and she so wanted that for them. They were smart, and unlike her, they wouldn't have to fight and claw for the American dream. Other than the incident with Katie, the *healings* hadn't affected them negatively; so why not benefit? None of those nineteen families would begrudge a few thousand dollars to cure their child.

Joshua gave her a last squeeze and stepped back. "Maybe we'll make enough money to move to a bigger house. Then Maya and me wouldn't have to share a room."

Good idea.

"Yes. It is a good idea, Mommy," Maya said.

CHAPTER 25

Like a sock puppet, Mark's grinning head poked over the partition of Riley's cubicle. "You comin' to lunch?"

Riley squeezed the bridge of his nose, rolled his shoulders, and leaned back in his office chair. He glanced at the wall clock. "Damn."

The videographer, in the cubicle now, waved an arm at Riley's work area. "What the hell happened?"

Riley blinked to clear the blur from three hours of intense online research. Multi-page extracts printed from dozens of web sites cluttered the desk and papered the floor. "She won't answer my calls, so I was digging for background on Lauren Doolan." He glanced at the papers and smiled. "I guess I fell down an Internet rabbit hole."

"No kidding. Anyway, focus on what's important—food?"

Riley stood, stretched his arms and hopscotched through the paper piles. "Great idea."

In the elevator, Mark asked, "Find anything?"

"Uh?"

"The chick with the twins who won't talk to you."

"Ah, the mysterious Ms. Doolan. Not sure. Maybe. She's a program operations assistant at a medical research company called Pharmacon. Back when her sister died, she worked for a Doctor Maya Arrunsen—now deceased."

Riley held the building's front door open, and they stepped onto the sidewalk. The excitement that had kept him digging all morning bubbled to the surface. "I think there might have been a deeper connection between her and the doctor. Maya's an unusual name. Lauren Doolan probably named her daughter after her boss. That's a big commitment."

"Not if they were good friends."

"Possible. But unlikely. Doolan only joined Pharmacon six months before Arrunsen died. And the doctor appears to have been a textbook solitary genius type."

At the café, they ordered sandwiches and coffees.

"Maybe she just liked the name," Mark said.

"Maybe. Anyway, it was Arrunsen who kept me going. Did you know she won a Nobel Prize for her work in evolutionary biology?"

"Seriously, dude. Everyone knows that." Mark rolled his eyes.

Riley laughed. "Me neither, but in her acceptance speech, Arrunsen postulated that her research might become the basis of a 'new medicine' that used targeted retroviruses to modify human DNA."

"Fascinating." Mark's dry tone implied the opposite. "Come on, Einstein. Collect thy sandwich and walk. Time to return to the grind." They headed for the exit. "One more question, though."

"Sure."

"How will you explain to Maxwell Priory that you wasted half a day researching a dead scientist?"

Riley held the café door for his friend, but not for long enough.

Mark got his arm up just in time to avoid a black eye. "Piss head!"

"Serves you right for mentioning he-who-shall-not-be-named during lunch break. I can't explain why I won't let this go. Except, well, you've met Freddie Morgan."

Mark lifted his voice to high-drama mode. "The very reverend Freddie." With an exaggerated sweep of his arm, he made a deep bowing motion. "Bless you, my son."

"Exactly. God had seven billion people to choose from. Why pick that guy to perform miracles?"

His friend shrugged. "Who cares? The church story made terrific TV, and it didn't do your career prospects any harm."

"Yeah. I guess."

Back in his paper-strewn office, Riley sketched a facsimile of Lauren Doolan on his notepad. He doodled her some curly hair. What if she wasn't protecting her children from the media? What if she was protecting herself? Lauren had visited the Booker twins and Shanice Mosely. And last Sunday, she had snuck out from the church's side curtains minutes before the service. How come the skeptical Ms. Doolan was suddenly on Team New Beginnings?

Then there was her daughter. Maya had been close to death, written off as a hopeless case. Dorothy, the hospital's patient advocate, hadn't said much, but she *had* called the baby's recovery a miracle, and that came from a woman familiar with infant mortality. Reverend Morgan had never laid hands on Maya; he'd never even seen her. But Lauren Doolan had. It was difficult enough to swallow Freddie Morgan as a healer, but to believe that prayers muttered on a stage twenty miles away could heal a terminally ill child beggared Riley's belief. Yet these children were cured somehow.

Riley didn't know *how* Lauren Doolan was involved, but the idea that she *was*, coupled with the possibility that science and not a pompous preacher was at the root of the cures, had kept his eyes wide and his pulse high since he arrived at work.

If science was doing the healing instead of faith, that would be a far bigger story; *that* would be a medical breakthrough of the magnitude envisaged by Maya Arrunsen when she published her Nobel prize-winning paper on *controlled symbiogenesis*.

It would also be illegal.

Riley followed up by phone with the children who had received the second, private healing. Nineteen had shown remarkable improvement in their health. Each child had experienced a change of eye color. He checked that box on his spreadsheet and muttered, "Why did God alter their eye color?" According to the reverend, it was a sign from on high, but New Beginnings Church had operated for ten years and he could find no previous mention of violet eyes.

Something had changed.

Maybe the anomaly could lead him to an answer—the twentieth child, Katie Cairns, still had brown eyes, and she still had cancer. He called her mother again. She was devastated when she learned of the other successes. She begged Riley to tell her what those parents had done differently. The woman blamed herself.

Where else could she look when her daughter alone had failed to improve? After he ended a very difficult call, Riley dialed Nina Morgan and asked why Katie was dying when the others were getting better. The deacon trotted out stock phrases about the family needing to have faith and patience—no help there.

Two of the cured children suffered from the same type of cancer that Katie did, and *they* were in remission. It made no sense.

He left messages for Lauren Doolan at home, then he connected with her at work, but before he could ask a question, she threatened him with a restraining order if he didn't stop harassing her. The more she blocked him, the more certain he became that she had the answers he sought. There was far more going on here than faith healing. His face was tingling and hot as he wrote a list of bullet points that supported his case. Then he called his boss's secretary, Florence.

"Is Mr. Priory available for ten minutes?"

"For what?"

She took her job as Maxwell Priory's gatekeeper very seriously.

"I have new information on the New Beginnings story. I think he'll want to hear what I've discovered."

"Hold."

The line went dead for twenty seconds before she came back. "He can spare you five minutes. Come up at four thirty." *Click.*

And thank you too, Florence. He used the wait time to polish his pitch and arrived at Florence's desk six minutes early. She glanced at him, scowled, and pointed to a metal chair. He sat. The chair wasn't comfortable; it wasn't meant to be.

At four thirty-five, Thomas Slattery let himself out of Priory's office. Thomas was News Channel 13's longest-serving and most well-known correspondent. He flashed over-white teeth at Florence, who smiled back—damn, this guy was such a creep. Nodding at Riley, he touched two fingers to his slicked-back hair in a mock salute then angled his head toward Priory's door. "Good luck," he said and breezed past without waiting for a response.

Riley tracked the man's departure and allowed himself a sly smile. *We'll see how cocky he is when my New Beginnings story turns into an exposé of an unregulated medical breakthrough.*

"Mr. Brown," Florence spat out his name.

He jerked upright and turned to receive her glare.

"Mr. Priory is waiting."

"Yes, ma'am." Riley sprang up and strode to Priory's office. With one hand on the knob, he paused for a fraction of a second and drew in a full breath. Then he opened the door and closed it behind him.

Maxwell Priory sat behind a paper-cluttered desk and locked lizard eyes on him. "This better be important. It's not been a good day."

The man looked as impatient as he sounded. And this from someone whose normal demeanor was pissed-off-station-chief. Riley considered backing out. But what could he say? Oops, wrong office. Or, sorry, I meant let's meet tomorrow when you look less like a raptor ready for a snack.

Riley handed him a copy of his bullet points. "I've summarized the opportunity. Based on my research, I—"

Priory put up his hand. His eyes scanned the single sheet for sixty silent seconds—Riley marked time in his head—and the longer it took, the more confident he became. His boss finally looked up. Riley searched the editor's face for a reaction, but came up blank.

"So you want the station to recant the faith healing story?"

"No. No. Not recant. See—" Riley leaned over the desk. He hadn't been offered a seat. "—the third bullet explains the new angle. The results are as we reported them. They are miraculous cures, but the preacher isn't doing the healing."

"He's a conman."

Riley grinned. He got that excited tingle of the chase again. Priory understood what this meant. "He's a conman, but that's not the story. I believe these children have been cured using an untested medical procedure."

Priory glanced at the paper again. His head moved slowly from side to side.

Riley was hitting stride. He leaned across the desk again and pointed to the photo he'd pasted at the bottom of the page—Dr. Maya Arrunsen standing at the lectern accepting her Nobel Prize. "Not only that—"

Priory slapped Riley's hand away and fixed him with icy blue eyes. "Have you told anyone else about"—he lifted the paper and waved it—"this?"

Riley smiled. "No, sir." He had mentioned it to Mark, but that wasn't what his boss was worried about. He was worried about losing exclusivity.

"That's the only thing you've got right. Now. Return to your desk. Do not pass GO. Do not speak to anyone of this." He was still waving the paper. "Transfer all of your New Beginnings files to Thomas Slattery. Then delete them from your PC and go home."

Riley lost the ability to breathe. He staggered back from the one-two punch of Priory's words. His mouth gaped open. He shut it and somehow grabbed enough air to talk. "Sir. That's unfair. I've done this research. This is my story."

Priory narrowed his eyes. And hissed, "This isn't a story." He crunched the paper into a ball and tossed it at Riley, hitting him in the chest. "This is a reason for us to lose our franchise." Priory took a few breaths, drummed his fingers on the desk. When he next spoke, his voice was calmer. "Look, Riley, you're a rookie. I get that. So listen and learn. Once you commit to a breaking story, once you start, it's like a snowball you've kicked down a hill. You can add to it, you can color it, you can show it from different angles, but you can't stop and take it back halfway down because it'll catch you and crush you and your credibility. The New Beginnings story has a couple weeks of life left. We'll follow up with any kids that recover and report on those."

"Sir, they've all recovered except one, but that's the point."

"I'm happy for them. But no, that's not *the point*." Priory slammed a fist on his desk. "The story has run its course. You can't rewrite it. If you do, it means we were wrong. We misled our viewers. And we can never admit to that. It was a good story. Let Thomas close it out next week. Go home. Come in fresh tomorrow, and I'll have something new for you." Priory stood and offered his hand across the desk. "You've done a good job. Don't screw it up now. Okay?"

Riley accepted the handshake. "Yes, sir."

He left in a daze. That was why Thomas had looked so smug. The decision to transfer his project had been made before he stepped into Priory's office. Mark must have blabbed about their lunchtime discussion. Back in his cubicle, Riley sat at his desk surrounded by his morning's research, and tears welled in his eyes. *Damn it!* He hated the editor for what he'd done. The news would be all over the office by morning—Thomas Slattery would make

185

sure of that. Priory had made a mistake. His boss had been sitting behind a desk too long; he'd lost his edge.

Riley sprang to his feet and stormed out of his cluttered cubicle. He glared at Mark when he passed his *friend's* desk and banged the outer office door as he exited. He strode to the parking garage, and by the time he reached his car, his mind was made up. On his drive home, he phoned Nina Morgan.

"Hi, Nina. Look, my boss wants me to cover next week's service. He's planning a follow-up story. Can you save a chair in the front row for me on Sunday?"

She said she would. Instead of bullet points and researched theories, Riley would bring hard proof to his boss. Then he'd see whether Thomas Slattery or Riley Brown owned the New Beginnings story.

CHAPTER 26

When Lauren arrived home from work on Friday, she heard a woman speaking to her mother in the kitchen—an unfamiliar voice. Convinced that Riley Brown had sent an emissary to question Margaret, she threw down her purse and stormed along the hall. That rookie needed to move on—yesterday! She yanked open the kitchen door and her mom sprang up from the table. "Lauren. You're home at last. This is Barbara Cairns. She's driven from Oklahoma to see you."

Cairns? The name rang a distant bell. Lauren let out the breath she'd been saving to blast Riley's accomplice. If Barbara came from Oklahoma, she wasn't with News Channel 13. She approached the woman who had gotten up. They shook hands. "I'm sorry, Barbara, should I know you?"

The woman was trembling; she glanced at Lauren and quickly averted her gaze.

"I'll leave you two to get acquainted," Margaret said.

"Where are the twins?" Lauren asked.

"TV dinner, tonight. Yours is warming in the oven." Margaret patted the woman's shoulder on her way past. "It was nice to meet you, Barbara. I hope Katie gets better soon. Remember what I told you. You must have faith."

"Thank you, Margaret."

Katie Cairns. Now Lauren knew who this was. Barbara glanced at her; chin twitching, she looked ready to fall apart. Lauren took her arm and guided her back to the table. "Let's sit?"

"Thank you." She took a seat and stared at the table.

"You came to see me. How can I help?"

"Katie's gotten worse. I—" Her face crumpled like a used sandwich wrapper. Sobs shook her shoulders. A feeble feline sound leaked from her lips and splashed an icy chill down Lauren's spine. Barbara's desperation transported Lauren back five years to Atlanta Medical Center, sitting beside Maya's incubator. This woman was staring into the black abyss of a life without her daughter. Lauren had seen that picture, felt that dread, lived that emptiness. She reached across and squeezed the woman's hand.

"I... I'm sorry. It's so hard."

"Take your time, Barbara."

The woman snatched a few shaky breaths. When she'd steadied herself sufficiently to look Lauren in the eyes, her face was drawn, her eyes glassy with grief. "This is rude of me, barging in here, but I have nowhere else to turn. For Katie, I have to try everything. You understand?"

"Yes, of course I do."

"I don't care what it is we've done wrong. But whatever it was, it was my fault. Not Katie's. I'm here to beg you to forgive me, for her sake."

Lauren's thoughts scrambled, flitted, grasped and lurched, trying to make sense of these words. The woman was upset. And apparently, it was an upset of Lauren's making, but how? Why? They had never met. There was nothing *to* forgive. Lauren squeezed the woman's fingers. "Barbara, I'm sorry. I don't understand what you want from me. Explain, and if I can fix it, I will."

A watery smile etched itself onto the woman's lips. Her eyebrows lifted. "Really? You mean it?"

"Of course. Just tell me what you need."

"I need a pill for Katie."

Barbara's answer hit Lauren like a rabbit punch, jerked her upright in the chair, forced her to take a five-count before speaking. "You mean the pill I gave the children at the church."

Barbara gave three huge, exaggerated nods, her grin at odds with her tear-glistened cheeks. She picked up her purse and set it on the table. "Look." Dipping into the bag, she brought out a wad of hundred-dollar bills wrapped with elastic bands. "That's four thousand dollars." She pushed the money across the table. "Steven, that's my husband, he thought, well because we only paid the tithe, that maybe the other parents had made, you know, a private gift to you personally."

"Oh. No."

There was a panicked madness in the way Barbara's eyes flitted over Lauren's face. The woman's arm snaked out and gripped Lauren's hand, squeezing, crushing her fingers. She lowered her voice, leaned in. "We'll never breathe a word. It's a secret we'll take to our graves." And with that dark word, so close to her fears for her daughter, she grimaced, released Lauren, and buried her face in her hands.

The raw grief radiating from Barbara Cairns shredded Lauren's heart and made her stomach churn. The woman must have contacted the other parents. Lauren imagined her torment when she realized Katie was the only child who hadn't recovered. The others would speak of the pill. The pill that Katie alone didn't receive.

Maya had been adamant that Katie Cairns was too "formed," too mature for the miracle cure to work. But Lauren couldn't explain that truth. Couldn't expose Maya. She waited until Barbara's sobs had subsided, and she had once again raised her head and jutted out her chin.

"Believe me, Barbara. If there was something I could do—"

"But—"

Lauren held up a hand, and the woman's mouth shut like a sprung trap, eyes tinged once again with hope. As though the words Lauren planned to utter would deliver the miracle that her daughter needed, the miracle granted to the other children.

"Wait here." Lauren left to retrieve the black medical bag from her bedroom. She returned to the kitchen and placed it on the table beside the woman's purse and the wad of money. A grin spread across Barbara's face. Clearly, someone had mentioned the bag.

"Open it."

Barbara's head jerked up and a curtain of fear passed across her eyes. She looked at the bag, then back at Lauren, who nodded. Barbara stood, opened the bag, and peered inside—a magician's assistant peering into a top hat, expecting to find a rabbit.

"What do you see?"

"There's a pillbox."

"Take it out."

She did.

"Open it."

Her hands trembled as she twisted off the top and laid it on the table beside the bag.

"Eat one," Lauren said.

"I… I'm not sick."

"If you were. That pill wouldn't help you. Those pills don't cure the children."

"I don't understand."

"Put one in your mouth and you will."

The woman did. "It's minty."

"It's a Tic Tac."

Forlorn, lost, hopeless. Barbara Cairn's eyes conveyed all those emotions and more. Lauren took a candy from the box and popped it in her mouth to reinforce the concept. "I'm so sorry, Barbara. If I could make Katie well, I'd do it, do it in a heartbeat." Pointing to the bag, she said, "There's no secret sauce. It's easier for the children to believe in a pill than for them to believe in faith healing."

Barbara's legs gave way, and she slumped into the chair, and then her body became boneless and she slid sideways; her head slapped the floor before Lauren could reach her—out cold.

Damn it.

"Mom!"

Her mother ran into the kitchen. "What is it—? Oh, my!"

"Help me with her." They levered her into a seated position on the floor and pushed her head between her legs. "I've got her," Lauren said. "Bring water."

"What happened?" her mom asked.

Barbara groaned and lifted her head.

"She thought it was me who cured the children."

"I explained it was Reverend Freddie's gift," her mom said.

"Well, you didn't convince her."

Barbara blinked herself awake and sipped the water. "I'm sorry," she said, and started sobbing.

Sitting beside Barbara on the floor, tears rolled down Lauren's cheeks, and she hugged the woman. "So am I, Barbara. So am I."

CHAPTER 27

An hour before the Sunday service, a Junior Healer stood at the center of the New Beginnings Church stage, directing his team as they filled leaflet dispensers, turned on lights, and straightened chairs. Riley approached him. "Hi, I'm Riley Brown from Channel 13 News." He pulled out his press card, but the boy waved it away.

"I recognize you, Mr. Brown. The deacon told me you were coming. Here." He handed Riley a card with VIP printed on the front. "Just put this on your seat."

"Thanks." He offered his hand, and the Junior Healer bent down and shook it. "I'm a little early," Riley said. "Okay if I sit over there and stay out of your way?" Riley pointed to the end of the row of chairs closest to the side of the stage where Lauren Doolan had appeared the previous Sunday.

"Sure."

When he was certain the staff were distracted, Riley skipped up the five steps and slipped through the curtain.

Lauren got them to the church forty minutes before the service. Maya studied her mom as she killed the engine and then turned to kneel in the driver's seat, facing her and Joshua. The tension line across the top of her mother's nose was showing. "Are you both sure you want to do this again? I won't be disappointed or upset if you say no."

The incident with Katie Cairns had shaken Lauren. Deacon Morgan had been instructed to only accept candidate children younger than ten years, but that didn't stop the worry. Maya appreciated that her mom was being protective, but the Sunday healings *had* to happen. Without them, there would be no money. No money meant no private tutors.

And private tutors were crucial.

Maya had already assimilated Ms. Hollinsworth's English and French language skills along with a smattering of Spanish. No kindergarten teacher could provide what Maya needed.

Yesterday, she asked her brother had he ever experienced the same dream twice. "You're weird," he said.

Maybe weird. Maybe something else. For the past month, when Maya closed her eyes each night, the same image awaited her. She was alone at the center of a black road that dipped and rose and wound away from her until it was swallowed by a distant horizon. Twenty yards along the tarmac stood a girl who, from the rear, looked like Maya. Maybe was Maya. Legs braced as though withstanding a buffeting from external forces, the Maya-like child stared forward with one arm extended, pointing the way.

Swirling gray mists that shrouded the panorama limited her to glimpses and inconclusive hints. The dream's full meaning extended far beyond her intellectual reach. Yet she sensed the scene had essential future purpose. She awoke each morning troubled by a loose jumble of ideas and possibilities. Her mother would listen, would try to help. But to Lauren, Maya was a five-year-old—an intelligent five-year-old—but a child nonetheless. Mention of a mysterious recurring dream would make her more likely to cancel the Sunday healings. There was no one else with whom Maya could discuss this riddle-me dream. Her brother thought her a weirdo; and her grandmother still believed Reverend Morgan possessed faith healing abilities. Maya craved new knowledge, fresh data to blow away the obscuring fog and reveal the significance of this all-consuming nightly vision. Above all, she yearned to know if the snippets she snatched as she stared from behind shut eyes foreshadowed a future that must be, or a future she could make. She hoped for the latter. But feared the first.

She unbuckled her car seat, reached forward, touched her mom's arm, and projected calmness through her fingertips. The lines on Lauren's forehead melted and a smile tweaked her lips. Maya conjured cuteness in her voice. "I *want* to help the sick children, Momma."

"And the money will pay for Maya's homeschooling, right?" Joshua said.

Maya whipped her head around and glared at her brother. She understood his purpose. Without her, Joshua would be the smartest kid in Hollinsworth's class. He didn't want to compete with his genius sister. It must be difficult always being the slow one, but pressing their mother wasn't the way forward. To continue on this path, Lauren must be convinced that the *healings* were the right thing to do.

Joshua's comment relit the concern in Lauren's mind. "Well, yes, Joshua, but—"

Maya covered Lauren's hand with hers, caressing doubt from her mother's thoughts, soothing and banishing worry. "I'm sure, Momma. Really."

"Come on then," Lauren said. "Let's get to our room before the church gets busy." She led them across the parking lot. An elderly woman to their left, wearing a summer frock and a white hat with a red feather tucked in the band, smiled and waved. Maya waved back. They must seem like the perfect American family on their way to Sunday service.

Walking down the center aisle, Lauren waved to Nina, who was on stage with the candidates for *healing*. Maya scanned the children. None were *formed*. Good. No one in the Doolan family wanted another house call from a distraught parent seeking a magic pill.

Lauren opened the door to their room, and Joshua walked through. "Hello, Mr. Brown," he said. "What are you doing here?"

A cold chill stirred in Maya's stomach. She followed her mom into the room, closed the door, and focused on the reporter who sat at the table, facing them, smiling and smug.

Lauren moved ahead of her and Joshua. Riley rose and stepped forward, offering his hand. "Hello, Ms. Doolan. I hoped I'd find you here."

She glared at the reporter and pointed, straight-armed, at the door. "Get out!"

Riley lowered his hand, but the grin remained. "I'll be happy to, but first why don't you tell me about Doctor Arrunsen's *new medicine?*"

Maya heard her mother's involuntary intake of breath. Riley's eyes widened and so did his smile.

"I'm sorry, new what?" But the lie was etched in her voice. To calm the tumult of panic cascading from her mother, Maya stepped forward and grasped her hand, dampening the fluttering in Lauren's chest until her mother regained composure. "Mr. Brown, I don't think this is the time or place to discuss my past working relationship with Maya Arrunsen. The doctor was a brilliant scientist and a good friend. I still mourn her passing."

He tilted his head and without a shred of sincerity said, "I'm sorry for your loss, but when *would* be a good time and place, Ms. Doolan? I've tried repeatedly to contact you."

Lauren stared at the reporter. Maya observed her search for an answer, any answer, that could get rid of the man and buy her time to think. Joshua moved closer and took Maya's other hand. *"He knows about you, Maya. He'll put it on TV. He'll ruin everything."*

"I can't allow that," Maya replied.

Lauren said, "Thank you, children. That's quite enough. Please leave this to me."

Joshua's head snapped around. He stared at Maya. *"How did Mom hear me?"*

Maya yanked her arm away from her brother and broke the mental connection, but the puzzle lines on Lauren's brow told her she was too late.

Riley still awaited an answer to his question.

"Well, Ms. Doolan? Why don't we set a meeting to discuss what's *really* going on at New Beginnings Church, and then I'll get out of your hair."

A tapping on the door broke the tension. "Are you ready?" Nina shouted.

The deacon opened the door and maneuvered a wheelchair into the room. Once through the doorway, she looked up and jerked to a halt. "Riley? What are you doing here?"

The reporter stepped past Lauren and crouched down next to the wheelchair. "And who do we have here?"

194

"I'm Michael." The boy was eight or nine and rail-thin. His head shook as though it were too heavy for his skinny neck. He squinted at the reporter.

"And why are *you* in this room, Michael?" Riley asked in a cloying voice.

Lauren stepped around the wheelchair and turned Michael away from the reporter. "That's enough! Mr. Brown is here uninvited, Deacon. I'd appreciate it if you would escort him from the church."

Riley straightened, smirking. "But, Ms. Doolan, it was Deacon Morgan who invited me. She kindly reserved me a VIP seat for today's service."

Lauren glared at Nina, who looked away, admitting her guilt.

Riley cleared his throat to regain Lauren's attention. "Answer my question about Maya Arrunsen, and I'll be on my way. Alternatively, let's meet after the service; although"—he nodded toward Michael— "I would love to stay and observe." He folded his arms and faced Lauren. "Are you certified to administer medical treatments, I wonder?"

"All right, Mr. Brown, you win. Leave us now, and I'll meet you after the service and explain."

"That's a good idea, Momma," Maya said. She flashed the reporter a sweet smile and offered him her hand. A cloud of uncertainty passed across his face, and his arm made an involuntary move away from her. She stepped in and took his fingers in hers. He was remembering the incident from his childhood when the tiger had frightened him. The same fear memory he experienced after he had poked his nose into their living room.

"It's okay, Mr. Brown." Maya poured calming thoughts into his mind. She resealed the big cat behind its glass wall, and his face relaxed. "Come, Mr. Brown, I'll show you to your seat. Momma will explain everything after the service." The reporter allowed Maya to lead him past the crippled boy, past Nina Morgan, and out of the room.

"Mr. Brown," she said, once they were in the hallway.

"Yes?"

"Who is Doctor Arrunsen?" Maya projected herself deep into his mind. Her extended consciousness formed a multitude of snaking silver tendrils, probing, seeking his information source. Below her, a Milky Way of Riley Brown's neurons sparked and flashed.

"She was a famous scientist who worked with your mom," he said.

Maya located the answer's origin in Riley's mind. Joshua was correct. Brown intended to expose Lauren as New Beginning's true healer. He didn't yet understand Maya's role, but he would. Now she understood why, most nights in her dream, the reporter stood at the first major intersection in her Vision Road—a dead-end side branch that offered no return to the main route. A Riley Brown exposé would force her down that road, and she would forfeit the opportunity to learn more about the future she believed was possible.

Like a burglar rifling through a sock drawer in search of a hidden jewel, Maya scrutinized his thoughts. Once relevant information was located, she cauterized the area, severed connections, deleted memories. Guilt stabbed at her. Never before had she interfered in another mind. Yet if Riley knew what was at stake, surely he would approve of her actions. She hoped that was true.

"Yes, I—" Riley stalled, mouth agape, as he struggled to retrieve information that was being erased from his mind.

"Is that why you came here today, Mr. Brown?"

"I suspect your mom of using Doctor Arrunsen's new medicine to cure children like Michael. Is she, Maya?"

She squeezed his hand and stopped walking. At the speed of thought, she streaked through his mind, snapping the links between Arrunsen and Lauren and New Beginnings Church, removing Riley's reasons to investigate. He turned and looked into her eyes, questioning.

"Is she what?" she asked.

"Excuse me?"

"I thought you asked a question about my mother and Doctor Arrunsen."

He exaggerated a frown and shook his head—clearly baffled.

She giggled. "Sorry," she said, "I got mixed up. It happens a lot to five-year-olds."

He patted her on the head. She was relieved. Brown didn't seem impaired after his impromptu brain surgery.

"You're a smart one," he said.

She resumed walking and pulled him along. When they reached the curtain leading to the church hall, she asked, "Are you going to stay for the service?"

He shook his head. "Not sure why I came, really. Anyway, there's no point. I'm moving on to another assignment tomorrow."

"That sounds exciting."

He beamed. "Yes it does."

Before Maya released his hand, she erased the memory of the tiger at the zoo. Riley Brown was a nice man. He didn't need to suffer that fear again.

He gave a wave and a smile and then climbed down the stage steps and made his way toward the exit.

Maya returned to the room and took her mother's hand. Lauren was frantically trying to figure how she had heard the twins' voices in her head.

"Shall I talk to Michael?" Maya asked.

Lauren nodded. "Nina, would you leave us please?"

Her daughter was already beside the wheelchair. "Hello, Michael, I'm Maya." She took the boy's hand. "When I was a baby I was ill like you, but Reverend Morgan *healed* me. If you have faith in him, he can help you, too."

Maya turned to her mom. Lauren's eyes were unfocused, far away. "Momma?" Maya said, "Do you have something for Michael?"

"Huh? Oh. Yes." Lauren placed her medical bag on the table and took a Tic Tac from the pillbox. "Here, Michael, this will make you feel better," she said, popping the pill onto the boy's tongue.

Joshua opened the door and the deacon came in. "Where's Brown?" Lauren asked her.

"Don't know, but his seat is empty. How did he get in here?"

"I should ask you that question. He ambushed us; he was waiting in the room when I arrived."

"Who's Maya Arrunsen?" Nina asked.

"It's a long story, but it might mean trouble." Lauren locked eyes with the deacon. "I'll deal with him, somehow." Then, accenting every word with a wagging finger, she said, "But any more publicity and this arrangement will terminate. Understood?"

The deacon's mouth twisted as though she were sucking a lime. She nodded. "Understood. We need to get moving. Are you ready for the next child?"

"Ready," she said.

The deacon wheeled Michael away.

"Maya, what just happened?" Lauren asked.

Maya moved to her mother's side and reached for her hand. Lauren pulled away.

"If I hold your hand, it'll be easier to explain," Maya said.

Lauren reached out. Their fingers touched. *Joshua and I talk like this all the time. You heard him because I was touching you.*

Lauren's eyes widened. On watery legs, she drifted to the center of the room and steadied herself against the table. "And can you both tell what I'm thinking?"

Only me.

A buzzing started in Lauren's ears. She stared at Maya and fear prickled her scalp. She was scared of her own daughter. Would she ever again see her as simply her daughter?

"Sit, Momma." Lauren slumped into the seat, gulping air, and lowered her head between her legs.

Maya stood beside her with one hand on her mother's back. She poured mental oil on Lauren's troubled thoughts, chasing her anxiety, bolstering her courage.

There was a knock. "It's the deacon," Maya said.

Joshua opened the door. A frail girl in a white dress stood next to Nina Morgan. The girl's pink hat covered a bald head.

"Hi, I'm Joshua, and this is Maya." He took the girl's hand and led her to his sister, still beside Lauren. The deacon left and closed the door. "I was once ill, just like you," Joshua said, "and Reverend Morgan *healed* me. If you have faith, he'll *heal* you too."

Maya took the girl's other hand and spoke softly, "Momma? Ready?"

Lauren shook out a Tic Tac and handed it to Maya without making eye contact.

Once the tenth child had received her magical mint and left the room, Lauren sat the twins at the table. Maya reached across the desk, seeking her hand, but Lauren withdrew. "I need to understand something first."

Her daughter sat upright in the chair, straight as a board, face implacable, and waited.

"How long have you been able to hear my thoughts?"

Maya returned her gaze—strong, open, confident. "At first I thought everyone could do it. Then one day, you and Grandma got into a silly argument just because you had misunderstood each other, and I worked it out. That's why it was so wonderful when Joshua got well, because then I could share."

That made sense. Any child would assume that she functioned as everyone else did until she found out she was different. "And you, Joshua?"

"I hear Maya if we're touching."

"Wow. Wait. What about the children you're *healing*? Can they—?"

"No," Maya said.

Lauren shook her head. What if Maya didn't fully understand her abilities? She might *seem* to be helping the children but doing them long-term harm. "I don't know how I feel about continuing if it's causing a fundamental change in these children's brains."

Joshua's chair screeched as he pushed away from the table and sprang to his feet. "But we have to continue."

Lauren softened her voice. "No. Joshua. We don't have to do any such thing."

"How else will you afford the tutors? Maya can't sit in that classroom with those stupid kids."

"Joshua. That's rude!" Lauren said.

"Well. It's true." He paced back and forth, frowning, using hand gestures. "Tell her, Maya. She listens to you."

Maya reached across the table and asked permission with her eyes. Lauren gave in. She yearned for the comfort that came with her daughter's touch. "Don't be frightened, Momma. Joshua doesn't mean to be cruel, but he's right. I can't change what I am."

Maya turned on a soothing heat lamp that bathed Lauren's body. Without that balm, Lauren would be freaking out right now. When did she become the child in this family?

"You're not the child. You're our mother and we need you to protect us. If people find out about Joshua and me, they will take us away from you and Grandma and study us like specimens... like Eureka."

Joshua nodded along. He took Lauren's other hand. "We'd be freaks," he said.

These thoughts had occurred to Lauren many times. That was why she persisted with the medical bag and the breath mints. It seemed her concerns had leaked to Maya. But what if she were mistaken about how they'd be received by the scientific community?

Maya shook her head. "You aren't mistaken."

"No, you aren't," Joshua said.

"We need you to shield us while we learn. When we're older, people won't be able to push us around. But until then—"

Lauren stood. "Maya. I want you to give me privacy to think things through. Can you do that?"

Maya withdrew her hand. "Of course."

"Promise me."

"I promise."

Lauren moved to the far corner, and even though it seemed weird, she turned her back on her children. She had no way to judge if Maya could still eavesdrop on her thoughts. How could she survive, knowing her daughter could tap into her mind? But what about the alternative? The children weren't wrong. They would have their lives taken from them, and the scientists who studied them would be simpletons compared to Maya. No. She would keep this within the family until Maya was able to determine her own path in life. Then surely, the sky was the limit for her daughter.

She turned and faced her children. "Maya? Is this how you learned French?"

"Ms. Hollinsworth thought in French all the time. It was fun. And I taught some to Joshua."

"Oui," he said.

Maya smiled. "That was when I learned about Adam—"

"Ms. Hollinsworth's nephew?"

"Yes," Joshua said. "He was smart. Although not Maya-smart."

Hollinsworth had talked about mental age and physical age as separate entities when dealing with higher-functioning children. How old was Maya already? How fast could she learn? What would she do with that knowledge?

"One more question. When you cured Joshua, you told me you sent a piece of you into him, but you didn't know how. Do you know how now?"

"No, Momma. But I want to learn. I can't touch all the sick children in the world. And I can't help them once they're *formed*." Sadness cloaked her eyes and her mouth drooped. "Remember poor Katie."

Lauren looked from Maya to Joshua and back again. She gave them a reassuring smile. Maybe through her namesake, Maya Arrunsen would achieve her dream after all, even if her "new medicine" came too late to save its inventor. If the doctor had been offered that deal on her deathbed, Arrunsen would have taken it without hesitation.

She narrowed her eyes and tried to see Maya not as her almost-six-year-old daughter, but as the most potent being alive, because, according to Hollinsworth, that was where her unmeasurable genius placed her, and that was before accounting for her other abilities. But no matter how unique she was, or perhaps because of that, Maya needed her, needed her protection and guidance. A heavy weight of responsibility draped her shoulders and brought forth a sigh. Maya may have an advanced mind and unique gifts, but to fulfill her potential, she needed a safe place to learn and grow.

She crouched and opened her arms. "Okay, come here you two." They ran to her. Joshua let out a woot. "I'll help you," she said, "but we have to work as a team. No more secrets." She leaned back and looked at each of them. "I'm not as smart as you two, but I *can* navigate the adult world. So you must be truthful with me from here on. Deal?"

Maya kissed Lauren's left cheek and Joshua kissed her on the right. The bargain was sealed, and the pressure drained away because they were finally being honest with each other.

Now, if only some miracle could get Riley Brown off their backs.

CHAPTER 28

Eight Years Later...

Sitting across the dining table from her tutor, Maya asked, "So, Professor Sterling, with a worldwide population of seven billion and counting, can we consider modern-day humans a plague?"

The expert in evolutionary biology lifted his left hand to stroke his mustache in a parody of contemplation, and his thought chains flooded Maya's memory banks. In seconds, she assimilated Sterling's upcoming answer plus its associated research—for him a lifetime of study, for her a fraction of a second.

"An unsupportable hypothesis, I'm afraid, Maya. Plague mammals—rabbits, mice, lemmings and so on—are small herbivores. Humans are large omnivores. We must work harder to obtain nutrition, and our territorial tendencies preclude multiple kin moving into our personal space. Even Thanksgiving can be a trial." Sterling peered over half-moon reading glasses and delivered a forced smile.

Like the seventeen tutors who had preceded him, Sterling had progressed through what she had come to know as the three phases of Maya-acceptance. At their first session, after twenty minutes of ninth-grade material, he had shifted to college-level concepts—phase one. Then, filled with wonderment at Maya's rapid progress, for a few months he considered her his *special* project—a fourteen-year-old prodigy whom he had "discovered" and planned to groom as a future member of his department— two. Her unique ability to connect and directly absorb information was, of course, unknown to him, but as soon she began to outthink him, his enthusiasm waned—phase three. Academics' egos always proved a complex conundrum to navigate. But she didn't require telepathy to read the professor's insincere smile as a defense mechanism.

"But we're no longer hunter-gatherers," Maya said. "Our cities have building codes and laws that support high population density. We harvest domesticated animals for protein. We've unleashed fertilizers and power tools on the land. Genetically modified plants provide increased yields. Our grocery stores and refrigerators are overflowing."

He shook his head. "Yes, but unlike rodents we don't breed rapidly and consume that bounty. Humans are predominantly monogamous with a long gestation period and a decade or more delay before our females achieve sexual maturity." He wagged his index finger. "That's two strikes for your hypothesis, I'm afraid."

Sterling didn't mention the impact of modern medicine on extending human life. Or that female chimps experienced only a dozen ovulations compared to four hundred in a healthy modern woman. It was more important for him to win the debate than it was to develop the argument.

Maya tapped the top of the graph that lay on the table between them. It showed population over the last six hundred years. After a brief dip in the mid-sixteen-hundreds, corresponding with The Great Plague, the line soared upward like a Fourth of July rocket. "Nature may not have equipped us for plague-level expansion, Professor, but *if* human interference has sufficiently changed the parameters, what would be the next stage."

He retrieved a clean handkerchief from his pocket, removed his glasses, and polished an invisible speck on the right lens. Maya observed his inner struggle as he endeavored to maintain a civil tone and answer what he considered a naïve request for information based on a fourteen-year-old girl's baseless hypothesis. In the end, money won out. He *was* being well paid. "Mammal plague scenarios are always unsustainable," he said. "Population increase eventually triggers an internal or an external agent that causes a rapid collapse, usually an extinction event."

"A deadly virus might be an internal agent."

"Yes, of course, amplified by the proximity of the expanding population it would spread rapidly."

"And an external agent?"

The professor glanced up from his polishing. He monitored her face, seeking assurance that she was serious and still engaged. The threat she posed to his intellect had created an untenable position for the man. Their relationship was toxic. This, she knew, would be their last meeting. "The population expands until it either consumes all available food or corrupts its own environmental requirements for survival. Then the mammals die en masse, although a few individuals may resort to cannibalism." He smirked. "Even herbivores will eat meat when faced with death."

"Or the animals must evolve."

"Well, genetic aberrations do sometimes orchestrate a more orderly collapse, for example, by lowering fertility. But—" He shook his head and tut-tutted, causing his disheveled, tobacco-stained mustache to twitch. "—surely not *evolution*, Maya. Plague events escalate rapidly and end suddenly. Evolution works across far broader timescales."

Then, shaken loose by the logic of her argument, a mental clamshell opened in Sterling's mind. Like a found pearl, his suppressed fears flooded into her. She saw his grandchildren—two small boys—playing on a lawn while the professor looked on with tear-glazed eyes and wondered would they survive the apocalypse he refused to acknowledge? Her assumption about Sterling's reticence had been incorrect. He wasn't trying to assert intellectual superiority. He was in denial.

The professor's studies confirmed what she had deduced. Modern civilization was doomed. The professor's family tree would wither. His genes would no longer spread and prosper. Not only did evolution lack time to deliver an escape route, evolution lacked motivation. Evolution would not benefit by continuing a human plague. Evolution despised plagues. Evolution honored diversity above all, and a species as dominant and destructive as humankind threatened the basic premise of evolutionary development. The human experiment would be dealt with as had all previous plagues—through an extinction event.

Maya observed Sterling's image of seven billion human-lemmings accelerating toward an evolutionary cliff. Constrained by inwardly focused societies and a selfish desire for personal aggrandizement, humankind could never accede to the massive disruptive changes required to return the planet to biodiversity. The population climax was inevitable. Only the means of the extinction remained in question. Sterling had pondered this topic long and often, and Maya wanted to suck him dry, even of knowledge-scraps he might not see as relevant.

"But consider this, Professor—" The words stuck in her throat. She gagged and gasped. A sudden, ferocious heat-flush prickled her scalp and throbbed through her cheeks. Hot needles stabbed their way down her neck. Fiery lava pulsed into her chest cavity and stole her breath then cascaded through her belly and scorched her thighs. Firecrackers exploded in her ears and stinging showers of sparks obscured her sight.

What?

Sterling's face swayed and blurred. His gaping mouth morphed into a parody of Munch's "Scream." Wincing and panting, she closed her eyes to block the unsettling image. The crack as her forehead hit the table rattled her teeth.

"Maya… Maya! Oh, dear." His chair scraped the floor. His voice, distant, echoing, called out, "Ms. Doolan! Lauren! Come quickly. Oh, dear."

With a soft hiss, Maya floated down to the center of the black road from her dreams. Above her, Sterling's last words floated as three-dimensional Sesame Street blocks. She bent and grabbed two handfuls of the mist that swirled around her feet. The gray wisps narrowed, and corded, gaining physical substance in her hands until she was able to plait them into a long, pliable rope. Maya shaped a lasso from her creation and cast it toward his words, snagging them. With a wrist flick, she tossed the blocks sideways. The blocks sped away as in a vacuum, dragging the rope, which pulled the fog from the plane like a silken sheet yanked with a flourish from a hidden prize. A startling white landscape was revealed, split down its center by the Vision Road. Unlike the hazy glimpses received in her dream state, this vista was stark and clear.

The road dipped and rose, disappearing into the plane and reappearing farther away as though stitched in place by a giant's needle. The way projected *from* Maya and was integral to her. A myriad of images fluttered and shimmered along its length—here an individual, there an uncountable multitude—they merged and moved and dissipated then reconstituted in a head-spinning and chaotic time-lapse movie.

To quell her dizziness, Maya focused on a point twenty yards ahead, where the black band first dipped out of sight. The child from her dreams stood at the center of the road. Dressed, as always, in a white robe and facing away. For once, her arms were at her sides. The girl turned, and Maya saw herself as a six-year-old, staring back. "What is this place?" she asked of her other self.

"Your life path." The voice possessed a metallic texture.

"My life is predestined?"

"If so, you would see all. Do you see all?"

Maya scanned the plane beyond the girl. As she searched out the farthest edge, more ribbon appeared. Responding to her gaze it lifted and snaked, always stretching toward the horizon. The farther the road progressed, the greater percentage that was hidden below the whiteness. The girl made to turn away.

"Wait." Maya looked behind. The tarmac veered from side to side but was fully exposed. She returned her focus to the future. "If you are me as a child, why aren't you back there?" She jerked her thumb over her shoulder.

"I am you…. And I am not you."

"Why haven't I seen this before?"

"Until now, you were a child and your path followed an evolutionary stable strategy."

"And now?"

"Now you are grown there are many futures." Young-Maya waved her arm in a grand gesture, and the road beyond her splintered and branched and then branched and splintered to form an incomprehensibly complex road map. "You must choose the path."

A cold shock jolted Maya upright. Like a glass sheet, the vision shattered, and the shards spun into blackness.

"Maya? Maya?"

She opened her eyes. The living room was dull and two-dimensional, unappealing. Her eyelids snapped shut. Maya was desperate to return to that fascinating place. To question. To learn. But only darkness met her.

Her mother rubbed a wet cloth over Maya's face and neck. Icy liquid dribbled down her back. Lauren's warm hands cupped

Maya's cheeks. She searched Maya's face from eighteen inches away. "What happened, sweetie?"

"My—" The word slurred; seemed foreign in her mouth. "I'm wet, Momma." Palms pressed into the table, Maya forced herself upright on rubber legs. She slid the chair away and took a backward step.

Her mom said, "It's just water from the cold compress. I... Oh!" Then in a no-nonsense tone, "Professor, thank you for your help, but can you please leave us now?"

"Of course. You will let me know how she is." He petted Maya's head like she was a puppy, but instead of her face, his wide eyes locked on her lower body. Maya followed his gaze, and sudden clarity sent an electric charge thrumming through her chest.

Her thighs were streaked with blood.

I am formed.

CHAPTER 29

Two weeks later...

As Joshua's hand poised to knock on her door, Maya called out, "Come in."

"That's still a little spooky, sis," he said as he came into the bedroom.

She put down her eyeliner and leaned back in her chair. Her brother was wearing his favorite T-shirt, clean shorts, and a generous application of aftershave. "What's her name again?" she asked.

"Caitlyn." The answer snapped from him.

She spun her chair and faced him. "So how may I assist you, *brother* dear?"

"A quick reading. You know. Do I have a chance with her?"

She wafted her hand at him. "What girl would pass up a date with the *hunky* Joshua Doolan."

"No need to be snarky. You don't understand. You're... Well... It's different for you." His shoulders drooped, and he fixed her with a sullen stare.

How right he was—more different than Joshua could ever comprehend. With his hair cropped short and the beginnings of a stubbly chin, he looked ready to date. Ready to mate. Joshua thought himself a self-determining being who had chosen to meet a female to whom he was attracted. But since her *forming*, Maya no longer viewed the world in such terms. Joshua did not control his actions. Never had. Never would. He was a temporary vehicle in which a set of narrowly evolved genes were scheduled to spend a few decades. Those genes controlled his emotions just as a conductor manages the instruments in an orchestra to animate a musical score. But unlike a baton-wielding maestro, her brother was unaware that he was playing someone else's music.

Maya's Vision Road had shown many routes by which civilization might end: war, famine, viral infection. It also pointed to a narrow path that leapt past the population plague without decimating mankind's knowledge base, without regressing to the dark ages. But the cost was huge, the process precarious, and success far from assured. Evolution was her enemy, not her ally. Nature was ready to discard the human experiment and start over.

Maya was not.

She moved to her brother and placed a hand his shoulder. Joshua's mind was a churning kaleidoscope of desire and uncertainty. His fear of failing to attract this fifteen-year-old girl was illogical, but right now intellect was forsaken. Her brother's animal ancestors held sway. Lust had turned his commonsense switch to the off position—the same position that had doomed the human race.

She tilted her head and delivered a wry smile. *"Most boys work this out for themselves."*

"Most boys don't have you for a sister."

She gave him a playful punch in the chest. *"There'll be payback."*

He smiled. *"Come on, Mom's waiting to see you dressed up."*

When she saw Maya's outfit, Lauren grinned like an actor in a toothpaste commercial. "You two look nice. Hurry. We're late." She hustled them to the car.

A pair of wrought iron gates set in an ornamental brick wall protected Caitlyn's home. Lauren lowered the driver's window, pushed a button, and spoke her name into a metal box. The gates opened. At the top of a tree-lined gravel road, the house came into view. "Wow," Lauren said.

"Caitlyn's father is a surgeon." Pride filled Joshua's voice.

Lauren dropped them at the front steps. "Message me when you're done." She locked eyes with Maya. "And… have… fun." Maya had more important things to focus on than her mother's dream for her daughter to find a "nice boy" and have fun. But she loved her mom, and Joshua had begged. So here she was.

A housekeeper led them along a hallway of shiny hardwood flooring and showed them through a set of French doors into the garden.

Forty or fifty high school kids milled around on a football-field-sized lawn bordered on one side by a line of mature pines and on the other by a lake dotted with ducks. A band played hip-hop inside a candy-striped tent. A few cliques hung out at a long, cloth-covered table laden with food.

Caitlyn spotted them. Although they'd only met her briefly at a school social, she shouted and waved as though her lifelong best pals had just arrived. Blond hair bouncing, she headed their way in strategically ripped designer jeans and a too-tight yellow top. "I'm *so* glad you came." The words were directed at Joshua, and he blushed. Caitlyn's eyes were mapping her brother's face.

"Happy birthday." Maya handed Caitlyn a greeting card.

While the birthday girl opened the envelope, Joshua placed a hand on Maya's arm and made contact: *"Well?"*

"She thinks you're a hunk, but she's dating Duncan, a senior on the football team, and he's here somewhere."

"A hunk, eh." Joshua grinned.

Caitlyn laughed at the card. "Very cute. Thanks... Oh. Is everything okay, Maya?"

Maya was focused on Joshua, logging the emotional frenzy in his mind. He wanted Caitlyn as surely as a well-flighted arrow wants to split the bull's-eye. Absent social norms and restrictions, her brother would drag this girl away by her shiny blond hair and have his way with her. And Caitlyn would be a willing dragee. The emotions controlling him right now had been embedded in human genes for millions of years. The desire was overarching, the selection of a mate totally random. That's what evolution demanded, biodiversity. That they both felt in control was an evolutionary trick—neither was. Amending this human desire paradigm was just one of Maya's challenges.

"I'm fine, thanks, Caitlyn," Maya said.

Joshua puffed out his chest. "I'm thinking of trying out for football in the fall."

"Have you played before?" Caitlyn asked.

"Quarterback. My last coach thought I had a good arm."

Caitlyn reached out and placed manicured fingers on his right biceps. Joshua tensed the muscle. Her eyebrows lifted.

Maya sensed the newcomer's arrival before his shadow appeared. "Did I hear someone talking football?" The voice was deep and masculine.

Caitlin's hand snapped to her side. She stepped back a half pace. "Duncan. This is Maya and Joshua. Joshua plans to try out for quarterback in the fall."

The two boys locked eyes for three long seconds.

Duncan broke the standoff. Almost as tall as Maya and ruggedly handsome with tousled black hair and milk chocolate eyes, he offered her his hand and grinned. "I don't think we've met. Do you go to Riverwood?"

"No. I'm homeschooled."

"Wow! That's awesome. What's it like?" The handshake had stopped, but he held on to her fingers and stared into her eyes. Maya observed the shift in his evolutionary decision making as he evaluated her as a potential mate.

Caitlyn said, "How about a drink or snack? We have loads." She pointed to the food table.

"Great," Joshua responded like an enthusiastic eight-year-old.

Duncan's body tensed. Maya observed his testosterone levels rise as he prepared to respond to Joshua's perceived challenge. Apparently, she would have to play bodyguard as well as pimp. She dazzled Duncan with a smile, flared her irises, plumped her lips slightly, and brushed a stray hair behind her ear. "You guys go ahead," she said.

"I... Okay," Duncan said. "I'll join you later. After I've picked Maya's brains about homeschooling."

Caitlyn hooked Joshua's arm with hers and pulled him toward the buffet.

The band cranked up the volume, and a cheer erupted from the marquee. Duncan pointed to a garden swing suspended from an oak tree fifty yards across the lawn and facing the lake. "Let's move so we can hear each other talk."

"Lead on," Maya said.

Duncan's heart rate lifted from eighty to ninety-five as they walked.

"Have you always been homeschooled?" he asked.

"Yes."

He swallowed and searched for another opening gambit. "How does that work?"

His pulse was a hundred and five. If she didn't throw him a lifeline, he'd run back to Caitlyn and end up fighting with Joshua. "Tutors come to the house. Spanish, English, math, science, et cetera. The same as you, really. Except I don't go to school; school comes to me." Maya didn't mention that she had recently finished with homeschooling, having sucked the marrow from eighteen different tutors, and was currently the youngest ever recipient of a "gifted child" scholarship to DeVry University; she started classes in two weeks. Ironically, the recommendation had come from Professor Sterling. Maybe the manner in which their last class ended had influenced him.

They reached the swing, and Duncan took his place beside her. In the small seat, his thigh muscle stretched and contracted against her leg as he rocked them. Maya saw his question before the words were spoken.

"Are you dating anyone?"

"No."

Duncan was fascinated by her eyes and turned on by her figure. He liked that she was tall, but he was conflicted by his obligation to Caitlyn. His impression of her was flattering to observe, but inconsequential. She broke the mental connection and returned to the physical world where she found Duncan inches from her face.

The band was on break, and a chorus of crickets filled the void. A breeze puffed across the lake and loosened a few leaves that spiraled to the lawn. His hand drifted to her neck, and he stroked her hair.

A red blaze of anger approaching from behind gave Maya advanced warning of Caitlyn's arrival. "What the hell are you doing?" Duncan's girlfriend whipped around the swing and positioned herself in front of them, left hand on hip and right index finger inches from Maya's nose.

Maya grabbed Caitlyn's fingers and squeezed. "It's rude to point."

"Ouch. Let go, bitch!" She tried to pull away, but Maya was too strong.

With her free hand, Caitlyn swung for Maya's face.

Duncan's arm shot up to block the slap. He shouted, "Don't try that again," and pushed her away.

Maya released, and her grip left red reminders on the girl's skin. Caitlyn staggered back a step, then twisted and yanked at the third finger of her right hand until she pulled off a silver ring. She threw it at Duncan. It bounced off his chest and landed in his lap.

"Cheater. Bastard!" She leaned in, spat in his face, and stormed off.

Duncan turned to Maya, concern smoldering in his eyes. "I'm so sorry. Are you okay?"

She found a tissue in her purse and cleaned Caitlyn's spittle off his cheek. "I think your girlfriend regrets inviting me to her party."

"Screw her. *I'm* real glad you came."

So, apparently, was Joshua, who had intercepted Caitlyn on her way back to the house and now had her cradled in his arms while she sobbed theatrically into his chest.

Duncan stared at his hands and toyed with his ring. "I don't care about Caitlyn," he murmured, before clamping the ring in one hand and swiveling toward her. Head angled and eyes closed, he leaned in. She saw the kiss coming, but not in time to prevent it.

Maya stood alone at the trailhead of a perilous route. In Darwinian terms, she *was* the fittest by far, but survival resided in her own hands. To succeed, she must propagate. But mingling her DNA with Duncan's would be a million-mile departure from her Vision Road. She perched so far above this boy on the evolutionary tree that she may as well mate with a sea sponge.

When he broke from the kiss, she stroked his head. Not since Riley Brown had she interfered directly, but time was short, and this situation had great potential for distraction. The last thing she needed was Duncan fawning over her. That would just feed her mother's desire for Maya to have a boyfriend like a "normal" teenager. She took his hand, stared into his doe eyes, and snaked a gossamer-thin silver tendril into his mind. His thoughts appeared to Maya as an intricate web that shimmered with a myriad of pulsing interconnections. She sought, located, and snip, snip, snipped away his desire for her. Then, in an act of sibling generosity, she severed his connection to Caitlyn—anyway, Duncan could do better.

213

His eyelids fluttered as though waking from a deep sleep. Clearly struggling to recognize his surroundings, he looked at the ring in his palm. Maya stood, and he glanced up shyly and blinked, then blinked again. "I'm sorry," he said, "did I offended you?"

"No, I think you're right. The ropes do look unsafe." She stared high into the tree, and he followed her lead. "You probably saved us from a nasty fall. But if you'll excuse me, I need to return to my brother. Weren't you saying you were hungry?"

"Famished."

She stroked his cheek. "Well, I enjoyed meeting you. Now, off you go before the massed hordes gobble the good stuff."

Joshua was sitting with Caitlyn on a low wall near the house. Walking across the lawn, Maya texted her mom: "We're ready. Had a great time. Come ASAP, please." When she neared her brother, Maya cleared her throat so he could disentangle from Caitlyn. "Joshua. I'm ready to leave."

"Haven't you done enough?" Caitlyn said. Her voice was raw from crying. A red nerve rash blotched her neck.

Joshua widened his eyes and gave a small shake of the head.

Caitlyn's chin quivered, but that was for Joshua's edification. Waves of jealousy gushed from the girl. She envied Maya's long legs, her perfect face, her figure, her height. "Just leave," she snapped. "My dad will drive your brother home later."

"Okay. I'll let Mom know. Have fun, Joshua. Happy birthday, and thanks for the invitation, Caitlyn." Maya offered her hand and Caitlyn recoiled as though it were a dog turd. For a nanosecond, Maya considered adjusting the spoiled brat's mind to instill some manners, but there was no benefit.

Caitlyn wasn't important.

The people at this party weren't important.

She loved her brother. But he wasn't important either.

Only the Vision Road mattered.

CHAPTER 30

Ten Years Later...

One week after he was freed from state prison, Clifford Jarvis slurped milk dregs from a bowl of cornflakes at the downtown Atlanta homeless shelter where he'd spent the night. He walked six blocks to the underground train station. Using dollars scrounged on the street, he bought a ticket for the Metropolitan Atlanta Rapid Transit and rode it north to Sandy Springs.

He was going to find his kids—ungrateful kids who hadn't visited him once during a twenty-four-year prison stretch. It was time they met their father, and he sure as hell wasn't planning to call ahead.

After exiting the MARTA station, Cliff oriented on a Google map he'd printed at the public library and started walking.

An hour later, he turned onto Madiston Avenue. Although it was late fall, and poplar trees stood like honor guards on both sides of the roadway, no leaves littered the sidewalks. Clearly, the local municipality took good care of the residents of Sandy Springs.

Cliff glowered at the million-dollar homes he passed; their pristine front yards decorated with freshly mulched flowerbeds, framing neat green lawns. A thirty-something woman with teased blond hair collected her mail and threw him a wary look before shimmying up her garden path in three-inch heels and a tight black skirt. A shiny BMW stood in her driveway beside a Prius. Hubby would be in the city, sitting in a corner office in a pinstriped blue suit, white shirt, and tie, no doubt getting paid a fortune for shuffling paper. He knew the type, knew the people who lived their protected lives in this neighborhood. And he hated them.

He stopped at a wrought iron gate that opened onto a gray slate path leading to number 1027. According to the Internet, this was where Lauren Doolan lived. Not what he had expected. Cliff stood on the sidewalk for a moment and took in the home: two stories with large bay windows on the lower level. Upstairs, he reckoned five, maybe six bedrooms, capped by a red slate roof with multiple peaks. Things had certainly looked up for Lauren. Perhaps she'd landed a wealthy husband.

Must have changed a lot, then. He let out a low chuckle. Lauren had never shown any interest in men. Cliff had tried his luck with her a couple times when Patsy wasn't looking—nothing. He'd always assumed she liked girls. *Perhaps she's landed a rich dyke.* He licked his lips and thought of a threesome.

A shiny Lincoln SUV stood in front of the closed doors of a three-car garage. The anger that had been building on the four-mile walk from the MARTA station flared. The yuppies who lived in this neighborhood didn't need a nearby station. They took cabs or had their trophy wives drive them to the train in seventy-thousand-dollar sedans. None of *them* would have done time over Patsy. They'd have paid a fancy lawyer, who'd have called in a favor from a friendly judge. That was their justice, but not his; his ugly-hag public defender had settled for a lousy plea bargain. Because the years weren't hers to serve.

Twenty-four years and not a word, not a call. Nothing. No chance to give his side of the story, to tell his kids what really happened to Patsy. Oh. No. They assumed he was guilty. Lauren and Patsy's bitch-mother had swooped in and stolen his babies—taken what they'd always wanted, without a please or thank you. What about *his* rights—a father's rights? The judge said he'd lost them. But *his* blood ran in those kids' veins. Well, according to this house and that SUV, his kids were doing just fine now, and their father wanted his piece.

He slipped the gate latch, marched up the path, climbed four redbrick steps to the polished oak front door, and pressed the bell. Chimes echoed inside. Footsteps click-clacked across a tiled floor. The door opened. "Can I help you?"

It took Cliff a couple seconds to be sure. But yes. It was Lauren—she had Patsy's eyes. She wore date-night makeup, and her nails were manicured and painted soft pink—quite the lady of the manor. Her starched blue top showed an inch of cleavage that sent a tingle through his crotch. It had been a long time since he'd been close to a woman who looked and smelled this classy. This was no lesbian. This was one fine piece of ass.

He grinned. "Don't you recognize your nearly-brother-in-law?"

She gasped, took a half step back, and began to close the door.

Too late.

He stepped up, jamming the door with his boot, and ran his left hand down her bare arm. Her silky skin ticked up his heart rate.

She jerked away, and he glimpsed a teasing tit-flash down the front of her blouse.

"Get out!"

"Now, Lauren, that's not very friendly." He grinned, enjoying the fear in her eyes—what a turn-on. His cock was straining against his pants. This could work. Why not? He knew the twins had survived and Lauren had adopted them. So she was their mother—more or less. But every kid needed a father, someone to take 'em in hand when they ran off the rails. He'd be happy to step into that role. Anyway, Lauren was closer to his age. It made more sense for *them* to be together than for him and Patsy.

"I'll call the police."

"I'm just here to see my kids." Behind her, an expensive-looking chandelier hung from a gold chain. Broad stairs curved up the wall to his right, leading to the bedrooms he supposed. Maybe she'd show him around. Maybe he'd show her a thing or two.

He slipped into the hall and leaned his back against the door until the latch clicked shut. He grinned and opened his arms. "What about a hug for old time's sake?" This was fun. Exciting. He reached forward and stroked the back of his fingers across her flushed cheek. She knocked his hand away. *Likes it rough. Good. Me too.*

"Mom?" A woman's voice—deep, husky, sensual—came from within the house.

Damn it. Someone's here.

Lauren took three paces back and grabbed on to the stair rail, body coiled, ready to escape, ready to run. But Cliff no longer cared. When the owner of the voice stepped through the doorway at the far end of the hall, his mouth gaped. He couldn't drag his eyes from the vision that seemed to glide toward him. Easily six feet tall, she was shaped like an hourglass. A tall, beautiful hourglass. Thigh-length white shorts hugged long tanned legs and flowed around smooth hips to end at a narrow waist. Her bare midriff showed a toned stomach below perky breasts that shaped a simple white T-shirt.

But it was her face. Her face transfixed him, imprisoned his gaze: soft full lips, peach skin, and bold cheekbones topped by huge almond-shaped violet eyes that locked onto him, anchoring him to the spot. He couldn't speak, couldn't move. Sex and confidence and power radiated from her. She glowed. Cliff gasped in a breath.

"Maya," Lauren said in a shaky voice, "meet your father."

His daughter stopped four feet from him. He opened his mouth to speak, but his throat locked up.

"What—" The word rang out, bounced from the walls as though it had substance and slammed into him. He clapped hands over his ears and staggered back a half step. "Did you do"—the girl's eyes impaled him—"to my mother?" She stepped closer and screamed, "Answer me!"

Cliff jerked his head sideways to escape her ferocious stare. Breaking eye contact stung as though he'd ripped out a cord stapled to his irises. "I—" He swallowed to moisten his throat. "I never done what they said. We had words, but she and the babies—I mean you and the boy—you was both fine when I left. And you're okay now, see?"

Maya's hand flashed out and clamped Cliff's wrist. Although he continued to stare at the floor, he felt her eyes boring into him; their heat seared through his skull, tore into his mind, and saw into his heart. Her grip tightened. Pain seared along his arm. "Ahh!" His hand tingled, going numb from lack of blood.

"Show me." Maya's words roared inside his head. His legs buckled, and he dropped to the floor, kneeling before her, eyes locked on her sneakers, too terrified to meet her gaze.

Then his eyelids slammed shut, clamped as if glued. A movie played in his mind: He was in bed, in the trailer—his and Patsy's trailer. It happened twenty-four years ago, but the scene was real. He was rubbing his morning hard-on against Patsy's back. He grabbed her legs, forced them open, pressed and probed and tried to get inside her, but she turned and pushed him away.

"Not now, Cliff."

"You don't say *no* to me, bitch!" He vaulted out of bed, grabbed her arm and yanked her after him. She flopped to the floor, her fat white belly poking out from an undersized pink nightdress. Ugly. She slid toward him and grabbed his calf, looked up with those pathetic puppy-dog eyes. "Cliff, baby, it won't be long now. Just a few weeks. Don't be angry. Come back to bed and snuggle. I love you."

Cliff didn't want to snuggle. Cliff was horny. Cliff wanted to screw. Why keep her around if he couldn't screw her? He hated when she got whiny, and lately all she did was whine about being hot, or hungry, or tired. He yanked his leg free. "I'm going out."

In a screechy voice, Patsy pleaded, "Don't leave me like this, baby. Help me up."

He turned away. She grabbed for his foot. He kicked out. His heel caught her in the face. She begged again, bloody snot bubbling at her nose, tears leaking down her stupid puffy pregnant face. He whipped around and kicked again, buried his foot in her fat belly. Teach her a lesson. That's what she needed. He went to work on her. Both feet swinging—one-two, one-two, one-two—until she lay still and quiet, curled in a ball, her bloody nightdress twisted and bunched over swollen breasts and a saggy belly. "Stupid fat cow. I'm outta here." He pulled on his jeans and slung his black biker jacket over his shoulder. "For good."

The movie ended. The pain in Cliff's wrist increased.

"Look at *me*, Father."

Maya's voice swamped his mind. Cliff thought his skull would burst, thought his brains would spurt from his nose. As though yanked by an invisible chain, his head tilted up. Venomous violet eyes scorched him. "Liar. Murderer. I *saw* what you did. Leave. Now."

When her hand opened, Cliff grabbed his arm, then recoiled. The flesh was indented, crushed as though clamped by a too-tight tourniquet. Pain pulsed along his arm. Blood seeped past a splintered bone that poked through the skin at his wrist. He couldn't move his fingers. He clambered to his feet and backed away. Eyes low, he fumbled the latch open. Bent forward, cradling his arm, he stumbled down the steps. Tear-glazed eyes made the sidewalk swim. He loped along the street not chancing a backward look, praying she didn't follow.

Cliff had served twenty-four years in a Georgia state prison, mixed and fought with hard men, murderers who would shiv your throat for a cigarette. Never had he felt fear like he had in that hallway. His daughter was a freak, a witch, a... something— something unnatural.

Maya watched her father's hunched back recede down the road. When she was sure he wouldn't return, she closed the front door and went to her mother. Lauren stood frozen at the bottom of the stairs, bloodless knuckles bleached white against the banister. Maya hugged her and projected soothing emotions that stopped the trembling and banished the fear.

Lauren pulled in a faltering breath. "I had no idea he was out of prison. I'm sorry."

Maya held her tightly. "Doesn't matter, Momma."

"What'll I do if he comes back? I mean, except on Sundays when you come for the services, it's just Mom and me in the house."

"He killed Patsy," Maya said. "He tried to kill Joshua and me."

"Cliff is an evil man. I'll take out a restraining order to keep him away."

Leaning back, Maya brushed a stray strand of silver hair from her mother's forehead and tidied it behind Lauren's ear. "He won't be back."

"How can you be so sure?"

"Before he left, I passed a *healing* into him."

Lauren's eyes widened. She swooned backward and landed with a tooth-jangling bump on the second stair. Maya understood the reaction. She had scythed a cardinal rule of civilized human behavior. She had broken the sixth commandment.

The fear flooding Lauren's mind brought tears to Maya's eyes. She hated to upset her mother. Without Lauren's selfless actions,

Clifford's brutality would have killed Maya before she was old enough to be born. Because of her adoptive mother's bravery, love, and protection, Maya had lived and grown up to become unique. Today, though, despite Lauren's assumption, the human contract of "thou shalt not kill one another" hadn't been breached. The rule did not apply. Maya's genomic sequence was as different from her father's as his was from an ancestral shrew.

But how could she explain to her mother that when the *healing* ended his life in a few hours, Maya wouldn't be guilty of patricide. She hadn't murdered her father, because only humans can murder humans.

And although Clifford Jarvis was human.

Maya was not.

THE END

Dear Reader,

Thank you for taking the time to read MAYA. If you enjoyed the tale, please consider telling your friends and posting an Amazon review. Word of mouth is an author's best friend and much appreciated.

If you'd like an email reminder when Symbiogenesis Book Two is released, please join my mailing list at PeteBarberFiction.com. I don't share and I don't SPAM. In fact, because I write so slowly, you'll hardly ever hear from me

… Thanks again. Pete.

FROM THE AUTHOR

Born into a blue-collar family in Liverpool, England, I immigrated to the US in the early 90s and settled in North Carolina.

I haven't always made the best life decisions. By age eighteen, I had narrowly survived two near death experiences and adopted a lifestyle that showed little promise for surviving to an old age.

In keeping with that ill-considered life-foundation, my work experience has been varied (haphazard?) and includes (among others) plumbing, computer programming, sales, marketing, construction, hotel operations, real-estate developing, and farming.

In 2005, through a mixture of luck and some good judgment (even a blind squirrel eventually finds a nut), I found myself with enough time on my hands to embark on a writing career.

The premise of Symbiogenesis has been driving me to distraction for many years. I have poured what skill I have acquired and all of my heart into the words in this novel. I hope it was enough, but mostly, I hope you enjoyed the journey.

ACKNOWLEDGMENTS

Edited by Laurie Boris. Art by TheCoverCollection.com.

This story would be far weaker without the input I received from a gallant crew of early readers. I am indebted to these folk who were both generous with their time and constructive with their comments. Thank you: Cherrie, Susan, Jonathan, Jeff, Al, Ray, Nicola, Jo, April, and Michael.

www.ingramcontent.com/pod-product-compliance
Lightning Source LLC
Chambersburg PA
CBHW031305120626
46554CB00001BA/297